Early acclaim for

Célestine Vait

Frangipani

"I read *Frangipani* in one sitting, falling in love with the characters. Célestine Vaite writes about the bond between mothers and daughters with such truth and tenderness. I loved reading about the struggle between Materena and Leilani, even when it made me cry. There are no hopes and dreams like those of a mother for her daughter, and Ms. Vaite made them so real, I found myself missing my mother terribly." — Luanne Rice

"Vaite uses words to paint a vivid Tahitian landscape worthy of a Gauguin painting and delivers a memorable story about big dreams on a small island. . . . She has crafted an unforgettable heroine: Matarena is passionate, clever, and never without words of wisdom or a bit of folklore to share with a troubled soul. By the end, the reader is left wanting more, more more. . . . A warm and lyrical look at the fabric of family life in Tahiti." — *Kirkus Reviews* (starred review)

"Vaite's work celebrates the vibrant fullness and humor of daily life in Tahiti and reflects her tremendous respect for the strength of the local women." — *Marie Claire* (Australia)

Frangipani

Frangipani

a novel

Célestine Vaite

BACK BAY BOOKS
Little, Brown and Company
New York Boston

Back Bay Books / Little, Brown and Company
Time Warner Book Group
1271 Avenue of the Americas, New York, NY 10020
Visit our Web site at www.twbookmark.com

First United States Edition: February 2006

Originally published in Australia in 2004 by The Text Publishing Company

Cover illustration and interior art by Philippe Lardy

Library of Congress Cataloging-in-Publication Data

Vaite, Célestine Hitiura.
Frangipani : a novel / Célestine Vaite. — 1st U.S. ed.
p. cm.
ISBN 0-316-11466-9
1. Tahiti — Fiction. 2. Women domestics — Fiction. 3. Mothers and daughters — Fiction. 4. Women in radio broadcasting — Fiction. I. Title.

PR9619.4.V35F73 2006
823'.92 — dc22 2005043598

10 9 8 7 6 5 4 3

Q-MART

Book design by Jo Anne Metsch

Printed in the United States of America

For my daughter, Turia Pitt, my inspiration,
my ally — bless the day you came into my life, girl!

And for my goddaughter Heitiare Faure,
I will always be there for you, darling.

Frangipani

The Day You Came to Me

When a woman doesn't collect her man's pay she gets zero francs because her man goes to the bar with his colleagues to celebrate the end of the week and you know how it is, eh? A drink for *les copains!* Then he comes home with empty pockets, but he's very happy. He tells his woman stories that don't stand straight to make her laugh, but she doesn't feel like laughing at all. She's cranky and she just wants her man to shut up.

Finally he falls asleep. He wakes up with a sore head and says that he'd like some slices of roast beef and lemonade.

Well, Materena is *fiu* of all this!

She's not asking Pito to give her all his pay down to the last franc. She just wants a few thousand francs, that's all. Just enough for food, gas, kerosene, washing powder, and bits and pieces for their son. That is why it is imperative that Materena collects Pito's pay, to which she believes she's absolutely entitled. She's Pito's cook, cleaner, listener, lover, and she's the mother of his son. It's not as if she does nothing all day.

Materena asks Pito if she could collect his pay, with sugar in her voice and tenderness in her smile.

"Don't even think about it, woman," Pito snaps, flicking a page of last week's newspaper. He tells Materena about his colleague whose woman collects his pay, and how all the others mock him. "Who's the man and who's the woman between you and your woman? Who's the noodle? Who wears the pants? Who wears the dress?" they taunt him. Pito doesn't want the same thing to happen to him. When you have no respect at work and the colleagues mock you from seven thirty in the morning to four in the afternoon, both behind your back and to your face, your life is hell. You don't get invited to the bar on Friday afternoon.

On Thursday night, Materena combs her hair wild-style, rubs coconut oil on her body, sprinkles perfume behind her ears, and attacks Pito with caresses just as he's about to drift off to sleep. Pito opens his eyes and chuckles. And while Pito is busy satisfying Materena, she's busy thinking about collecting Pito's pay, filling her *garde-manger,* painting the house, buying a new oven. The future and not just tomorrow.

Materena often imagines herself old, with her gray hair tied up in a thin and tidy bun. She's sitting in a colonial chair and Pito, old too but still handsome, is standing behind with one hand on Materena's shoulder and the other leaning on a walking stick. They are in a photo studio.

Materena moans with pleasure because Pito sure knows what he's doing. She loves him so much right now. She adores him. He's the king of the sexy loving.

"Pito, I love you!"

With a grunt, his nipples harden, Pito sows his seeds.

After the romance, Materena tenderly and lovingly strokes Pito's hair as he falls asleep with a smile, his head nested on

Materena's chest. Materena hurries to ask Pito about his pay before he falls unconscious. "Pito, *chéri* . . . You're so wonderful . . . your muscles are so big . . . Can I collect your pay?"

Pito's answer is a tired whisper. "*Non.*"

That *con,* that jerk! Materena yells in her head. He only says *oui* when it suits him! Well, sweet water is over. Materena lifts Pito's head off her chest and plonks it onto his pillow.

The following Thursday Materena (one hand around nine-month-old baby Tamatoa sitting on her hip and the other stirring the breadfruit stew) asks Pito, who's just walked into the house, about his pay.

"Are you going to leave off about that pay?" Pito growls.

"*Non!*" Materena's answer is loud and clear.

"You want the colleagues to laugh at me?" Pito professes again how he sure doesn't want the colleagues to laugh at him. He doesn't want the colleagues to say behind his back: "Between Pito and his woman, who's the noodle? Who's the boss? His woman, she wears the pants? Who slaves by the machine five days a week? Pito or his half?"

Materena, who didn't even have enough money to buy a can of tomatoes for the stew, explodes, "Ah! It's your mates who decide these days? It's not you? It's your mates who wash your clothes, who cook your food? It's your mates who open their legs when you need?"

Pito gives Materena a cranky look and stomps out of the house.

"Pito?" Materena calls out, rushing to him. "You're not eating?"

But he's gone.

Materena and Pito have a miserable week. There's no yelling — no drama. Pito doesn't talk to Materena, and he sleeps on the sofa.

A few times Materena tries to lighten up the atmosphere, but Pito refuses to cooperate. When Materena tells Pito, "It's hot, eh?" he doesn't reply. When she irons his clothes in front of him, Pito looks at the ceiling. When she asks him if he'd like to eat corned beef with peas and tomato sauce or corned beef with breadfruit and tomato sauce, he shrugs. But he eats everything. He even has second servings.

Four times Materena says, "Pito . . . ," and waits for him to say a word, but he's lost his tongue.

Days pass.

A week . . .

Gradually things get back to normal. Pito sleeps in the bed again. He agrees with Materena that it's hot. He smiles. He rakes the leaves. Materena forgets about his pay. Materena smiles.

Then Materena finds out she's pregnant. She cries her eyes out because she's happy but at the same time she's devastated. Another child, with the pay situation still the same! Materena can't believe what's happening. *Aue eh* . . . eh well, the baby is conceived, she tells herself. Welcome into my womb and into my life. Now, Materena decides, she will simply have to collect Pito's pay.

Materena is very nervous as she opens the office door. She's wearing her old faded brown dress. She wants to make the right impression.

"*Iaorana.*" Materena does her *air de pitié* to the young woman at the reception.

"*Iaorana.*" The woman's greeting is polite and professional. A bit abrupt too because, so Materena understands, the woman doesn't know who she is and maybe she's mistaking Materena for someone who's here to sell something to eat. So Materena reveals her identity (I'm with Pito Tehana, he works here, we live in Faa'a behind the petrol station, we have a ten-month-old son, he's with my mother today for a few hours, etc., etc., etc., and how are you today?).

Minutes later Materena knows that Josephine has a *tane* and a fifteen-month-old son. She lives with her *tane*'s parents but that's only temporary, she's looking for a house to rent. Josephine's mother-in-law is a bitch woman. Josephine's father is a postman. Josephine's mother died a long time ago, she fell out of a tree. Josephine was in labor for forty-eight hours with her son, Patrick. Josephine's *tane* just stopped smoking . . .

Finally there is a silence and Materena can explain her delicate situation.

Josephine immediately understands. "*Aue oui,* of course," she says. "There's food to put on the table . . . There's bills to pay . . . No problems."

She gives Materena the envelope with Pito's name written on it and Pito's pay in it and asks Materena to sign her name in full in a black book — the picking-up-pay procedure. After the procedure, Materena opens the envelope and takes Pito's pay out. Then she puts back one thousand francs. There, that should be enough for Pito to buy himself three beers at the bar tonight.

Less than two hours later Materena is in her house feeling very happy as she puts away the cans of corned beef, the packets of rice, the washing powder, and the chocolate biscuits for Pito. The family-size can of Milo that was on special and . . . what else did Materena get? Ah, mosquito coils, two cans of salmon for Pito, a bottle of Faragui red wine for Pito, soap, aluminum foil, shaving cream for Pito. Materena's arms are sore from carrying the shopping bags, but she's not complaining. It hurts more walking home from the Chinese store carrying just one can.

After putting away all the goodies, Materena steps back to

admire her pantry stacked to the maximum. Nothing compares to a pantry that is stacked to the maximum; an empty pantry is so sad to look at. Materena hopes Pito is not going to be too cranky with her. She hopes he's going to be very happy about the salmon, the chocolate biscuits . . . and the baby inside her belly.

At quarter past midnight, the baked chicken is still on the table, but it is now cold and stiff, and Materena is still waiting for Pito to come home.

He's absent the whole weekend and by Wednesday he's still missing. To explain things to the relatives who ask where Pito is hiding, Materena invents a story about Pito looking after his sick mother. Six relatives, including Materena's mother, say, "Ah, that's nice of Pito to be with his mama when she's sick. I didn't know he was like that. We learn things every day."

Pito makes a brief appearance one Friday morning very early to inform Materena he's leaving her, and she can keep his sofa, but he's taking his shorts, his shirts, and his thongs. Materena, half awake and standing still like a coconut tree in the living room, wants to shout, "Stay! I'm pregnant and I love you! I'm never going to pick up your pay again! I swear it on top of my grandmother's grave!" But she just looks at Pito from under her eyelashes as he turns around and leaves.

She remembers herself with him in the shower and they're embracing like they're under the rain. She pushes the soap away with her foot. The last thing she needs right now is to slip on the soap and crack her head open.

She's with Pito under the frangipani tree behind the bank and he rips her sexy black underpants with his teeth before she has the chance to tell him that they're not her underpants, they're her mother's from a long time ago when she wasn't religious.

Pito busts a wall to install a shutter so that more light and fresh air come into the bedroom. Materena passes him the nails. He doesn't know what he's doing and she tells him what she thinks. He gets cranky and yells at her. She yells back at him.

Pito is gone now, and Materena walks to the kitchen to get her broom. She starts sweeping long, sad strokes.

She doesn't know what else to do.

What Is the Needle Going to Say?

Some women like to keep the sex of their baby in the dark until the midwife shouts, "It's a boy!" or, "It's a girl!" Other women, like Materena, want to know right from the start if they're talking to a son or a daughter.

Holding a needle attached to a thread above her belly button, Materena waits for the verdict. After a while the needle starts to move. Clockwise one time, in a tiny circle, a big circle, a bigger circle, another and bigger circle. Tears fall out of Materena's eyes. It's a girl! Materena is going to have a daughter! What emotion! Oh, even if the baby were another boy, Materena would still be crying, but a girl, eh? A daughter, what a responsibility!

Materena isn't saying that a boy isn't a responsibility. A child, no matter the sex, is a responsibility. True, Materena understands that when you sow you assume responsibility. From the day the child is conceived till the day the child leaves home you're responsible for its well-being. Actually, you feel responsible until you die. Even then it's not guaranteed the children are going to stop needing you and leave you alone. A child is a gift for eternity.

Materena lovingly rubs her belly, thinking of her daughter. First she sees a little girl with plaits who looks like her when she was little. Next she sees a confident and strong woman with a degree, a good job, a driver's license, a briefcase. A champion with words and mathematics — a schoolteacher, a professor, a *somebody.*

She realizes that children don't always fulfill their mother's dream, but Materena will definitely aim to raise a woman who knows what she wants and makes it happen. When you're this way, it means you believe in yourself, which is not a bad way to be when you're a woman. Materena is determined her daughter will never worry that she's not good enough. She will know that she is, end of argument.

As the days go by Materena talks to her daughter in her womb. "And how are you today, girl? You're fine? You're comfortable? It's Mamie here talking to you . . ."

Materena talks about Tahiti to give her unborn baby girl a general idea of her soon-to-be home. That place is the scorching sun at midday, the heavy and still humidity before the rain. "So? It's going to rain or not?" Materena asks her baby girl and describes to her the sweet smell of flowers as they are opening up early in the morning, the aroma of coffee brewing in kitchens, and fresh bread being baked at the bakery nearby. She talks about the bright colors everywhere you look; the red and orange hibiscus edges, the yellow *monettes* — "They make the gardens so pretty, little one, you're going to like them!" — the white tiare Tahiti flowers people wear behind their ears, the right one meaning "I'm free," the left one, "Sorry, I'm taken."

She points out the trees planted to mark the day a child comes into the world, the day someone we love goes away, a day people will talk about in one hundred years. Frangipani, kava, *mape,* tamarind, lime, orange, carambolas, *quenettes,* the list is endless because the soil here is so fertile. You throw a seed and it grows. But the tree Materena prefers, she confides to her unborn daughter, is by far the breadfruit, because it is beautiful with its large green leaves; strong too, and what's more, it is a tree that feeds — always there for you when money is low.

"Our island is so beautiful, girl, it's paradise," Materena gushes, listing off all the things that people come here to see — the mountains, the white-sanded beaches, rivers, waterfalls . . . "But I've never been to these places," she admits. "Why? Well, because I love it so much here."

And as she continues the baby's guided tour, Materena sees her place with new eyes herself. Faa'a PK 5 — behind a petrol station, not far from the Chinese store, the church, the cemetery, and the international airport. It is mismatched painted fibro shacks, church bells calling out the faithful on Sunday morning, the endless narrow paths leading to relatives, quilts adorning walls, diaper cloths drying on clotheslines, and someone in the neighborhood raking brown leaves.

Here is also women talking stories by the side of the road, barefoot children chasing chickens or flying kites, babies falling asleep at their mother's breast, men gathered outside the Chinese store counting the few cars driving past.

"It's our ways, our island," Materena says with a tender pat for her belly, and keeps on talking. About the weather today, what she ate this morning, who the baby's father is, what happened with him three days ago, how she met him, the two years she waited for him when he went away for military service in France, and how he never sent her a parcel, not even a postcard. She talks about the baby's family — the brother is Tamatoa, the grandmother is Loana, the other grandmother is Mama Roti, and the uncles are . . . And the aunties are . . . One by one, Materena tells her unborn daughter who is who in the family, who is nice, who is not so nice, who is dead.

When baby Tamatoa has his nap Materena talks to her unborn daughter about herself. Well, for a start she likes to broom. When she's cranky she brooms (rapidly), when she's sad she brooms (slowly), when she's lost she brooms (half rapidly and half slowly). The result is the same, though. The floor is clean and Materena is happy. She's also happy when the *garde-manger* is full, when she gets a little compliment about her cooking; love, respect, a bit of rain now and then.

She's sad when people and animals die, someone she loves yells at her, money is low. She likes to listen to people talk and she doesn't mind raking the leaves.

She left school at fourteen years old and has been working ever since. She's sold peanuts and lemonade at a football stadium, washed dishes in a restaurant, made sandwiches at a snack, where she met Pito, cleaned houses, and now she's a housewife.

She doesn't have a coconut tree in her hand, that's for sure. She's not lazy. And she's very proud to have been born a woman because women are the strongest creatures on Earth. And speaking of women, the two women Materena admires the most in life are her mother and her godmother, Imelda. Her favorite cousin is Rita. Her favorite color is blue. Her favorite singer is Gabilou. And she used to have a dog.

Materena keeps on talking cheerfully as she makes her son's bottle. He wakes up minutes later.

"Your brother is awake," she says out loud, walking to his room to get him. "*Oh, la-la,* he's so cranky today! Can you hear him?" By the time Materena opens the door, Tamatoa, sitting upright, is yelling his head off.

"But, *chéri?*" Materena cackles as she bends over to pick her son up. "What's the matter? You had a little nightmare?" She gives him a big kiss on his head to reassure him, but the baby keeps on yelling.

"What is it?" Materena asks, checking her son for mosquito bites on his arms. She finds none. She lifts his shirt. There are no bites. She puts baby Tamatoa back on the mattress and takes off his wet diaper. "There," she sighs. "Feel much better now?"

Tamatoa is still yelling his head off.

"Oh," Materena says. "Don't panic, Mamie has got your bottle ready."

She hurries to the kitchen and takes Tamatoa's bottle, being heated in a pot on the stove. She squeezes a bit of milk on the palm of her hand. "Look at what Mamie has got for you," she sings, showing her son his bottle. But instead of smiling with relief, baby Tamatoa yells even louder. When Materena gives him the bottle, he throws it back at her. When she picks it up and puts the teat in Tamatoa's mouth, he spits it out.

"What's the matter with you today?" she asks, thinking that the whole neighborhood must be wondering what she's doing to her baby for him to yell like this. Materena picks him up and gently pats him on the bottom. "Good baby," she says, and he buries his head in his mother's chest and starts to sob.

"But, *chéri,*" Materena whispers, "it's not like you to cry like this. What's wrong?" The baby, now whimpering, lifts his beautiful sad eyes to his mother and suddenly she thinks she understands the situation.

She squeezes her baby tight. "I forbid you to cry for him, you hear? I forbid you. I'm all that you need." And for the first time since Pito has left, Materena bursts into tears, her head falling onto her son's shoulder, her heart beating with profound sorrow.

Side by Side

Even if your heart feels like it is being crucified you still have to wave to relatives.

Materena, on her way to visit her mother from the Chinese store, carrying a bottle of cooking oil and a crucified heart, waves to her cousin Tapeta on the other side of the road. Tapeta waves back and hurries to cross the road as fast as her big pregnant belly allows her, all the while calling out, "*Iaorana,* Cousin! I need to ask you something!"

Materena waits, hoping Tapeta's request requires a simple yes-or-no answer. Her mother is waiting for the cooking oil to start frying fish for dinner.

The two cousins embrace, gently tapping each other on the shoulder.

"How's baby?" asks Materena.

"Oh, *bébé* Rose is fine," Tapeta replies, rubbing her enormous belly, "but she's getting heavy."

"Eh, eh." Materena smiles, eyeing her cousin's belly, thinking, How is that baby ever going to come out?

Tapeta, mistaking Materena's smile for a smile of envy, chuckles. "Eh! Don't you get clucky on me now! You've got to wait until Tamatoa is two years old to get pregnant again, you don't want your children to be too close. Don't do what I've done three times!"

Materena laughs a faint laugh, and she's just about to excuse herself when Tapeta takes her hand and leads her to the shade of the mango tree near the petrol station. She needs to ask something, she says, and it won't take too long, she promises.

"*Oui,* because Mamie is waiting for her cooking oil," Materena says.

"Sure, five minutes. I just need a little advice, but first I have to tell you the full story." When Tapeta, comfortable under the mango tree, says the full story, she means the full story — the story from the very beginning.

"You know I had a brother," Tapeta begins.

"*Oui, oui,* he died before you were born."

"Correct, five years before I was born, and you know on which island he's buried."

Aue, Materena thinks. She knows it's an island far away, but which one is it? "Raiatea?" Materena says, hesitantly.

"Apataki!"

"*Ah oui!* Apataki . . . I don't know why I said Raiatea."

"Well, you forgot where my mother is from, that's all. Now, I hope you remember where she's buried."

Yes, this Materena remembers. Tapeta's mother is buried in the Faa'a cemetery, in the Mahi burial plot, underneath her husband, one grave up from Mama Jose's grave and one grave down from Papa Penu's grave. When it comes to the people buried in the Faa'a cemetery, Materena knows all the details. Even if by some horrible twist the names on the crosses were wiped out, Materena would still be able to tell you who's buried here and who's buried there.

Tapeta gives Materena a big smile of gratitude, her eyes getting tearier by the second, and asks, "You know how my brother died, eh?"

Materena, hoping she's remembering correctly, tells Tapeta that her brother died in his sleep.

Tapeta confirms this with a sad nod. "*Eh oui,*" she sighs. "Three months old. One day he was alive and the next . . . eh-eh, poor Mama." Tapeta talks about how her mother carried the memory of her beautiful son in her heart right till the day she died. She had a lock of his hair in her pendant, his pillow on her bed, his baptism robe in a glass frame, his little white shoes in her sewing box. "She could never love me like she loved him," Tapeta says, her head down. "I suffered, you know . . . the alive can't compete with the dead."

"Cousin." Materena takes Tapeta's hand in hers. "Don't think about stories like that when you're pregnant, it's not good."

"I know, but bloody Mama came into my dream last night! I've been calling out to Mama for years, but she never came. She just bloody ignored me. And then last night, just like that, she decides to visit me. She comes into my dream to tell me she wants to be next to her son."

"*Aue.*" Materena has goose bumps.

"She says this to me," Tapeta continues, shaking her head with disbelief, "but she doesn't give me instructions. It's up to me to guess who has to be moved! Who do I dig out, eh? Mama? Private as she was? I don't think she's going to be too happy having people going through her bones. I move my brother, then? But he's already been moved once. I don't want my little brother to be disturbed again."

"Really? Your brother has already been moved?"

"Ah, you didn't know?" Tapeta informs Materena that her parents, Reri and Julien, were in Makatea working in the nickel mine when her brother died, so the boy was buried there. But two years later, when they returned to Apataki, Reri took her son along even though it was, at the time, against the law that says you can't move a dead body for fifty years. The mama furiously dug the little coffin out in the middle of the night, all the while muttering, "I'm not leaving my son behind."

Years later, the husband decided to come back to Tahiti, and Reri was prepared to do the same thing, but he said, "What for? We're going home to Apataki soon. Your island is my island."

God decided otherwise.

"I understand that Mama wants to be next to her son," Tapeta tells Materena. "She only had him for three months when he was alive, so it's normal she wants him for hundreds of years dead. I understand, I'm a mother too."

Silent tears roll down Materena's cheeks. Materena also understands, but it doesn't mean she knows whom Tapeta should move. Part of Materena thinks the baby should be moved so that he can be with both his parents, and part of Materena thinks the mother should be moved so she can be with all her family. But then Tapeta won't be able to visit her mother every Saturday as she's been doing for years. Ah, it's a shame Auntie Reri wasn't more specific in the dream. What about Uncle Julien?

"Have you asked your father for advice?" Materena asks.

"He's a man," Tapeta snorts. "You don't talk about babies to men. You talk about the gas bottle and the lawn, not babies."

Materena sighs a long, sad sigh. She would probably have laughed at Tapeta's comment if her man hadn't abandoned her with one son born and one daughter on the way. She would have said, "Ah, you're right, Cousin, men are hopeless with babies. All they know is how to make them, eh?" Materena and Tapeta would have had a good chuckle. But right now, Materena is crying.

"Cousin?" Tapeta looks at Materena closely. "Ah well, it's a sad story, I'm sorry I told you about it. But don't worry, I'm going to see Mama at the cemetery today and ask her to give me a few more details next time." Tapeta explains that her mother has always been vague anyway. When Tapeta would ask her mother where the soap was, she'd say, "There." If Tapeta had the bad luck to ask, "There? Where?" she'd earn herself a hand on the back. "She's never been able to tell me things as they are," Tapeta says. "It's about time she learns."

And with this Tapeta apologizes to her cousin for having kept her for too long.

One Step Forward

Pito has been gone for eighteen days now. It's time to get up and move on.

To give herself strength Materena thinks about Auntie Antoinette, the mother of Rita, Materena's favorite cousin. Antoinette fell on the ground and cried her eyes out when her husband went to get the newspaper and didn't come back for days. But when Antoinette's sister, Mama George, saw him at the market with another woman (they were holding hands and kissing like crazy people) and told the whole population, Antoinette stopped crying.

After she stopped crying, Antoinette shoved all of her ex-husband's things (shirts, shaving brush, ties, thongs, shorts, etc.) into a box and left it by the side of the road with a note saying Free, Please Take. The box was gone within seconds. She then painted the doors in her house blue, took down the white curtains her ex-husband had insisted on, and replaced them with colorful curtains as her sister Teresia had told her to do years ago. She bought a vase and made a bouquet of flowers for the first time in her life. Before, when Antoinette had seen a bouquet of flowers in a vase, she'd say, "Eh well, poor flowers, I wouldn't like to be you." For Antoinette, at the time, anyway, flowers were for the earth and not for the vase. But now she displayed her bouquet of flowers in the living room for everyone to see, facing the front door so that the first thing she'd see when she opened it would be her beautiful bouquet. Antoinette got up after her fall and moved on with her life.

Materena intends to do this, but she's not having Father Unknown written on her daughter's birth certificate. That's the only reason Materena has to see Pito. She doesn't care if there's another woman on Pito's horizon. It isn't going to change the situation.

Materena admits to her daughter in the womb that she's a bit worried about being a single mother. When she smells Pito's pillow her heart aches, it is a crucifix for her. But women are real strong creatures, she assures the baby, they can survive anything — flood, fatigue, separation, single parenthood. They're tough.

So her man has abandoned her and their baby son, Tamatoa, and, yes, she's heartbroken. But it doesn't mean she's going to lie on the ground for days and days. It's time to get up and march on! For some reason, Materena suddenly feels very strong. It's like someone is whispering into her ears, "Eh, don't worry, everything is going to be all right."

The previous week Materena had been prepared to go and see Pito at his work to say sorry and ask him to come home, kiss him and hold him tight. She got all dressed up. But a voice inside her head shouted, "Materena, don't you dare do that! If Pito loves you he'll come back. Let him show you what he really feels for you." To resist the temptation Materena raked the leaves, she needed to do that, there were yellow breadfruit leaves all over the place, and no dignified Tahitian would have leaves rotting away in the garden. Leaves must be raked and then burned, which is exactly what Materena did. The smoke did her good, it was like she was burning the past, moving on. After that, she planted a tamarind tree, she marked the day, the day when she got up and walked.

"Men . . . they're such *cons,*" Materena goes on to her daughter. But all the same there's no need to turn into a man hater like Auntie Antoinette.

Even all these years after losing her man, every day Auntie Antoinette has a reason to exclaim, "Ah, men! They're such *cons!*" If she sees a man walking in front with a woman following a few steps behind, she'll say, "Watch that *con,* he has to walk in front, he has to show to the whole population that he's the king, that it's him who decides." She never thinks that maybe the man is walking in front because his woman told him off last night. That she screamed at him that he was an idiot and that she should have listened to her mother. Maybe the man and the woman don't even know each other.

A man and a woman have eight children, Auntie Antoinette declares how the man is an animal, how he forced his woman and all she wanted to do was sleep. What a *con!* A man falls asleep during Mass, what a *con,* continue to live in obscurity.

Never complain to Auntie Antoinette about your man. She'll only say to you, "Well, it's you who's the idiot. What are you doing with him? What have you got in your head? Rocks?"

Materena is determined not to turn into a man hater. She knows that not all men are *cons.* Materena certainly hopes that she and Pito will remain good friends. It's important for the children.

That is what she told Pito's best friend, Ati, when he came to visit yesterday after having been away for a month in the islands. He's the only person who knows that Pito has left (and for a question of pay). Ati was so cranky with Pito. When he visited her he said, "Materena, Pito is blind, he doesn't know what he's got." Then Ati took Materena in his arms and held her tight. A bit too tight, Materena thought, and who knows what would have happened if Tamatoa hadn't started to cry.

Before Ati left, he told Materena that he was going to visit her again later on in the evening, but Materena told him it was better that he didn't. She didn't want people to start talking. She had to tell the family about Pito and everything first.

Aue, Materena says to her baby. She can't keep lying to the family that Pito is looking after his sick mama. Sooner or later the relatives are going to put two and two together, smell the rat, start talking, investigate, hold meetings outside the Chinese store and whisper to one another. As soon as Materena walks past they'll talk louder about a curry recipe, wave to her and call out, "Eh, Cousin! You're fine? Pito's mama is still sick?" Later on, with Materena far away enough, the investigation will continue. "Like I was saying to you," they'll whisper.

Materena is well aware of this. She's not Tahitian for nothing.

Oh, it's not as if her relatives are after a juicy story because they're so bored. But they want to know where they stand. They're getting a bit sick of calling out to Materena to see if Pito's mama is fine, not counting the fact that they're by now very concerned for Mama Roti.

There will be many shocked relatives when Materena confesses the truth, how Pito left for a question of pay. How he left because he didn't want his mates at work to make fun of him. So many relatives have said to Pito, "Ah, Pito . . . the day Materena packs your bags and sends you back to your mama, I'm not going to be surprised."

But here, he packed his bags himself and took off. He disappeared.

As for Mama Roti, she's in very good health.

It's time to inform the population, starting with her mother, although Materena suspects her mother already knows the situation. Loana has been around a few times lately, bringing boxes of food along. She's also slept over twice. She said, "Ah, it's so nice for me to have a bit of company, it's so much better than to listen to that guy with the nice voice talk on the radio." Loana went on about how some mothers can't live with their children once they've moved out, but she could, and easily too. Materena feels the same way about this, but she'd still rather live with the father of her children than her mother.

Well anyway, it's time to tell the truth.

But first Materena is going to put Pito's Akim comics in the trash along with his toothbrush and his old things. Then she's going to move the sofa to where the wardrobe is and move the wardrobe to where the sofa is. No need to change the curtains, they're already colorful. Materena would never have white curtains, they get dirty too easily. As for a bouquet of flowers . . . well, there's a plant. It's been there from day one in this house, and Materena likes to see it the moment she opens the front door, and so she intends to leave it as it is because it's not good to move plants around. If they're happy where they are, leave them alone. She might replace the linoleum with carpet. But first, she must see Pito.

Baby Tamatoa is with Loana, who said, "Don't rush coming home, girl . . . If you want to go to the cinema, go to the cinema, here's a bit of money. If you want to go visit your mother-in-law, go visit your mother-in-law, no worries."

There, Materena is ready to confront Pito. She checks herself in front of the mirror one more time. Yes, she tells herself, she looks fine, not too much rouge on the cheeks, hair neat in a bun, and . . . Materena looks closer into the mirror. She can't believe how pretty she is today . . . But! She's really blossoming!

Okay, off she goes.

She swirls out of the house, closes the door, and marches ahead, and . . . is that Mama Roti under the mango tree next to the petrol station? In a coat? But *oui!* And she's talking to Mama George and Auntie Stella and a few of Materena's other aunties. No doubt they're asking her if she's feeling better. And no doubt Mama Roti is telling them that she doesn't know what they're going on about.

Oh, la-la, Materena is just about to turn around and run back inside the house when Mama George spots her.

"Materena!"

Now Mama Roti also starts calling out to Materena.

In fact, they're all calling out to Materena, so Materena keeps on walking to face the music.

"*Iaorana,* Aunties," Materena sings, kissing each of them, starting with the eldest auntie.

Now the ex-mother-in-law. "*Iaorana,* Mama Roti. You're fine?"

Mama Roti does her *air de pitié* and moans that *oui,* she's fine, but yesterday she thought she was going to die. She had a 104-degree temperature, and she was so cold, and the day before yesterday she had a 102-degree temperature, and she was so cold. She is still cold, that's why she's wearing a coat. It belongs to one of her cousins, who was married to a Frenchman, though they're divorced now. On and on Mama Roti goes about her fever, 102 degrees, 107 degrees. Luckily her son Pito was looking after his poor dying mama. He cooked her soups, he buttered her bread, checked her temperature in the middle of the night.

"*Ah oui?*" Materena says, thinking that Pito is so nice.

"*Oui,*" Mama Roti confirms, looking for a moment like she's about to cry. Then, doing her cranky look, she continues. "My other sons? Them! They're a bunch of no-hearts." She gives more information about how Pito looked after her so tenderly . . . Ah . . . bless the day he was born . . . bless the day he was conceived, etc., etc. . . . "Okay, *au revoir,*" Mama Roti says suddenly to Materena's aunties in the middle of her praises for her son, dismissing them with the back of her hand. Then, grabbing Materena by the shoulder: "I need to ask you to do something for me, girl, let's go inside the house."

Materena and Mama Roti go inside the house and sit on the sofa.

"How's Pito?" Materena asks.

"Oh, he's fine, I told him to stop worrying about me and to go back to you and his son, but he said, 'Mama, you gave birth to me, I'm staying here until you feel better.'"

"Ah . . . and . . ." But Materena is not going to ask Mama Roti if Pito has told her about their fight. "Why do you need to talk to me, Mama Roti?" Materena asks.

"*Aue . . . ,*" Mama Roti moans. "Men sometimes . . . nothing in the coconut."

Here's the reason why Mama Roti needs Materena.

There's a confrontation planned this afternoon at the Pic Rouge between the Tehanas and the Piris, and Pito is getting ready to defend the honor of the family. *Aue,* Mama Roti laments, she has done all she could to stop her son from going to the confrontation. She cried, she begged, she yelled, and Pito yelled back. So Mama Roti got out of her sickbed, borrowed her cousin's coat, and hopped in the truck to come and talk to Materena. There was no point in Mama Roti asking the relatives for their help. All the women in the neighborhood were busy dealing with a son or a husband going off to war. Well anyway, Mama Roti is here because she counts on Materena to stop Pito from going to the confrontation.

"Eh, girl?" she says. "Come with me to the house and do your tricks on my son."

Mama Roti cries silent tears, shaking her head and mumbling how men have nothing in the coconut sometimes. It's not enough for Pito that his father broke his back at a confrontation, that he couldn't play soccer anymore. When Mama Roti met Frank Tehana he was a soccer star. Months later she was pregnant and her man was in the hospital for an operation on his back. From that day on till the day he died Frank complained about his back every day, driving Mama Roti crazy . . . *Aue eh* . . .

Materena joins Mama Roti in her desperation. She knows all about confrontations.

A confrontation is when two enemy families meet in the dark and hit out at each other until the last man falls. A confrontation usually happens because one person from one family said something nasty (or did something nasty) to a person from the other family, and before you know it cousins and uncles from both families are involved, and next thing there's a confrontation. Anyone can participate, there's no age limit. But most of the participants are young. The older men have better things to do.

Anything can happen in a confrontation. Well, first, you can die, and second, you can get paralyzed for life. The enemy comes behind you and snaps a thick piece of wood on your back, and the result? You're in a wheelchair or you have a bad back for the rest of your life.

And while the men are at war, the women stay at home and pray.

Materena gets up. "Mama Roti, let's go and save Pito."

Mama Roti holds Materena's hand in the truck all the way back to her house, caressing it now and then, making Materena very uncomfortable. Mama Roti has never held her hand before — Materena understands Mama Roti's message, all right, and she's feeling the pressure.

Mama Roti stops yards away from her house to undo Materena's bun and run her fingers through Materena's hair. "There, you look much better like that." She advises Materena to let her hair out more often because hair is a woman's greatest asset and a bun makes Materena look so old and prim.

She's unbelievable, that woman! Materena shrieks in her head.

Pito is pumping his muscles when Materena walks in. Eyes meet eyes . . . Materena wants to run to her man, hold him tight and kiss him hard, but Mama Roti is behind her, sighing. It's strange, but when you haven't seen your man for a while he somehow improves. Materena has always found Pito handsome, but today she finds him irresistible. He actually looks like an actor. She can tell from the expression in Pito's eyes that he is thinking the same about her too.

"Pito." This is Mama Roti talking in between two long sighs. "I went to get Materena like I told you."

Pito ignores his mother to ask Materena where Tamatoa is.

"He's with Mamie."

"Ah . . . and he's fine?" Pito says.

"He's going to have a new tooth soon, at the front."

"*Ah oui!*" Pito exclaims, smiling. Then with pride he adds, "That's my boy." Then to his mother he says, "Mama, can I speak to my woman in private?"

My woman? Materena thinks to herself. Does this mean reconciliation? He's not cranky with me anymore?

As soon as Mama Roti leaves the living room, Pito walks to Materena and Materena walks to Pito, and next minute they're jumping on each other. In the middle of all the heat and the passion Materena urges Pito not to go to the confrontation and Pito explains that he has to because his family needs him.

"I'm your family now, Pito," Materena says. "Me and your son . . . and I'm pregnant . . . It's a girl . . . I did the needle test." It all rushes out before she can think.

The first time Pito found out he was going to be a father he stood still like a coconut tree and said nothing. He does the same today. That's just the way Pito reacts to this kind of news.

"Come home, eh?" continues Materena. She promises Pito to cook him chicken curry and to give him a massage if he comes now.

But their conversation is interrupted by a car tooting and men's voices calling out, "Cousin! You're ready?"

In a flash Mama Roti comes out of her hiding spot, shrieking, "Pito! You stay right where you are." She holds on to him just to make sure.

Two young men come to the door, and Materena vaguely recognizes them. She might have met them at a baptism the previous year but she's not 100 percent sure. The young men's faces are covered with green and red stripes and they are dressed in a khaki military uniform. The last and only time Materena met these two young men they were dressed in their wedding-and-funeral suit and they were drunk.

"*Iaorana,* Mama Roti," Pito's cousins say together.

"*Iaorana,* what?" By now Mama Roti is firing angry sparkles from her eyes to her nephews. She yells at them that they look stupid with all that war paint on their face and goes on about how she looked after them when they were babies, changed their diapers, fed them the bottle. "What's this?" Mama Roti continues. "You've got nothing else better to do, eh?" With giant strides she's at the door, grabbing one of her nephews by the hair. "Mama Roti, *aita . . . ,*" he shouts. She grabs the other nephew by the hair. "Pito . . . control your mama," the nephew shrieks. Pito heads for the door, but not before his mama catches him, a fiery look on her face. The more Pito tries to unlock himself from his mother's mad embrace, the tighter Mama Roti holds on to her son. In the end the cousins come to Pito's rescue. It's three against one. Mama Roti has zero chance.

"Materena!" Mama Roti shouts as Pito slips between her fingers. "Help me!" But Materena is still immobile, like a statue. She's thinking.

She hears the car driving away and Mama Roti's angry yell, "Pito! If you get paralyzed, don't you come running crying to me!"

After a while Mama Roti stomps inside the house, and the first thing she does is give Materena a cranky look. "I didn't see you try to stop my son," she says. "If my son comes back in a wheelchair, you better look after him . . . Eh well, I don't know what you're going to do, but I'm going to pray."

Materena nods and sets off to the nearest gendarmerie without a word. When you can't talk people you love out of doing stupid things, you've got to swallow your pride and appeal to the gendarmes for help, because praying is not enough.

Materena opens the door of the gendarmerie office feeling like turning around and running. But an invisible hand is on her back, thrusting her forward. Before she knows it, she's standing and smiling at the front desk, where a young gendarme is typing a letter.

He lifts his head and, beaming with delight, asks her how he can be of assistance.

Materena quickly realizes she's dealing with a gendarme who's new to Tahiti. He doesn't have that look gendarmes who are not new to Tahiti have (frown and cranky eyes). But then again Materena understands how extremely rare it is to see Tahitians walk into the gendarmerie office of their own free will — what's more, relaxed and smiling. Tahitians are usually dragged in kicking and cursing by French people. The young gendarme must be relieved to be dealing with a smiling Tahitian. Still smiling, he waits for Materena to let him know how he can be of assistance, and so she tells him the whole story about the confrontation.

The gendarme, smiling a bit less, asks Materena if she knows what kind of weapons the fighters would be using. Any guns?

"*Non,*" Materena reassures the gendarme. "In Tahiti people only use thick pieces of wood and machetes to fight. They don't shoot each other. They just hit each other's limbs."

The gendarme thanks Materena for the information and promises to look into the matter. A very proud Materena walks out of the gendarmerie. She can't believe her audacity! Her courage! Ah, she must not want Pito back paralyzed. Or perhaps her baby girl is playing tricks on her. People do say women change when they're pregnant. They do things that are completely out of the ordinary.

What Materena knows from reading Pito's newspapers is that gendarmes use *bâtonnets* and tear gas when they have to stop trouble. As far as Materena is concerned, the warriors are going to be surprised to see the gendarmes. They'll run all over the place like chickens without a head.

That's what happened all right, so Pito informs Materena the next morning as he walks into the house with his haggard face and puffy eyes, casually picking up his son as if he's been away for only ten minutes. The baby cries because his father has been away for almost two weeks, a long time when you're a baby, enough time to forget your father's face. Pito quickly passes Tamatoa back into his mother's arms and gives her the whole story.

Yesterday, he explains, right in the middle of the confrontation, gendarmes crept from behind the bushes, yelling, and surprised the warriors with *bâtonnets* and tear gas. All the warriors ran back to their vehicle of transportation (car, bicycle, truck, Vespa) except for Pito. He was still in shock over the news Materena had told him. That he was going to be a father again and the baby was a girl. A girl! What was he going to do with a daughter?

So he stood still and the gendarmes grabbed him and shoved him in the police wagon, direction, the police station, where he spent the night in a stinky prison cell sleeping on a concrete floor. But all is okay, Pito goes on, the gendarmes didn't take his fingerprints, so he doesn't have a police record. He's not a criminal, and he's not going to lose his job.

Anyway, Pito was released half an hour ago and he caught the truck straight to Faa'a. Materena, relieved to see him in one piece, puts her son on his mattress and cooks her man an omelet.

Less than five minutes later Pito's best friend, Ati, arrives to visit, just as he promised Materena the previous night.

A Written Contract

The newspaper is on the kitchen table opened to page 17. The ad is below the winning numbers of last week's *tombola.* It's in a square with a postal box address in capital letters. It's an ad for a position as a cleaner.

Materena, six months pregnant, has decided to apply for it. She feels it's time to get back into the workforce.

"There's going to be a tough battle," says Loana, who's come to help Materena write the letter. "The whole island has seen that ad." Meaning Materena won't be battling *just* against the relatives.

That's the problem when an ad is in the newspapers and not taped to the front window of the Chinese store. What's more, the ad is below the winning numbers of last week's *tombola.* There's going to be a tough battle, all right; but then again, Materena points out to her mother, the position is not just for a cleaner, it's for a *professional* cleaner.

"Where's the difference?" asks Loana. "A cleaner is a cleaner. She cleans, she scrubs, she mops."

"*Oui,* but it says here Professional Cleaner."

"*Professional* doesn't mean anything, Materena! It's just a word."

Materena nods in agreement, but in her mind there's a big difference between a cleaner and a professional cleaner. She's not going to start an argument with her mother about the meaning of the word *professional,* though. She didn't ask her mother over to argue. She asked her mother over to help her write the letter of application.

That's what Madame Colette Dumonnier wants. She wants a letter, a reference, an interview. She wants a professional cleaner for two years, and there will be a contract.

This is highly unusual. Most Frenchwomen don't have contracts with their cleaner. They hire and fire as they wish. And cleaners don't mind a loose agreement. They're free to walk out the door the day the boss starts to be too bitchy, the day they decide they're *fiu* of cleaning houses, and anyway, they prefer to clean hotel rooms and meet tourists.

All right, back to the letter. Materena rubs her hands together.

She's never written a letter in her life, but it doesn't mean she can't begin today. In her opinion, writing is like talking, except that she has to worry about spelling mistakes. Materena bought a dictionary today to make sure her letter is perfect. She also bought a felt pen and nice writing paper.

"Dear Madame Colette Dumonnier?" Materena asks, looking up to her mother.

Loana gives her approval with a sharp nod and watches her daughter neatly write it down. "Now, first sentence: I'm a cleaner."

Materena grimaces and tells her mother that it is such a weak first line. Why should she tell Madame Colette she's a cleaner? If she's applying for the position as a cleaner it is because she is a cleaner, *non?* Why tell Madame Colette Dumonnier what she already knows?

"Materena," Loana snaps, "have you lived longer than me? How many letters have you written in your life?"

"Mamie . . ."

"*Non,* just tell me."

"Zero?"

"I've written three letters in my life, okay?"

Oui, true, Materena thinks, but they weren't letters to a potential boss, they were letters to a potential lover. It's very different, you can't compare. But Materena doesn't say this to her mother, it is only going to make her cranky.

"And what do you want to say in the first line?" asks Loana.

"I don't know."

"Well, what about, How are you today?" Loana says.

How are you today? Materena thinks. *Non.* It doesn't sound professional, and it sounds too much like she's trying to be friendly.

"What about, I hope all is well with you?" suggests Loana, seeing Materena's reaction. Materena isn't happy with this suggestion either.

"My name is Materena. I'm responding to an ad in the *Journal?*"

Materena puts her pen down and thanks her mother for all her wonderful ideas.

Loana gets up. "If my ideas are so wonderful, how come you're not writing them down? *Aue,* you write your letter yourself. I've got plants to water."

By nine o'clock that night Materena is still searching for her first line.

The first line in a letter is as important as the first line in a story. In Materena's experience as a listener, when people tell her stories, the first line can make her think, I can't wait to hear the rest of the story, or, What am I going to cook for dinner tonight? Then again, Materena knows many stories that start with a weak line only to become wonderful stories later on. You never know with stories.

But when you're writing a letter for a job you really want, you've got to instantly win over the person reading it. When you're writing a letter for a job you really want, you've got to be prepared to spend hours and hours on it.

Materena wants that job. She can clean with her eyes closed and she doesn't mind the two-year contract. A two-year contract means she won't get fired the day she goes into labor. It means Madame Colette Dumonnier understands that when a woman has a baby, she can't work for at least two weeks because she's got to recuperate from the birth and take care of all the Tahitian Welcome into the World rituals. Madame Colette Dumonnier is also going to understand that Materena will be taking her newborn to work for a few months.

If Madame Colette Dumonnier understands all of this, Materena really doesn't mind having a two-year contract with that woman.

Pito lets Materena collect his pay these days, but when your man lets you collect his pay, he expects to eat what he likes to eat. He expects to have razor blades available when he shaves. He expects, expects, expects. And when you buy yourself a tiny little thing, like a pair of cheap plastic earrings, you worry he's going to be cranky with you, he's going to ask you how much the earrings cost, etc., etc. It's quite nerve-racking spoiling yourself even a little with the money your man lets you have. Well anyway, for Materena it is. She'd like to be able to buy things without feeling guilty: lavender-scented soaps, a two-sided vinyl tablecloth reduced by 50 percent, and so forth.

Work is health, that song says. No work, eat stones.

Okay then, first line. The first line has to make Madame Colette Dumonnier exclaim, "I don't need to interview twenty-five people, I've found my professional cleaner!"

Materena thinks and thinks . . . She's thinking so much she gives herself a headache. It is now nine thirty. How hard is it to come up with a line that has less than ten words? You stupid, Materena tells herself as she gets up. She grabs the broom. She's got to do something with her hands to help her think clearly. She brooms, mops, scrubs the bathroom, wipes the kitchen walls . . . she rearranges the *garde-manger.*

It is twenty to one in the morning when, finally, the line Materena has been searching for comes into her mind. All excited, Materena sits back at the kitchen table and writes: "I've been cleaning houses since I was eight years old to help my mother." That first line, the magical line, unleashes the rest of the letter. Materena writes away furiously. She's going to check the spelling later on.

She writes that people can eat off her mother's floor. She says how the cleaning of a house always starts from the top and not the bottom, how a professional cleaner must be able to keep secrets because she's bound to see things, find things, hear things, things that don't concern anyone else but the boss. She writes that she's six months pregnant and all is well with her and the baby.

Once she's satisfied with her words Materena checks the spelling and writes a clean copy. And another. And another. Until she's finally happy her letter is as perfect as she can possibly make it.

Next morning, Materena kisses the envelope containing the very important letter before posting it with the words, "Okay, letter, off you go. Good luck."

The waiting begins . . . One day, two days, four. A whole week. Each day when the postman approaches, Materena's heart starts to go *thump-thump* with hope. When the postman walks past her house Materena's heart goes *thump-thump* with dejection.

By the second week Materena is sure Madame Colette Dumonnier threw her letter in the trash the second she read it because it was so stupid. She didn't care that you could eat off Materena's mother's floor.

Loana says, "It's God's plan for you not to work at that woman's house. God always has a plan."

This isn't making Materena feel any better. She's thinking, If I can't even get an interview for a cleaning job, what am I good for?

Just as Materena is about to give up on Madame Colette Dumonnier, the postman slides a letter under the door. Materena shrieks with delight, does a little dance with her son, rubs her belly, and tells her daughter, "Eh, girl? Guess what? Mamie has got an interview!" She smells the letter, waves it in the air, she puts the letter on the kitchen table and looks at it for a while.

What if Madame Colette Dumonnier has written to say thank you, but no thank you?

Ouh, that is the last time Materena is applying for a job in writing! She much prefers the usual system. You stand in a line with all the applicants, you talk to the woman who wants a cleaner, you get told on the spot if you have the job or not. There's no waiting in agony.

Materena has applied for a position as a cleaner three times that way and she was successful three times. For some reason Frenchwomen like the look of her. They like the fact that she dresses like a cleaner. She doesn't wear short dresses and makeup. She doesn't look like a cleaner who steals rich husbands.

One of Materena's bosses went back to her country, one boss moved to another island, and the other cried when Materena resigned so that she could be a full-time mother.

Materena opens the envelope, sighing with anxiety.

Inside is a two-page letter. Materena wonders what Madame Colette Dumonnier has to tell her. She glances at the messy writing, the words crossed out with a line, the spelling mistakes, the exclamation marks. She reads that Madame Colette

Dumonnier has been in Tahiti for six months and she still doesn't understand this island! The last time Madame Colette Dumonnier needed a plumber she had to wait four days!

Many people here shouldn't be holding a driver's license! she continues. Not many people here wear shoes! The cemeteries are rather splendid! Many people here go to church! Women here have a lot of children! Men here drink a lot! The sound of the ukulele is rather nice! The mosquitoes here are very vicious! It is very hot here!

Anyway, she also writes that Materena was the only person who responded to the ad. And since Madame Colette Dumonnier is only days from going into labor with her first child, Materena's got the job. Congratulations. The address is . . . See you on Monday.

There won't be any contract, as Madame Colette Dumonnier is not sure she'll last that long on this strange island.

The Everyday Life

Materena's baby was expected to arrive in this world two weeks ago, but she doesn't want to come out of her mother's belly yet. Materena isn't too worried. Some babies arrive before the due date, like Tapeta's daughter Rose, some babies arrive right on time, like Madame Colette's son, Marc, and some babies arrive after the due date.

Loana doesn't feel too happy about her granddaughter's delayed arrival. She is panicking. She visits Materena every day to see how things are and to ask, "Can you feel the baby kicking?"

She's here again tonight, on her way to a prayer meeting, to see how things are and to ask, "Can you feel the baby kicking?"

Tonight for some reason the baby is sound asleep. To reassure her mother, Materena shakes her belly a little and gently taps on it several times. The baby kicks Materena in the ribs, stopping Materena's breath for a few seconds, and Loana sighs with relief. Before she leaves, though, Loana makes Materena promise to go and see the doctor the next day to check that all is fine with the baby. "You don't want the baby to be strangled by the umbilical cord," she says.

The next day Materena goes to see her doctor, because a promise to her mother is sacred.

He's very busy, says the doctor's secretary. The best he can do is to see Materena in four days. Materena thanks the doctor's secretary and walks out of the office, but five steps later she stops to think. No, it doesn't suit her to see the doctor in four days, she wants to see him today. Materena has always accepted whatever appointments her doctor's secretary has given her, but not this time.

She marches back to the doctor's office and, adopting a pitiful air, she asks for an earlier appointment.

The doctor's secretary sighs. "Are you having contractions?" she asks.

"*Non,*" admits Materena sweetly, so as not to aggravate the doctor's secretary. Everybody knows that if you want an appointment with the doctor when it suits you, you better be nice to the woman who makes the appointments. Materena explains how she's very worried about the umbilical cord strangling her baby. Another sigh from the doctor's secretary. "Well, how about tomorrow morning at seven o'clock? Dr. Marshall is very busy."

This is more suitable for Materena. "Eh, eh, *merci beaucoup,*" she says. "Tomorrow is good."

At seven o'clock in the morning precisely, on Wednesday the twenty-sixth of July, Materena is in the doctor's waiting room with Loana, who has Materena's suitcase for the hospital just in case there's going to be an emergency. Loana also has with her the coconut for Materena to drink from to make the baby slide out with ease.

The waiting room is already filled with patients: three

pregnant women, two old men, and seven young men after a medical certificate.

At twenty past nine, Dr. Marshall is finally free to see Materena. He takes her pulse, he listens to her heartbeat and to the baby's heartbeat, then gently taps Materena's belly several times, reads Materena's medical card, does some calculations on a piece of paper. Then he looks into Materena's eyes and says, "Give me one minute." He grabs his telephone and dials. Materena turns her head the other way so that Dr. Marshall doesn't think she's listening.

She opens her ears.

Dr. Marshall is talking and talking, and Materena understands in between the medical *charabia* words that she's going to the hospital. Dr. Marshall puts the telephone down and tells her that they are going to activate the birth.

Well, doctors know best. But she does ask her doctor if there will be a problem with the umbilical cord strangling her baby. Dr. Marshall starts to chuckle, but when he sees Materena's very serious face he puts his serious face back on. "*Non,*" he says. "I'm not anticipating any problems."

When Materena tells her mother of Dr. Marshall's decision, Loana gets cranky. "See now! Lucky I told you to go and see Doctor! *Aue,* children, eh! We think that when they're grown up we don't have to worry anymore, but the worrying never stops!"

Loana thinks they are going to the hospital in the ambulance, and when she finds out that there is no ambulance, she gets crankier. "And how are we supposed to go the hospital? On foot?"

After two trucks and forty stairs to the maternity ward, Materena, with her mother carrying the suitcase, rings the labor room's buzzer, and the nurse tells her to wait in the corridor. Sitting on the bench directly opposite the labor room, Loana starts to cry as she holds her daughter's hand, stroking it lovingly. "Be strong, girl . . . you're a woman . . . we're strong."

It is about eleven o'clock. To make the minutes go faster Materena and Loana talk. They talk about this and that: Materena's being born with swollen eyelids on a concrete table with Auntie Stella bending Loana to make the baby come out; Loana's being born with slanted eyes in a bamboo hut . . . They talk and talk, and meanwhile the minutes turn into an hour.

They stop talking to look at a young pregnant girl doing the hundred steps with her mother by her side. Then the door of the labor room opens and out walks a nurse wheeling a mother and her newborn, and they hear the screams from behind the door: the screams of suffering, the moans, the screams of joy.

At two o'clock Loana says out loud, "Eh well, we could die in this hospital and no one would come!"

At half past two, Loana rushes over to the nurse wheeling another mother and her newborn out of the labor room. "Nurse?" she says. "My daughter has been here since eleven o'clock, she's here to have her birth activated, and she hasn't eaten anything since this morning."

"It's not our fault everybody decided to give birth today!" the nurse snaps. "They all went to the same party, or what?" And she hurries away with her squeaky shoes, pushing that wheelchair.

Loana, hands on her hips, shoots her in the back with her cranky eyes.

Not long after, another nurse walks out of the labor room, but this time with an empty wheelchair. Materena hurries to that nurse to explain the story about the umbilical cord. The nurse, smiling with compassion, replies, "Don't worry, you're next."

An excited Loana hurries to the telephone to call the family: Pito at work, Mama Roti at her cousin's, Cousin Rita, who is looking after Tamatoa, an auntie and another auntie, and a few favorite cousins.

Little by little the relatives arrive and get comfortable on the bench and on the ground and they joke around to make the pregnant woman laugh, to give her strength before she goes into the labor room. But when the minutes turn into another hour, everybody gets tired of joking around and laughing and everybody becomes silent. Mama Roti and her cousin get the cards out.

Another hour passes and another, and at about five thirty Pito takes off with one of his cousins to get some breadsticks and cheese for the family.

"And you, *chérie?*" Pito asks Materena. "You want something special?"

"*Oui,* please."

Materena wants a packet of Twisties, the green ones.

"The green ones?" says Pito, puzzled.

"*Oui,* the chicken-flavored ones, you see? Not the red packet, the green one."

As soon as he disappears, a nurse walks out of the labor room with a notepad and calls out, "Materena Mahi!"

The relatives start to cry, wishing Materena good luck. Loana runs to get Pito, hoping to catch him in time, as Materena follows the nurse into the labor room, feeling very anxious now. It's not the same when you walk into the labor room in pain, then you can't wait to start pushing. When you walk into the labor room not in pain, you ask yourself, What are they going to do to me?

Materena is made to lie down on the bed in one of the delivery rooms. In the delivery room on the left side of the curtain, a woman is yelling her head off, but in the other delivery room, on the right, a woman is asking the midwife (in between pushing) if she's earning good money.

Materena takes a deep breath, trying to distract herself by remembering all the traditional Tahitian rules about giving birth.

First rule: no shouting as you push the baby into the world, because when you shout the baby inside gets frightened, and it's not wise to be born frightened. It's enough that one second the baby is in his mama's belly and it's dark and comfortable and warm, and next minute he's in this strange place he doesn't know. And the light is hurting his eyes, he can't breathe, and it's cold.

Second rule: no crying out loud as you push the baby into the world, because when you cry out loud, the baby about to be born gets all sad, and it's not wise to be born sad. The baby is going to be a crying-for-no-reason baby, and then that baby is going to grow into a crying-for-no-reason person. And when you're a crying-for-no-reason person and you're a woman, life is just going to be one misery after the next. One little pain, and that's it, you'll cry your eyes out. It's much better for you to be a woman who cries only for big pains.

Third rule: no cursing and screaming words of insult as you push your baby into the world, because when you curse and scream words of insult, the baby inside gets all cranky, and it's not wise to be born cranky. That baby is going to be a cranky-for-no-reason baby, and then that baby is going to grow into a cranky-for-no-reason person.

Materena is trying to remember all these rules while a nurse, all smiling and friendly, puts a drip into her arm. For a long while after the drip is inserted nothing happens, and Materena is starting to get really bored until, at last, she gets a contraction. She's so happy! At least something is happening. The next contraction is a bit more painful, but it is still comfortable. Within an hour the contractions are so painful that Materena is moaning, "*Aue!* When is this going to stop?"

Three times she calls out to the nurse that she is ready to push and three times the nurse says, "You've got a long way to go yet," and poor Materena is left all alone to deal with her suffering.

And what suffering, eh? Materena feels like smacking her

cousin Tapeta, who told her, "Don't worry, giving birth gets easier and easier with each child."

Easier!

"*Aue!*" Materena yells. By now, Materena is in too much pain to follow the traditional Tahitian rules about giving birth. In between contractions, she tries to get out of bed, but her head is spinning, not counting the tubes and everything. She falls back on the bed, moaning, with a fist shoved in her mouth as another contraction comes on and goes on and on and on. Materena feels like eating her hand. Right that moment she would give anything to have one leg (both legs) amputated instead of this torture. Even to have all her teeth taken out with pliers would be a pleasure. Her whole body tenses, her legs tremble, until at last the contraction eases up and Materena sighs with relief, though she knows that everything is going to start up all over again in less than thirty seconds.

"She's having a baby girl," Materena hears a woman say. "Girls hurt their mother from the day they come into the world. It's like that. I can talk because I've got six girls . . . Girls are a curse, trust me."

"*Oui,* she's having a girl, all right," another woman is saying. "It's more painful to push girls into the world because they don't want to be born. They resist. They know what they're in for in this world of miseries."

Another contraction comes up and Materena loses track of the conversation, too busy dealing with her suffering. "*Aue!*"

The curtain is suddenly pulled open and a big mama midwife, smiling and introducing herself as Mary, walks in and closes the curtain behind her. She checks how everything is going and is very pleased to inform Materena that it is time to push. Grinding her teeth, Materena pushes and pushes, but nothing is coming out.

"Push!" Mary the midwife commands.

"That's what I'm doing!" Materena growls.

She pushes and pushes, she pushes and yells her head off for twenty excruciating minutes. But still nothing comes out.

Mary thinks her hand will hurry things up. That hand (the whole lot) goes in and Materena shrieks so loud that the hand quickly retreats.

"You're not helping, mama," Mary says.

"Just take that baby out of me!"

"Let's calm ourselves, okay?" Mary, looking slightly worried now, commands, "Push. Come on, push . . . Give me that baby!"

Materena pushes. Nothing happens.

The curtain is pulled open, and what a relief it is for Materena to see Auntie Stella, long regarded as the best midwife on the island.

"Auntie Stella," Materena cries. "My baby doesn't want to come out."

Stella kisses Materena's forehead and tells her to be strong and not to worry. Then she begins her inspection and concludes that the only way for the baby to come out is for Materena to push standing up. Let gravity help. Stella frees Materena of the tubes and helps her get out of bed.

At that precise moment, Pito walks in, red-eyed, with Materena's packet of Twisties.

"But!" Stella exclaims. "You've smoked *paka,* or what? Unbelievable! All you men are the same!" Materena is in too much pain to say anything. She feels like all her insides are going to fall out. But she can't believe Pito bought her the red packet of Twisties when she asked for the green one.

"Come here," Stella orders Pito. "Make yourself useful and put that packet of Twisties on the bed, you idiot."

Pito puts the packet of Twisties on the bed.

"Stand behind your woman."

Pito stands behind Materena.

"Put your hands under her arms."

Pito puts his hands under Materena's arms.

"Hold her good!"

Pito holds Materena good.

"Mary . . . quick, grab a pillow and put it on the floor here," Stella goes on with her orders. And to Materena she adds, "Next contraction, I want you to push real hard. Don't stop until I tell you, okay? Don't worry if you rip. Baby has got to come out *now.*"

They all wait for the next contraction as Materena begs her baby to please come out. Then it comes, and Materena pushes with all her heart and soul and her baby daughter makes her entrance into the world upside down, with her mother's hands underneath her head in case the baby falls, but there's no need. Stella has it all under control. When the baby slides out, there she is with her hands open, ready to catch.

Leilani Loana Rita Imelda comes into the world the week her cousin Rose is baptized and the week her older brother falls off the table and breaks his arm. She comes into the world frowning and with her eyes wide open.

Auntie Stella, relieved that all is well, laughs and says, "Oh, but we have a thinker here. We have a professor." Then, to Mary, she asks, "What's the time?"

It's twenty-nine past eight precisely.

And Materena cries out with joy, "Welcome into the world, girl!"

There and then she feels that magical bond mothers feel when they see their child for the very first time. Materena gets back onto the bed with great difficulty while Stella holds the newborn and Pito follows Mary, keeping an eye on where he's putting his feet. Materena can't wait to embrace her beautiful, greased baby girl.

At last, the newborn is placed on her mother's belly. "My baby," Materena cries out with joy. "My beautiful baby girl . . . look at all that hair you've got . . . my *chérie* . . . my friend."

"Eh well, that's one very lucky baby," Stella says as she cuts the umbilical cord.

"Look at your daughter," Materena tells Pito. "Look how beautiful she is." Perhaps the *paka* is affecting Pito's vision, but he really can't see what Materena is seeing.

Over the next few days Materena tries very hard to breast-feed her daughter, but there's a problem with her breasts. They are hard like cement and swollen like grapefruit, with veins popping out everywhere along with lumps and cracks. Breast-feeding is a real torture, but Materena keeps on trying. She puts hot compresses on her breasts, and cabbage leaves, and she massages her breasts all day long.

In the end, the hungry crying baby girl is offered a bottle, and the nurse on duty is pleased to see her drink it all in one go. After that first bottle, Leilani seals her lips real tight whenever Materena's nipple comes near her mouth.

Materena is so devastated. For her, breast-feeding is the reward that comes after the pain of the birth. Breast-feeding is what makes the mother and child get close, bond. She tells her mother that.

Loana's reply is a reprimand. "Stop talking nonsense . . . It's not breast-feeding that makes a mother and her child bond. It's everyday life."

The everyday day life Tahitian-style begins with the Welcome into the World rituals. So here is Materena, accompanied by her mother, introducing *bébé* Leilani to her relatives, and everyone has something *gentil* to say about Loana's granddaughter, who came into the world upside down. That she has beautiful eyes, long legs, a wide nose, the only kind of nose to have when you're a woman. Then it's off to the cemetery to introduce the little one to the dead.

After that, all Materena wants to do is rest, but she catches the truck to Punaauia instead to meet her mother-in-law so that she can introduce Pito's daughter to the family. And what a pain Mama Roti is! Mama Roti is hopeless at introducing newborns. Instead of talking about her newborn granddaughter, she talks about herself. "Eh, Uncle, come and look at Pito's daughter!" Then, next minute, "Uncle, I've got to do some tests for my eyesight tomorrow. Can you believe it! My doctor is saying I'm going blind!" Materena is so annoyed, even more annoyed to hear one of Mama Roti's cousins comment on how Leilani is so small, that *her* granddaughter was so much bigger when she was born — 8½ pounds. You don't make comparisons when a baby is being introduced to you! You just give compliments!

That day Mama Roti gives Materena a lime tree to be Leilani's tree, but Materena already chose Leilani's tree, a beautiful frangipani tree, to be planted after the baptism next week along with Leilani's placenta. Materena also chose Leilani's baptism robe and the godparents (Ati and his girlfriend, Marieta, who left him two weeks later to marry a legionnaire).

The night before the baptism Materena cuddles her baby all night long because Leilani is crying nonstop. It's always like that before a baptism. The baby cries because the devil is cranky at the thought of losing another soul, and so he makes the baby cry. But it could be that Materena is really stressed tonight and her baby can feel it. Materena is stressed because her daughter's baptism is heading toward a night of drinking, and Materena doesn't want that. Just looking at Pito and his cousins drinking and joking around is making her heart twitch into a knot. Materena doesn't mind drinking at weddings, but at baptisms, come on, where's the civilization? Why do we have to drink every time there's something to celebrate?

Materena is so annoyed, but for her daughter's sake (it's enough that Leilani has to deal with the devil) she settles down. She wraps her baby tight in a cloth, holds her close to her heart, and recites prayers. Never carry baby with her head over your shoulder, looking out into darkness, because the devil is lurking around. Hold baby tight with her head buried in your chest.

Hold baby tight and love your baby with all your *mana,* the power within you.

The Encyclopedia

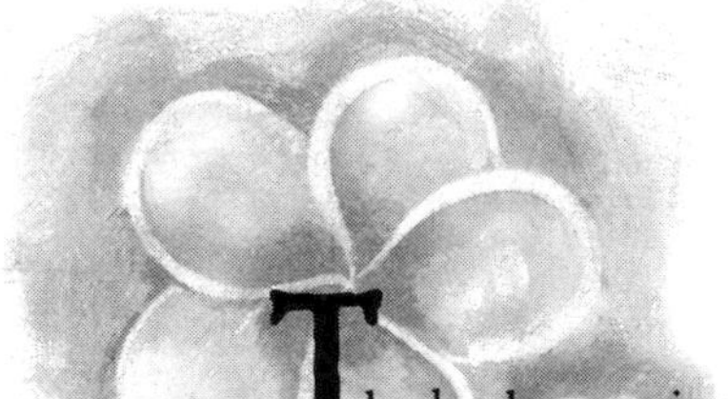

The bathroom is scrubbed every day in Materena's house because Materena can't stand her bathroom dirty. Soap scum makes her cranky and so does hair in the bathroom drain, toothpaste smeared on the tap, grime around the tap rings . . . Well anyway, Materena scrubs her bathroom every day.

She's scrubbing, scrubbing really hard and wishing her twelve-year-old daughter, also scrubbing, would stop talking, but when your daughter helps you with the housework you don't criticize. You just smile and nod, you answer her questions, or you say nothing because you don't know what to say.

"Mamie?" Leilani taps her mother's hand. "Did you hear me?" She's waiting for her mother to explain why it doesn't snow in Tahiti, and once again, Materena will have to say that she doesn't know.

This is happening more and more these days. Let's just say that Materena can't keep up with Leilani's complicated questions. Who started the French Revolution? What's the medical term for the neck? There's a limit to what Materena knows. People can't know everything.

Aue, Materena was much more comfortable with her daughter's questions when they weren't complicated: Who invented the broom? (A woman.) Is it true that eating charcoal makes the teeth white? (Absolutely not — brushing your teeth every day with toothpaste makes them white.) Who invented the rake? (A woman.) What time does the first star appear? (The first star appears at quarter past six.) Who invented the wheelbarrow? (A woman.) Is God a woman or a man? (God is everything that is beautiful.)

Leilani used to say how clever her mother was, but these days Leilani doesn't say this anymore. So, why doesn't it snow in Tahiti? How would Materena know this? "Girl," she sighs, "I don't know why it doesn't snow in Tahiti."

"Ah . . . I knew you wouldn't."

"Why did you ask me, then, if you knew I didn't know?" asks Materena, a bit cranky.

"I just hoped you knew."

"Well, stop hoping. Ask me about the ancestors, the old days, cleaning tricks, budgeting, who's who in the family album and at the cemetery, plants, words of wisdom Tahitian-style, traditions. Don't ask me why it doesn't snow in Tahiti. Ask your teacher."

"I do, but Madame always says, 'That's not what this lesson is about, Leilani.' " Leilani drops her scrubbing brush and stomps out of the bathroom complaining that she doesn't know anybody who can answer her questions, and that all she gets is "Be quiet, Leilani."

Aue! Materena feels so guilty now. Here, she's going to give her daughter a kiss . . . and some coins to get herself an ice block at the Chinese store. My poor girl, Materena thinks. She's always stuck at home with me.

Materena finds Leilani reading yesterday's newspapers at the kitchen table, elbows on the table. "Girl?" Materena isn't going to say anything about the elbows on the table, how it's rude and everything. "You want to get yourself an ice block at the Chinese store?"

"*Non,* I'm fine."

"You're sure, *chérie?*" Materena kisses the top of Leilani's head.

"I'm just having a rest. I'll come and help you again in a minute, okay?"

"*Non,* just relax."

"*Non,* I want to help you," Leilani insists.

"All right, then . . . But don't worry if you can't help me, you help me enough as it is." And with this Materena escapes to her bathroom and locks the door. Ah, what peace. Materena can sure do with a few minutes of silence.

A few minutes later: "Mamie?" It's Leilani calling again.

"*Oui.*" Materena chuckles, thinking, Already?

"There's someone at the door."

"Who is it?" Materena steps out of the bathroom, scrubbing brush in hand.

"It's a woman with a briefcase."

"*Eh hia.*" Materena is annoyed. That woman at the door is here to sell her something, like perfumes, or to talk about religion, and Materena is in the mood for neither. "Tell that woman I'm not here."

"Mamie, just go and say good afternoon to her, I feel so sorry for her." Leilani explains how she's been watching from behind the curtains the woman door-knocking in the neighborhood. Two relatives closed their door on her, one relative opened the door and waved the woman away, and one relative walked out without a word and went on to water her plants.

"What are you doing spying on the relatives?" cackles Materena. "It's to give you ideas for your memoirs?"

"I was just looking," protests Leilani. "Mamie, the woman is waiting for you."

"She asked to speak to me?"

"*Non,* she said, 'Is your mother home?' "

"And what did you say?"

"I said, *oui,* my mother is home, she's scrubbing the bathroom."

"Couldn't you say I was asleep?" Materena puts her scrubbing brush down and rearranges her chignon and her pareu. "People should know we're Catholics around here and that we've got no money," Materena says, walking to the door. "You only have to look at the houses."

"Good afternoon," Materena greets the Frenchwoman, who can't be more than twenty years old and who looks a bit like a gypsy with her floral dress, sandals, and loose hair.

"Oh, good afternoon, madame," the young woman says with a rather strange yet beautiful accent.

"Are you from France, girl?" Materena asks.

"*Oui,* from Marseilles." The young woman smiles.

"Ah, Marseilles." Materena nods knowingly.

"Have you been to Marseilles?" The young woman asks Materena eagerly.

"Girl, I've never been out of Tahiti in my whole life." Materena laughs.

"Where's Marseilles?" asks Leilani.

"It is in the south of France . . . I could show you on a map if you like."

Before Materena has the chance to tell the young woman not to worry about it and to go on with her mission, Leilani gives her consent. Yes, she'd like to see where Marseilles is on the map of France. In a flash an encyclopedia comes out of the woman's briefcase as she explains that she always has an encyclopedia with her to show people what the encyclopedia set looks like. And it's just by chance that she has volume 7, F–H, with her.

"You sell encyclopedias?" Materena asks.

In one breath the young woman confirms that she is selling encyclopedias, and there's a promotion (a 20 percent reduction). She goes on about how much she loves encyclopedias, she's had an encyclopedia set since she was eight years old, she's on holiday in Tahiti (one of the most beautiful countries in the world), she arrived two days ago.

Ouf, that's a lot to spill in one go, Materena thinks. But how nice to say that Tahiti is one of the most beautiful countries in the world. "Come inside the house," Materena says. "Let's sit at the kitchen table." The young woman doesn't need to be asked twice. With one giant step she's in the house before Materena can ask her (politely) to take her shoes off. It isn't a Tahitian custom to take your shoes off before walking into a house, but it's nice when you do, that way you don't bring dirt into the house. Well anyway, it's too late for Materena to tell that woman about shoes and everything. But for Leilani it isn't. "You can't come in the house with your shoes on," she says, her eyes widening in stupefaction. "You're going to put dirt on Mamie's carpet."

The young woman, her face red with embarrassment, hurries back outside. She takes her shoes off and neatly places them next to the row of thongs by the door. "I'm very sorry," she says. "I've just arrived, you see. I'm not aware of this country's customs as yet." Walking in, she adds, "Oh, it's so lovely here."

"It's comfortable, girl." Materena smiles, relieved her house is very clean today. Materena's house is always clean, but today it really shines. Everything has been dusted, there are no cobwebs on the ceiling and there is no fluff on the carpet.

"Oh," the woman exclaims, stopping right in front of the potted plant placed in the middle of the living room. "Is this a real plant?" she asks, stroking the leaves. Before Materena can say, "Of course it's a real plant!" the woman inquires if it is a Tahitian custom to place a potted plant in the middle of the living room.

"Well," Materena replies, "*oui* and *non.* In Tahiti, we believe that a potted plant —"

"It's to hide the missing carpet square." Here, Leilani has informed the visitor. And right before her mother's horrified eyes, she lifts the pot so that the visitor can see for herself, and explains that everybody does this in Tahiti. They use potted plants to hide missing carpet squares, holes in walls, anything.

"I see." The woman nods. "It's a very intelligent way of doing things." She walks to the wall to admire a quilt pinned to the wall. "*Magnifique!* Whoever made that quilt is talented. This quilt is truly a piece of art." She goes on about the intensity of the bright flowers, the intricate patterns, the balance of it all, the use of geometry.

"My mother made that quilt when I got married," Materena says, caressing it tenderly.

"Mamie is going to be wrapped in that quilt in her coffin," Leilani adds.

Materena gives her daughter a quick, cranky look. You don't tell strangers stories that only concern the family! The woman looks to Materena. "Is this a custom in Tahiti?"

"An old custom, girl. Not many people are wrapped in quilts when they're dead these days, but I want to be wrapped in a quilt my mother made just for me because, you know, once you're linked with your mother through the umbilical cord you're linked for the eternity."

"These are such beautiful words, madame . . . I'm so honored to meet you."

Materena cackles, thinking this girl has got to be the best seller she's ever met in her life. She is now looking at the framed photographs below the quilt, and Materena doesn't mind. If photographs are on the wall it means it's fine for people to look at them, you don't need permission. You only need permission to look through a photo album.

"This is my beautiful oldest son, Tamatoa, at his confirmation," Materena tells the interested visitor. "He's playing soccer at the moment with his father and uncle. And this is my youngest son, Moana, at his confirmation. He's also playing soccer with his father and uncle at the moment. This is my mother when she was young, this is me when I was young, and this is my husband when he was young. This is my husband and me when we got married six months ago . . . with our beautiful children."

"Is it the custom to marry late in Tahiti?"

"Oh, *oui* and *non,*" replies Materena. "In Tahiti we believe that it's unwise to marry before —"

"Men don't like to get married in Tahiti. They always give women excuses and they're lazy."

Again, Materena gives her big-mouth daughter a discreet look to be quiet.

"And is that you?" the woman asks Leilani, pointing to a framed newspaper clip.

"*Oui,* that's my girl." Materena sighs with pride. "It was after a running competition. She came in fiftieth, but there were thousands of competitors."

"One hundred and twenty, Mamie."

"And this is a school award Leilani got when she was ten years old," Materena says, ignoring Leilani's last comment. "For a story she wrote."

"Do you like to write?" asks the woman, smiling at Leilani.

"Oh *oui,* she loves to write!" Materena exclaims. "She's always writing, that one, she writes, she reads, she's very intelligent, all my children are intelligent, and to think that I'm just a professional cleaner."

"Oh, you're a cleaner!"

"A professional cleaner," Materena corrects. Because there *is* a difference.

"I admire professional cleaners!" the woman exclaims. "My mother is a professional cleaner, I believe professional cleaners ought to be decorated!" Materena looks at the young woman with little eyes. What's this? she thinks. It's to make me buy an encyclopedia set?

"I admire professional cleaners too," says Leilani. "It's so hard to clean. Last time I helped Mamie clean Madame Colette's house, I was so tired. I had to sleep in the truck on the way home."

"You didn't help me," Materena hurries to add. She just doesn't want the encyclopedia woman to start thinking things. "When you told me you wanted to be a cleaner, I had to show you how hard cleaning is." Materena explains to the Frenchwoman that it is definitely not her plan for her daughter to become a cleaner. In fact, she's always pushed her daughter to see beyond cleaning and to get a job that has nothing to do with a broom and a scrubbing brush.

"You are a clever woman," the encyclopedia woman says. "May I show you the encyclopedia?"

"Sure. What's your name, by the way, girl?"

"Chantal."

"Ah, what a beautiful name you have, Chantal. Okay then, Chantal, you and Leilani make yourself comfortable at the table, I'm going to make us a lemonade."

"And what is your name, madame?" Chantal asks with a genuine smile.

"Materena."

"You have a beautiful name too, and," turning to Leilani, Chantal adds, "your name is lovely as well."

Leilani informs the visitor that she was called after a Hawaiian ancestor, but not Leilani Lexter, whose husband (Tinirau Mahi) soon regretted having married her because she liked partying too much. "I was called after Leilani Bodie," Leilani says. "She was very serious. She was a medicine woman."

"Oh . . . well, you might become a medicine woman too," says Chantal.

"I don't think so. I don't like sick people."

"We never know!" Chantal exclaims as she sits at the kitchen table.

"May I ask you a few questions?" Materena, cutting the lemons for the lemonade, hears Leilani ask. Chantal invites Leilani to ask her as many questions as she wants. She's in no hurry at all. Materena cackles. Chantal, you have no idea what you've just gotten yourself into.

"Why doesn't it snow in Tahiti?" Chantal repeats Leilani's question. "That is a very intelligent question, and the answer is that Tahiti is too close to the equator." She asks for some papers and a pen, which Leilani hurries to get, and next minute, Leilani is getting a free geography lesson.

Now Leilani would like to know, What is the medical term for the neck?

Easy, the Frenchwoman quickly draws a human body, and next minute, Leilani is getting a free biology lesson.

And who started the French Revolution?

Easy . . .

And do fish sleep?

Of course — Chantal smiles — but because fish don't have eyelids they can't close their eyes. But fish do sleep.

On and on and on Chantal shares her knowledge with a delighted Leilani, the knowledge she insists she got after years of reading encyclopedias and other books of interest.

The main salt in the sea is the same as the salt people put on their food. Its chemical name is sodium chloride.

Plants make much of their food from water, carbon dioxide, and sunlight. This process, called photosynthesis, produces oxygen.

When we're sick our body temperature goes up above normal, which is 98.6 degrees. This rise in temperature is called a fever and is triggered by the germs that cause the illness. They release chemicals that act on the part of the brain whose job it is to control temperature. This in turn produces other chemicals that make us feel cold.

The human body has more than six hundred muscles, which together make up more than 40 percent of the body's weight.

Sixty percent of the body consists of water.

Hiccups are caused when our diaphragm (the wall of muscle between the abdomen and the chest) goes into spasm.

Fingernails grow four times as fast as toenails.

By the time Materena is signing her name at the bottom of the form binding her to thirty-six repayments for the encyclopedias, Chantal looks very drained.

She earned her commission, that's for sure.

Bedsheets, Onions, Coconut Milk, and Women

Materena's deal with the children is: Read the encyclopedias and you won't have to lift a finger around the house. But Leilani is the only one who has taken up Materena's offer. You won't see Leilani with a scrubbing brush these days. She's too busy reading her encyclopedias, which she has personally covered so that they won't get dirty. Leilani also washes her hands before opening a page of her precious books, and you won't catch her reading and eating at the same time.

Materena is certainly pleased with her daughter's fondness for the encyclopedias, but she really wishes her sons were fond of them too. So far, ever since the encyclopedias made their theatrical entrance into the house two weeks ago (in front of the entire curious neighborhood), Tamatoa has opened one single page to see what the word *sex* had to say. He was so disappointed he shoved the book back in the bookcase. He had expected to see explicit drawings. As for Moana, he makes an effort now and then to read the encyclopedias, but Materena knows it is only to make her happy. Moana sits on the sofa with an encyclopedia opened, but his eyes are on the wall.

Presently the boys are doing push-ups outside, right in front of their father and Uncle Ati, who are sitting comfortably in a chair with a beer in hand, counting from one to ten. When Pito and Ati get to the number ten, the boys have a quick rest, long enough for Papi and Uncle to take a couple of sips.

Materena peeps outside from behind the curtains and shakes her head with disapproval, but what is bothering her more now is to watch her youngest son crumple onto the ground as soon as his set of ten push-ups is finished.

My poor baby, Materena thinks.

"One!" Pito and Ati call out, and the brothers go on pumping their muscles again.

Moana is red in the face, sweating and suffering, not keeping up at all with his older brother, who, to make matters worse, decides to clap his hands together as he lifts his body up. Tamatoa just has to show off that he's unbeatable.

"Ten!"

Tamatoa keeps going as his brother sags to the ground. Pito and Ati take a couple of sips.

"One!"

Aue, Materena can't bear to watch. "Pito!" she calls. "I want the boys inside the house for a bit of reading."

Pito glances at Ati and shakes his head. "What did I tell you," he says. "She's obsessed with her encyclopedias."

"Well," Ati says, "we've got to see beyond our nose."

"*Merci,* Ati." Materena smiles a sweet smile to her husband's best friend, who smiles back, winking.

"Come on, boys, chop-chop, on your feet."

"Mamie," Tamatoa protests, "I just want to be strong."

"Me too," Moana follows.

"One!" Pito begins.

The training continues. Materena can't believe her eyes! Where's the respect for the mother?

"Five!"

It's like I'm invisible, Materena yells in her head. What I say doesn't count!

"Ten." Pito adds that he'd like now to see sit-ups. "Go and get a towel." The boys run into the house and are back within seconds, but Materena is not going to let her boys put clean towels on the bloody ground.

"Eh, ho," she says, grabbing the towels off her boys. "Do you think I'm a washing machine?"

"Materena, stop annoying us. Go and dust your encyclopedias and give me those towels." This is Pito's order. Materena marches to the house, her clean towels safely tucked under her arm before Pito has the chance to snatch them off her, and as she puts them back where they belong, an idea comes into her mind. Well, if it's so important for Tamatoa and Moana to be strong, they can start making their own bed, washing their own clothes, and cooking.

"So you want to be strong?" Materena asks her boys the next day when they are arm wrestling at the kitchen table.

"Yeah," Tamatoa replies, looking his mother straight in the eye and flattening his brother's arm on the table.

"And you?" Materena asks Moana, who's rubbing his arm. "You want to be strong?"

He nods, grimacing a little.

So far, so good. Now to Materena's mission, but first here's a packet of Delta Cream cookies to make sure the boys don't run off. They're into those cookies in a flash, and so Materena makes herself comfortable at the kitchen table and begins. "You know how Papi always says you can't teach an old dog new tricks?

Well, it's not true. It's never too late to learn new tricks. It's only too late when you're dead. You understand?" Tamatoa laughs his head off and nearly chokes on his cookie.

"What's so funny?" Materena asks.

"It's your voice, Mamie, it's so *serioso.*"

"Well, this is a *serioso* situation."

Both of the boys are now laughing. "Boys!" Materena can't stop laughing either, but she better, because the cookies are disappearing fast and once they're gone, she'll be talking to the chairs. "Boys . . . come on . . . I just want one minute of your time, okay . . . just one minute. The world has changed. Women are doing lots of things they didn't do in my day, like driving trucks. So men have to change too." Materena informs her sons that women of today are only interested in men who know how to do women's things, like ironing, hanging clothes on the line, folding clothes, sweeping, making the bed, cooking . . . Men who know nothing about these things can't get a woman. "And I'm telling both of you," says Materena in her *serioso* voice, "I'm not going to be your wife, okay? As soon as you're men, you have to look after yourselves. Mama Roti gave me a man who couldn't cook, couldn't do zero, and I'm not going to do this to my daughters-in-law."

"Mamie." Tamatoa is up. "You're on a different planet now, I've got things to do."

"Tamatoa! I haven't finished!" But Tamatoa walks away, because the last person he fears in this world is his mother.

Moana stays, because the person he loves the most in this world is his mother. "Mamie," he says, taking his mother's hand, "I'll listen to you . . . so women like when men cook?"

"Oh *oui!*" she exclaims. "You want me to teach you how to cook?"

"Okay."

Later, in front of the *garde-manger,* Moana gets his first cooking lesson.

"A good cook," Materena tells him, "can cook anything with whatever is in the *garde-manger,* but always make sure to have cans of tomatoes and coconut milk, onions, and rice in your *garde-manger.*"

And to Tamatoa, standing at the fridge snorting, Materena says, "As for you, you can change your own bed from now on. You're going to be fourteen years old soon, and I sure don't want to be changing your bedsheets by then."

On the Subject of Cleaners

In the Mahi family you're never going to hear a woman say about another woman that the reason she cleans houses for a living is because she's got rocks in her head, that she's stupid.

For the Mahi women, cleaning is one of the best jobs to have and it is as good as any job in an office, if not better.

Cleaning houses helps you be independent (you don't have to rely on your man's pay so much) and, what's more, you're your own boss. You walk into a house, you clean, and you get out. There are no papers to sign.

The only downfall is that when you're sick, when you're stuck in bed on your back and you can't go to work, you don't get paid. But the boss still gets her house cleaned because you've sent a cousin to replace you for the day. The boss is happy, the cousin is happy, and even you're happy because you didn't let your boss down. Your conscience is clear.

It's impossible to count on the fingers how many Mahi women are cleaners. But one thing's for sure, Materena is the champion cleaner of them all. She's the only cleaner in the family who's been cleaning the same house, the house of Madame Colette Dumonnier, for more than twelve years. And that is no small achievement, considering that there are more women willing to clean houses than there are women willing to pay for that service.

So that's why Materena is always the relative that young women thinking of a career as a professional cleaner go and see.

Not only does Materena know all the tricks of the cleaning trade, but she also knows what makes a boss really happy, so happy that even if another cleaner came tomorrow to propose her services for 30 percent less pay, the boss would say, "I've already got a cleaner, thank you."

In Materena's mind, cleaning is not only about cleaning, because anyone can clean, but not just anyone can be trusted and keep secrets. You see, a cleaner is bound to see things, and find things — things that she might be tempted to take or that are so bizarre she'd want to tell the whole population about it.

With Materena, no matter how much the relatives ask her questions about her boss, the boss's family, the boss's husband, the boss's house, she has only one answer to give: "It's not your onions."

Other relatives aren't so discreet.

One relative, not long ago, told the whole population about how her boss was having an affair with a man she called her architect. Apparently, as soon as the boss's husband left for work, the lover appeared to pick up the boss. The boss would say to her cleaner, "I have a meeting with my architect, I will be back at three o'clock." But one morning the relative (who was already suspicious of her boss's story) saw her boss and the architect kissing like crazy in the car, and she said to the whole population (right outside the church), " 'My architect,' my eye! We kiss our architect in the car, eh? We kiss our architect on the mouth?"

Another relative also told the whole population about her boss having an affair.

Another relative told the whole population about her boss going to the hospital to have an abortion.

Another relative told the whole population about her boss writing a very mean letter to her mother.

You're never going to hear these kinds of secrets coming out of Materena's mouth about her boss. She's taking every single secret about her boss and her family to the grave. Still, she agrees that some information about the boss can be passed on to the whole population.

Just like a relative passed on the information about how her boss ate only soups. Carrot soup, turnip soup, leek soup, soup after soup after soup, soup day and night. Worse than Mama George. And another relative passed on the information about how her boss hated living in Tahiti, she hated the heat, the mosquitoes, she always begged her husband to go home where they belonged. The husband would just snap, "Enough!"

Another relative talked about her two bosses who were sisters. Their house was always clean and always tidy and the relative had to try to find something to do. But most of the time, the sisters would ask their cleaner to join them around the piano and sing. The relative always accepted the invitation. Singing is less boring than pretending to be cleaning.

Now, there's no harm in passing that kind of information on to the whole population. But still, you're never going to get any information out of Materena about her boss (and boss's family, house, etc.) because, as far as she's concerned, everything about her boss (and boss's family, house, etc.) is top secret. The fact is that when Materena cleans, she cleans, she doesn't snoop around looking for secrets. She only does this with her children.

What matters more to Materena is that her boss's house

shines, the clothes are washed and ironed, the books put away, the plants watered . . . Materena really takes pride in her work. She's the only cleaner in the family who gets Christmas and birthday presents from her boss.

That's another reason why young women thinking of a career as a professional cleaner come to see Auntie Materena, and this is what Materena tells these young women, the future cleaners of Tahiti.

First, if the young woman has only just left school because she was too bored there, Materena tells her to forget about a career in cleaning, because there's too many cleaners as it is. Go back to school, get your degree. But if the young woman has left school a long time ago and she's got a couple of children and a man who doesn't have a job, or a man who's tight with his money, a man who wants his woman to be nice to him twenty-four hours a day before he gives her one banknote, well, this is what Materena says:

Always start from the top and work your way down to the bottom.

Look for chances to show your boss you're more than a cleaner. For example, remind her that the food in her fridge is about to go out of date, or if you see that one of your boss's plants is not doing too well, find out why. The plant may be a plant that needs shade and your boss has planted it in full sun. Tell your boss about it. Materena has saved many of her boss's plants that way.

Grab every single opportunity to show your boss that you're honest. Let's say you find a banknote in your boss's husband's shirt, well, don't you go slipping that banknote in your wallet. Slip that banknote in an envelope instead and write the boss's name on the envelope so that the boss's children don't open the envelope and take the money. Write a short note to explain the situation about that banknote to the boss.

Always remember that your boss is just another woman and that she's got feelings. If you find a love letter in your boss's husband's pants, don't you go showing it to your boss. Flush the love letter down the toilet instead. When Materena gets to that rule, the nieces always ask her if she has ever done this and Materena always says, "Of course not!"

All in all . . . when it comes to being a professional cleaner, Materena is unbeatable. That is why she's always pushed her daughter to see beyond the scrubbing brush and the broom. Cleaners never recommend their children to follow their path. You're more likely to hear cleaners tell their children, "Don't you dare be a cleaner like me." Materena said this to her daughter many times, and it seems Leilani understands her mother's message.

Today she told her mother what she'd like to do when she finishes school.

She'd like to be a pilot. Materena said, "And why not? We're not living next to the airport for nothing!" But deep down Materena thinks, "I hope Leilani isn't going to be a pilot. Planes are so dangerous."

Leilani would also like to be a psychiatrist. Materena said, "Ah, that's nice." But deep down Materena thinks, "She's not going to have a lot of business in Tahiti — we talk to a favorite cousin or to the priest. Tahitians who pour their troubles out to a psychiatrist don't exist."

Leilani would also like to be a *mutoi* (She's going to see the worst in people as a cop, thinks Materena) and a *militaire* (What about the war?). Leilani wants to be so many things. Ideas keep on coming into her mind and she can't decide, unlike her younger brother, Moana, whose mind is set on becoming a chef.

Then Leilani asked her mother if she always wanted to be a cleaner. She was very shocked to hear her mother exclaim, "Of course not!"

"How come you're a cleaner, then?" asked Leilani, puzzled.

Materena didn't feel like replying to this question. Instead she went to get the washing off the line, and now, shampooing her hair under the shower, she thinks about how it wasn't her plan to be scrubbing and sweeping for years and years and years. She visualizes herself scrubbing walls when she's sixty years old. Her hair, all gray, is thin and falling in her eyes. And she's muttering under her breath with a croaky voice, "Ah, scrubbing and scrubbing, a woman's job is never done."

But at least it pays the bills.

Catholic Girls

Anne-Marie Javouhey is the Catholic girls' school facing the magnificent cathedral in Papeete. It's hidden behind a high concrete wall with an iron-grilled gate.

Although the school looks like a prison, it is not. It is the best school in Tahiti. In this school, young girls are trained to become independent, free women, and although it costs much more than the Catholic school in Faa'a, Materena doesn't care.

Her cousin Tapeta's daughter Rose attends Anne-Marie Javouhey. The whole family is on a constant breadfruit diet so that Rose gets her chance to become somebody. That is what her mother wishes for with all her heart and soul.

Tapeta complains to Materena that every now and then Rose puts on airs like she's a rich little daddy's girl, and Tapeta just slaps her daughter back to reality. And when Rose gets teased at school about her plain dress, thongs, and pandanus bag, Tapeta tells her that she can do with a bit of suffering. In Tapeta's opinion, people need a bit of suffering to become better people.

Tapeta is determined her daughter will always work hard at school so that she will not be poor when she grows up. She wants her to get a top job that pays big money, or marry a man who has a top job that pays big money. And then Rose will be able to pay her hardworking mother back and perhaps take her to Rome too. It is Tapeta's dream to see the popes' graves and to stand in the arena where the first Christians sang their faith as lions devoured them raw.

The last time Materena saw Tapeta she asked her how Rose was doing at school. "She's not first," Tapeta said, "but she's not last. My Rose, she's in the middle and it's not bad at all to be in the middle."

The two cousins spoke for a while and Materena found out that Rose had been on the waiting list for Anne-Marie Javouhey ever since she was in primary school. Tapeta would visit Anne-Marie Javouhey four times a year to remind the headmistress or the headmistress's secretary that her daughter deserved a chance just as much as any other woman's daughter. Tapeta also reminded the headmistress or the headmistress's secretary that she always paid her bills. And Tapeta's daughter Rose got in.

Today, at two thirty, Materena has an appointment with the headmistress at Anne-Marie Javouhey.

It is now two fifteen and Materena is waiting inside the cathedral. Wanting to make the right impression, she is wearing a white missionary dress that falls right near her ankles. In her pandanus bag Materena has Leilani's exceptional school reports and a Colorful Imagination School Merit Award Leilani won for her story about a young girl who lost her *savate.* Materena thought about wearing her gold necklace with the gold Virgin Mary pendant, but that necklace, blessed by the archbishop himself, is reserved for special occasions like baptisms, communions, and confirmations. Not that she needs such a necklace to prove to the headmistress that she regularly goes to mass. Tapeta did say that the only two things the headmistress cares about are:

You can pay.

Your daughter is not going to jump over the wall to go meet boys lurking on the other side.

Six girls in Rose's class aren't even Catholics. But it really helps if you are one.

At twenty-five past two, Materena walks onto the grounds of the Anne-Marie Javouhey College. There's concrete everywhere except for a tiny patch of green immaculate lawn, and there's a covered hall with tables and chairs and a life-size statue of the Virgin Mary, Understanding Woman.

The school office is even more immaculate. The pristine white walls are plastered with framed black-and-white photographs of serious-looking nuns, and Jesus Christ is nailed to the cross in the middle of them all.

The woman at the front desk is busy putting a letter into an envelope. Materena, standing straight and tall, goes on admiring the nuns in the photographs as she waits for the front-desk woman to acknowledge her presence. The woman, after a half a second glance at Materena, opens a drawer, gets a stamp, licks it, rubs it on the envelope, closes the envelope, places it in an office basket, and buttons up her crocheted white sweater. She does all of these things very slowly and Materena would like to shake that rude woman a little.

At last the front-desk woman lifts her eyes to Materena and looks at her as if she has no idea what Materena is doing in her office. "May I help you?"

Smiling a polite smile, Materena replies, "Good afternoon. I have an appointment with the headmistress at two thirty today."

"What is it in regard to?"

Smiling still, Materena says, "It is in regard to my daughter, Leilani."

The front-desk woman gives Materena a blank look.

"I'm here to enroll my daughter, Leilani."

The front-desk woman sighs and painfully reaches out to a thick book, opens it to a page filled with names. "Name, please, school details, and contact details." After writing the information down, the front-desk woman tells Materena that she will be advised should a place become available. But Materena is not leaving before showing off Leilani's school reports.

"You can see the school reports of my daughter, she's a . . ."

The woman is not interested in the reports that Materena is almost shoving in front of her face. "That won't be necessary, madame." She goes back to her envelope ritual and completely ignores Materena.

"Thank you." Materena walks out, smiling. But once outside the school, the smile drops off, and twenty yards later, Materena loudly tells the front-desk woman off.

Well, at least Leilani has her name in on the waiting list, and that is a start. Materena certainly intends to visit Anne-Marie Javouhey College four times a year, rain, shine, or cyclone. To celebrate, Materena buys a watermelon at the market.

Mother and daughter, in the kitchen, are now enjoying the sweet watermelon together. The boys are outside flying their kites.

"Girl," Materena says, "I did something today."

"Something naughty?" Leilani asks, giggling.

"But!" Materena can't believe that Leilani sometimes! It's funny, though. "*Aue,*" Materena says, chuckling, "I'm too old for that kind of trick." Then seriously, "*Non,* I went to Anne-Marie Javouhey College today and put your name on the waiting list."

Leilani widens her eyes. "And the money? It's expensive!"

"Eh, money we can always find." Materena smiles to her

daughter. "The money is not your concern, girl. You just keep working good at school, okay?"

"I promise, I swear!" Ah, Materena feels so happy. It's always good when your kids show their appreciation. She's at the stove stirring the stew with Moana carefully watching when Pito, in the company of Ati, walks in.

"Something smells good, woman!" Pito is in a happy mood. He pinches Materena on the bottom and, turning to his son, he says, "What are you doing in the bloody kitchen again? You're always skulking around in here these days. Go and play outside."

"Pito." Materena brushes Moana's shoulder to show him not to worry about anything. Mamie has got everything under control. "We're not going to start again."

She's getting sick of having to defend Moana's ambition to be a chef. His older brother, Tamatoa, doesn't get teased at all for his ambition to be a bodybuilder, but poor Moana takes it all the time. It's like it is a crime for a boy to cook, but it is fine for a boy to spend hours and hours building his muscles and oiling his body in front of the mirror. When Materena bought Moana a ceramic bowl last week, Pito shrieked, "A bowl! What's next? An apron? I'm not having one of my sons wearing an apron!"

But today, Pito chuckles and messes Moana's hair. This is as good as his saying, "Oh, all right, then, stay in the bloody kitchen."

Materena laughs with relief and invites Ati to stay for dinner. Without waiting for him to accept the invitation she gets another plate. The fact is that Ati always stays for dinner when he visits around dinnertime, but Materena doesn't necessarily always invite him to stay.

"So," she says, winking to Ati, "what have you two been up to?"

But here's Leilani charging into the kitchen. "Papi! Guess

what? I'm going to Anne-Marie Javouhey College. Mamie went to see today!"

Materena looks over at Pito. She expects him to say something like, "What a good mother you are." Instead he says, "I'm not sure about that."

Materena, thinking he's making allusion to the money, exclaims, "I will sell my body if I have to! I will find the money!"

Pito gets a beer from the fridge. "*Ah hia,* relax, don't go jumping on your horse. I wasn't talking about the money. I just don't like Catholic schools."

"I went to a Catholic school and there's nothing wrong with me!" Well, Materena feels she's a bit of a martyr sometimes, because when you're Catholic, you're not supposed to enjoy yourself. You're supposed to think about all the people in the world who are suffering. That is what the nuns at Notre Dame des Anges School have taught her. "I'm a good and caring person and it's very good to be that way."

"Catholic girls," Pito says, smirking, "they're . . ." He looks over to Ati, who starts chuckling. And the men go on drinking their beer.

"What?" Materena would like to be informed. "What about Catholic girls?"

Pito gives Leilani the signal to make a disappearance, and Leilani stomps out of the kitchen, mumbling, "Why can't I listen if Moana can? You're talking about *my* future!"

She is gone now, and Materena orders Pito to go on about Catholic girls, but all he does is chuckle.

"They're what, Catholic girls?" Materena eagerly asks again. "They're too nice, they're too martyrish? They're what?"

Pito and Ati look at each other and smirk.

"What do you think, mate?" Pito asks with a smile that says many stories.

"Oh . . ." Ati glances at Materena for a brief second. "Well . . . I'll have to say that . . ." Ati glances at Materena again. "Maybe what I think is not what you think."

"I'm thinking what you're thinking," Pito says.

"*Ah oui?*" Ati asks, feigning surprise.

"*Ah oui,*" Pito confirms, cackling.

Meanwhile Materena is still waiting for an answer about Catholic girls, but all she's getting here is a story that's going around the pot. Typical men, she thinks.

"*Aue bof!*" she says, waving a hand in the air. "Anyway, for me, Catholic girls are really nice girls."

Ati and Pito look at each other and burst out laughing, with Materena looking on, puzzled. She asks her son if he understands these two clowns.

He says, "I wasn't listening."

Standing in front of the intimidating iron gates a few months later, Materena rearranges her daughter's immaculate plaits and says, "Show respect to the nuns, girl. Don't get into trouble." As she straightens Leilani's long brown dress, Materena adds, "You're very lucky you can go to this school for free. I'm very proud of you getting that scholarship. Be good, okay? Don't talk back to the nuns."

Then, to her son, whom Materena is taking to the hospital for his cast to get taken off, Materena asks, "Tamatoa, say something nice to your sister."

"Your school looks like a prison," he says.

All right, time to walk in.

The place is swarming with girls running all over the place. They all eye Tamatoa (the only male around) and giggle into their books. The two nuns on duty don't seem like they're in control.

Here they are calling one name after another, and nobody is listening. But it's madness here this Monday morning!

Meanwhile, as Tamatoa is shaking his head and telling his mother how the girls here are so ugly, they walk into the office for the formalities. The headmistress, a large black woman with the most beautiful teeth Materena has ever seen, officially welcomes Leilani into the school and introduces her to another young girl, a small cute brown girl with hazel eyes, freckles, crooked teeth, and flaming red hair.

"Vahine," the headmistress says, "this is Leilani. Say good morning."

"Good morning." The young girl smiles, blushing in front of Tamatoa, who is looking her up and down.

"Good morning," Leilani says. "How are you?"

"I'm fine, thank you. And how are you?"

"Fine, thank you."

The headmistress places her hands on her chest and smiles. "Go on, girls," she says. "Off to class."

Materena thanks the headmistress profusely and follows her daughter and her daughter's new friend outside.

She watches them walk away.

She hears them say, "You like pancakes? So do I!" "You believe in aliens? So do I!"

Into Womanhood

A girl is officially a woman the day she has her period. Tears fall out of the mama's eyes when she welcomes her daughter into womanhood. There are nonstop lamentations. *Aue!* I can't believe you're a woman! Life goes so fast! It seems like only yesterday that I was pushing you into the world! I'm still the boss!

After the crying, the lamentations, and the embrace, traditionally mother and daughter sit at the kitchen table for the Welcome into Womanhood talk, beginning with the rules that are passed on from generation to generation, from mother to daughter, and on and on. The mama talks, keeping in mind that the purpose of the Welcome into Womanhood talk is to enlighten the new woman, pass on her experience as a woman of many years so that her daughter's life will be a bit easier.

Cleaning tricks may be revealed, secrets that are not meant for the grave, recipes that fill the stomach and take less than ten minutes to prepare, advice on curtains, plants, men, life in general.

It generally starts with: Don't wash your hair during your

period, otherwise the blood is going to turn into ice and you're going to go mad. Don't touch plants, trees, or flowers during your period, otherwise they're going to die. Make sure to rest. You lose pints of blood when you have your period . . .

The daughter is supposed to listen dutifully and nod. Comments are not required.

But Materena is not going to give her daughter, who became a woman about ten minutes ago, the traditional Welcome into Womanhood talk. She's going to do it the new way. Let's move on to the new century!

So what is she going to say?

"Mamie?" Leilani is waiting for her mother to begin talking. "Are you dreaming?"

"I'm thinking, girl."

"And my Kotex?"

"Don't panic, I'm going to get you a packet of Kotex at the Chinese store soon." Materena wipes the corner of her eyes with the back of her hand.

"Mamie," Leilani says, cackling, as she affectionately takes her mother's hand in hers, "stop crying."

"I'm not crying because I'm sad, I'm crying because I'm moved, I'm happy." Materena smiles through her tears. "You're going to understand when you're a mother . . . Just give me one minute."

"Toilet paper is really uncomfortable."

"*Aue!* Is that all you can think about? Your Kotex? I use toilet paper and it's not uncomfortable for me. Let me think a little . . ."

There's a silence until finally Materena is ready.

"I admire you." There, Materena spoke.

"*Merci,* Mamie! I admire you too."

"*Ah oui?*" Materena feels honored. "And why do you admire me?"

"I admire you for lots of reasons . . . but shouldn't you be the one telling me why you admire me?"

"*Oui,* of course . . . sorry, this is *your* day . . . Well, I admire you because . . ." And Materena lists the reasons.

She admires her daughter because she can point north just like that, name all the countries in the atlas, she can write pages and pages without checking the spelling in the dictionary, she knows if we lose pints of blood we're dead, she can . . .

Give the medical word for every part of the body. Read books thicker than the Bible. Not eat for two days to raise money for the starving children of Africa. Materena admires how her daughter is courageous enough to tell anyone jumping in front of her at the Chinese store, "Excuse me, but I think I was before you." Or yell at people for throwing rubbish out of their car window. She can speak four languages (French, English, Spanish, and a bit of Tahitian). Ask strangers questions.

Materena has never ever been called the Walking Encyclopedia by the relatives. Leilani has.

Materena finally finishes. That's enough compliments for today.

"Now," she continues, "I'm not going to tell you not to wash your hair during your period, otherwise the blood is going to turn into ice, because . . . eh well, I was right, you're laughing . . . I knew you were going to laugh . . . eh oh, let's calm ourselves, okay? I didn't invent this talk. See what happens when you read too many books? When you've got encyclopedias? You don't believe in Tahitian ways anymore! Stop, you're making me laugh! I know it sounds stupid . . . Blood turning into ice, can you imagine? *Aue!* If your grandmother Mamie Loana heard us laugh . . . Okay that's enough, let me continue . . ." Materena takes a deep breath. You're not supposed to be laughing during the Welcome into Womanhood talk.

You're supposed to be very serious because it's serious, all of this! Materena adopts a serious face.

"Be proud to have been born a woman," Materena says.

"*Oui,*" Leilani sighs.

"Don't you sigh on me!" Materena talks about how it's important for mothers to tell their daughters to be proud to have been born a woman. Being born a woman doesn't mean you have to be the one stuck with the cooking and the cleaning and looking after the children for the rest of your life. Women can do anything. Being a woman also means you add something magical and special to this world. "You know that book you were reading last week," Materena says, "about that Chinese woman who prayed to her God not to make her come back as a woman?"

"*Oui.* She preferred to be reincarnated as a dog than as a woman."

"Well, I don't think it's awful to be a woman anymore."

"Oh" — Leilani shakes her head — "women do have a harder life. You can't deny that."

"I don't deny it," Materena says. "But why do you think God gave us all these hardships, eh? It's not because he knows we're capable? We're strong? We're tough?"

"Mamie, I don't want to talk about God today, please."

"All right . . . no God today . . ." Materena knows that Leilani is a bit cranky with God at the moment because He's allowing children in Africa to starve, He's making people die young, He's doing many things Leilani doesn't approve of. And plus, God doesn't make any sense to Leilani. She finds it easier to believe in the existence of aliens. Materena has tried to defend God and His existence several times, but each time Leilani has said, "Don't talk to me about God."

Today Materena won't say anything about God, but she does

say that she feels very lucky that it was she whom God chose to carry and raise Leilani, and Leilani smiles.

"Now," Materena says, also smiling at her daughter, "always believe in yourself, okay?"

"I will."

"It is very important to believe in yourself," Materena continues. "You can have thousands of people believing in you, but if you" — Materena points a finger to her daughter — "if you don't believe in yourself, you're not going to be able to take that step forward you need to take to be a truly happy person. It's all in here." Materena places a hand on her heart. "And in here." The hand goes to the head. "Remember, only you can make it happen. You follow me?"

"I follow you, Mamie."

"Know what you want and make it happen."

"*Oui.*"

"Mamie is always going to be here for you, remember that."

"I'll remember."

"Keep on working hard at school, don't get distracted. Get your papers — degrees — and then get a good job. When a woman has a good job, she doesn't have to rely on anyone, you understand?"

"I understand."

"Don't be a nobody like me."

"I don't think you're a nobody, Mamie."

Materena smiles and pats her daughter's hand. "You're so intelligent, girl."

"You're intelligent."

"I'm intelligent?"

"You are *very* intelligent."

"*Merci,* girl." Materena cackles. "I can always count on you to give me compliments."

"It's not a compliment, it's a fact." Leilani takes her mother's hand in hers. "You also can have a new, exciting future ahead of you. All you need is to know what you want."

"I know what I want!"

"And what do you want?" asks Leilani, interested.

"I want . . ." Materena stops talking to look at her daughter closely. "Why am I talking about myself?" She chuckles. "Today is not my day, today is your day, I'm not the daughter bleeding for the first time in my life, I'm the mother with years of experience . . . Last thing, don't you dare make me a grandmother before I'm forty," Materena says, trying to lighten up the conversation.

"I'm not interested in boys."

"We all say that, but when the hormones —"

"Mamie, I'll tell you, don't worry."

"Promise?"

"Promise."

"You tell me and I'll get you the contraceptive pill *illico presto,* okay?"

"The pill? My boyfriend will be wearing a condom."

"Oh, I don't know any Tahitian man who wears a condom."

"Well, my boyfriend will. No condom — no sexy loving."

Materena widens her eyes. She can't believe the conversation she's having with her daughter today! Well, this is what happens when you don't follow the tradition, you pay the price.

Okay, it's time to move away from the subject of boys and condoms. "I really believe you're capable of doing whatever you want with your life," Materena says.

There's no response from Leilani.

"Leilani? Did you hear what I've just told you?"

Leilani seems lost in a private reverie. Her eyes are staring straight ahead . . . at Materena's chest.

"Leilani!" Materena exclaims, waving her hands in front of Leilani's face. "*Ouh ouh!* Come back to Earth!"

Leilani comes out of her reverie to reveal that she's never noticed her mother's breasts were so small.

"Eh? Why are you talking about my breasts?"

"Did you always have small breasts, Mamie?"

"Well *oui!* Mamie Loana has small breasts, I've got the size of my breasts from her."

"Am I going to have small breasts too?" Leilani asks, clearly worried.

Materena glances at her daughter's chest. At fourteen years old, Leilani still doesn't need to wear a bra, but she wears one anyway. She's been wearing a bra for the past two years. Yes, Materena thinks, it is very likely that Leilani is going to have small breasts, like her mother and her grandmother. And so what? Small breasts are convenient. They don't get in the way. It doesn't hurt when you run.

"Mamie?" Leilani wants an answer about her breasts. "My breasts? Are they going to stay small?

"Maybe," Materena replies, "but I can't say . . . I know women who have big breasts whose mothers have small breasts, and the other way around too. Anyway, you're clever, you have long legs, beautiful eyes, and beautiful teeth, you can't have everything . . . Now, let's go back to the Welcome into Womanhood talk . . . Why are you sighing? You want your Kotex? *Aue!* Are you obsessed or something? All right, then, but when I come back from the Chinese store you're listening to me for two hours, okay?"

"Sure."

"You're only saying that because you want me to go to the Chinese store now, it's not true?"

"*Oui,* it is true."

"You're unbelievable, you." Cackling, Materena gets up and grabs her purse. She understands that young girls are too embarrassed to buy pads at the Chinese store. Materena even knows grown women who are too embarrassed to buy pads. There are always a lot of relatives at the Chinese store and when they see the pads wrapped in newspaper for privacy, the whole population knows you've got your period, the whole population can say, "Here's one who's not going to wash her hair for the next four days."

Sitting at the kitchen table with the transistor in front of her hours later, Materena is ready to record the Welcome into Womanhood talk. This is the talk her mother gave her twenty-four years ago, the talk Materena now feels she should have given her daughter, if only to follow the tradition that certain things should be passed from mother to daughter and on and on. Certain things such as good habits, family stories, the everyday life. Well, Materena is just about to do this — on a tape, so that Leilani can listen to it over and over again, and she can even write the precious information in her notebook. If she hasn't already done so, after years of watching her mother do things the way she does, and hearing her say the things she says.

It's quarter past eleven and everyone is asleep, the perfect time for a recording session.

Materena presses the record button.

> Curtains don't just stop the rays of sunshine and the eyes of the curious coming into the house. They uplift the soul of a woman too, but to do that they've got to be colorful and pretty. Never cut costs with your curtains, Leilani.
>
> Breadfruit fills the stomach, is nice to eat, and can be

cooked in many different ways: barbecued, baked, in the stew. Plant a breadfruit tree if you don't have one growing where you live. You won't regret it.

Clothes are hung first thing in the morning and taken off at least half an hour before it gets dark, otherwise they will be dampened. Clothes are folded as soon as they are taken off the line, otherwise they will be creased. Babies' clothes are never washed with adults' clothes. Shirts are hung upside down but pants are hung right-side up. Sheets need four pegs. Bras and underpants are hung in the house, not on the clothesline for the whole population to admire.

Lemon squeezed on the dishes gets rid of odors like fish, garlic, and onions. Dirty dishes left by the sink overnight attract cockroaches.

Only buy two-sided tablecloths, that way you'll have two tablecloths for the price of one. Only buy dresses that can be taken down.

Tidy your house before going to bed because when the first thing you see in the morning is *bordel,* you get cranky.

Always put the soap back in the soap holder. When it's on the ground somebody might step on it one day and crack his head open.

When you visit somebody, stop five yards away from the house and call out. Don't walk into the house in case somebody is doing something you don't want to see or something you don't need to see. Call but don't call like somebody died, call with a normal voice. If nobody answers your call after the third call it means nobody's home or maybe the relative you want to see doesn't want to see you.

To get rid of unwanted guests without hurting their feelings, broom around their feet.

Don't eat in front of people if you can't share.

When someone tells you a secret for the grave, it means you have to take that secret with you to the grave. Reveal a secret for the grave and bad luck is sure to strike you minutes later. Your tongue will swell and suffocate you.

Don't visit people at eating times unless you've been invited.

Show respect to old people.

Never say anything to a bad mouth because everything you say is going to be used against you later on.

Don't get married before you have at least one child with your man. Children are the hardest part in a couple's life. When there are no children, everything is easy, everybody wants to get married. Once there are children, everything changes.

Check the woman who raised the man you want as your husband. Men like to say to their sons, "How's the mama? A big pork chop? That's your girlfriend in twenty years." Well, girl, check your boyfriend's mama, see how she raised her son. Was she still changing her son's bedsheets after he turned fourteen years old, when boys start to do things in their bed their mama doesn't need to know about?

It is taboo, forbidden, to fall in love with a cousin, remember that. Your family is not going to speak to you, attend your children's baptism, communion, confirmation, etc. Your name will no longer mean anything, and your children will be born deformed.

Don't fall in love with a man from an enemy family either. You'll be caught between your family and his family, torn this way, torn that way. Your life will be nothing but misery.

Forget about falling in love with a man from another religion. There's always going to be an argument about this and that, God, the Virgin Mary, where the children are going to be baptized.

Avoid foreigners at all costs. Foreigners always go back to their country and they don't always ask the woman to follow. If your foreigner by some miracle asks you to follow him back to his country, you better make sure your passport is always valid so that you can come home to your mother's funeral.

Foreigners eat raw fish with salad dressing.

Stay away from typical Tahitian men. A typical Tahitian man will make you earn your wedding ring. Expect to wait years for a typical Tahitian man to commit. One day he'll tell you, "*Oui,* I'm ready to marry you." The next day his song will be different, "*Non,* I can't marry you yet, maybe next year."

A typical Tahitian man must have three nocturnal meetings a week, at least, with his mates. They drink, listen to music, smoke, and sometimes they talk. More often, though, they just look into each other's eyes and laugh. Or they tell jokes.

If you're depressed, lost, crying, your typical Tahitian man pretends he can't see your suffering. He walks straight past you as you stand in the room with tears streaming down your face.

A typical Tahitian man holds his baby as if it were a pack of taro. He's very proud to show off his baby to his mates, he's grinning as if he's pushed that baby out into the world. When the baby becomes a child and starts asking questions, your typical Tahitian man says, "You can't see I'm busy, eh? Go see your mama."

A typical Tahitian man believes that it is beneath his dignity to show his woman affection. You ask a typical Tahitian man, "Am I beautiful, *chéri?*" he answers, "You're not ugly."

Enough about men. Now, to make a fruit tree produce you bash it around with a stick and say, "You're going to give me a fruit or what? Eh? You ungrateful tree! I water you, I give you fertilizer, and all you give me is a great big zero!"

When somebody gives you something in a bowl, give the

bowl back as soon as possible, and give it back with something in it. It doesn't matter whether or not you ate whatever was in the bowl in the first place. Let's say it was ripe lemons and let's say you didn't get the chance to use these lemons and they rotted on you, well, you still can't give the bowl back empty. It's not the relative's fault you didn't use her lemons.

Never visit a woman who's just given birth looking your best.

You can put up a six-foot-high fence around your house if you want to. It's not against the law to put up a six-foot-high fence. But a six-foot-high fence is like saying to the relatives, "I don't want anything to do with you lot." So, next time you're going to be in the shit up to here, you can cry until midnight for the relatives to come and save you. It's fair. It's the Tahitian way. You're in or you're out, you can't just accept what suits you.

Soups are always better the next day. So are stews.

A man with missing teeth means he's been in a fight. A woman with missing teeth means her man beat her. If a man ever knocks out any of your beautiful teeth I'll cut his balls.

It's better to put a bandage over a black eye and have people think you've just had an operation on your eye than reveal your black eye and have people believe a man beat you. If a man ever gives you a black eye I'll cut his balls.

When we die it doesn't mean that we don't exist anymore. True, we are buried, we become a skeleton, then we become soil, but all that we have left behind is still there. Whenever people talk about us, well, we come alive again.

When a man gives a woman a ring she must immediately drop the ring on the ground and listen up for a *ting* sound, the sound of gold. No *ting* sound means the ring is *camelotte,* fake, and you've been fooled.

A dead man's last wishes are law and must be followed.

You can ask a quilt maker to put anything you want on your quilt (leaves, birds, fruit, vegetables . . .) but do not ask her to change how things are in real life. Examples: purple limes, red breadfruit, green frangipani flowers, black tomatoes . . .

Don't start thinking you know more than I do.

Materena presses the stop button, puts the tape in an envelope, writes Leilani a note, and slips the envelope under Leilani's bedroom door. Then she checks that the gas is closed, switches the lights off, and goes to bed.

Secrets for the Grave

There are secrets which can never be told. They are called secrets for the grave. And there are secrets that can be told one day, it's just a question of waiting for the right moment. They are called secrets, pure and simple.

With the secrets for the grave, we promise to never reveal them on the head of somebody we love and who is dead, we promise before God, and above all we promise to the person who trusted us with her secret. These kinds of secrets die with us.

With the secrets pure and simple, we don't promise anybody to never tell. We just wait for the right time to spill the bucket. Sometimes, though, it happens that secrets come out into the open at the wrong time. This happened to Materena when her mother told her the truth about her dog. Materena's dog was named Prince and Materena loved him so much. But one sunny morning he ran away. For years Materena was so confused. She kept thinking, What did I do to Prince for him to go and abandon me like that?

One day she asked her mother that question and Loana said, "Eh, what? Who are you talking about?"

Materena said, "My dog. Prince?"

Loana just shrugged and said, "Eh, who knows what goes on inside a dog's head." It was years later that her mother told her the truth. It just slipped out of her mouth. Materena had been going on about Prince and all that, how she couldn't believe he had abandoned her, and Loana said, "*Aue!* Prince didn't abandon you . . . stop going on about Prince . . . Richard Lexter sold it to some Chinese people, they wanted to eat your dog."

When secrets come out at the wrong time people can be hurt. That's why Materena is going to reveal a few secrets to her daughter today, because today is the right time.

Leilani is drinking her chicken soup with ginger that Materena has made just for her. And plus, nobody else is home. Today is a good day to say a few more things to the new woman.

"Girl?" Materena begins as she sits at the kitchen table facing Leilani. "I have a few things to tell you."

"A few things?" asks Leilani. "Like what?"

"Like secrets."

"Secrets about who?"

"About you." Then Materena hurries to add, "But these are not secrets for the grave."

"Oh, a secret is a secret," says Leilani, shrugging.

"*Non,* Leilani." Materena proceeds to explain the two types of secret to her daughter: the secrets we take to our grave, and the secrets we can tell.

Leilani attentively listens, then puts her spoon down, and arching one of her eyebrows, she looks into her mother's eyes and says, "Go on, then, spill the bucket."

Materena takes a deep breath and begins.

Her first secret is about how she lied that her French father had died in the Second World War defending his country. Materena explains to Leilani that she was just too young that day she asked about her French grandfather to know the truth. That he'd left after military service in Tahiti. That Materena had never met him. Materena expects Leilani to get a bit cranky, but Leilani cackles. "Oh, Mamie, I've known the truth for years." Leilani explains to her mother that it was impossible for her grandfather to have died in the Second World War. She'd done some calculations and concluded that Tom was about eleven years old (the same age as Materena's mother) when the Second World War broke out.

And now Materena is really embarrassed. "Ah," she says. "Ah . . . I didn't think you were going to do some calculations."

"Mamie" — Leilani laughs, enjoying herself — "have you forgotten that I have a scientific mind? People with scientific minds always question things. They never assume."

"Ah," Materena says again.

"What's your next secret?" Leilani asks cheekily.

But first Materena would like her daughter to promise that she won't get cranky, because it's quite a big secret. Leilani puts a hand up and promises that she won't get cranky. So Materena tells her daughter about that pink bicycle Mama Roti had given her for her seventh birthday. But first, let's have a bit of recapitulation.

That day Mama Roti couldn't stop raving how the pink bicycle had cost her the eyes of her head. Mama Roti was so happy her granddaughter loved the bicycle more than she loved the quilt her other grandmother had made working day and night for a whole week. But Materena was not happy at all about that bicycle. In her opinion, you just don't give vehicles to other people's children. Materena really believes you should see the parents and ask them if it's okay with them for you to give their child a vehicle. But even back then Mama Roti never asked

Materena what she thought about her ideas. Here she was, clapping her hands at Leilani riding that bicycle, and every time she fell, she yelled, "Watch out for your brand-new bicycle!"

The second Leilani fell and split her chin open, Materena understood God was giving her a sign, and so she decided to make that bicycle disappear. Later on that night Materena wrapped the bicycle in a bedsheet and hid it on top of a wardrobe in her bedroom at her mother's house. Her mother said, "My eyes didn't see what you've just put on top of the wardrobe."

There, here's the story about Leilani's pink bicycle, and Materena waits for a reaction, hoping Leilani won't get too cranky. She cried for days when Materena told her somebody had stolen her bicycle.

Right now Leilani is laughing. "Mamie," she says, "I've known the truth for years!" Leilani explains to her mother that the day she saw that big thing wrapped in a bedsheet on top of the wardrobe she knew straightaway it was her bicycle. She could see the shape of the handlebars.

So she got a chair, climbed on top of it, grabbed her bicycle, and started to ride it in her grandmother's garden. Loana was weeding that day. When she saw Leilani riding her bicycle she said, "It's best you don't tell your mother about that bike."

"I rode my bicycle in Mamie Loana's garden for years," says Leilani, clearly enjoying watching her mother's eyes pop out of her head. "You're not the only person with secrets, you know." Leilani cackles.

"What other secrets have you got for me?" Materena asks, shaking her head with disbelief.

Leilani puts her spoon down and starts to think. "Okay, do you remember how I used to go to school with four slices of banana cake to eat at recreation?"

Materena nods. *Oui,* she remembers the two years Leilani

went to school with four slices of banana cake to eat at recreation, before lunch at the school canteen. Materena was always making banana cakes. She couldn't keep up with Leilani's growing appetite. Then one day Leilani said, "I don't need four slices of cake anymore. One is enough. I think I've stopped growing."

"What about those slices of banana cake?" Materena asks. "Don't you dare tell me you were chucking them in the trash!" Materena is already getting cranky.

"Me, chuck food in the trash?" Leilani exclaims, also cranky. "Do you know to whom you're speaking? I would never, ever chuck food in the trash! I gave those slices of cake to a girl who had nothing to eat."

"Oh, *chérie.*" Materena smiles. "Oh . . . that was so nice of you to do that . . ." But what happened to that girl, Materena wonders. How come she stopped eating Materena's banana cake?

Materena asks her daughter this.

"She backstabbed me," Leilani says. "She told everyone in our classroom I was a show-off, that I wanted to be the teacher's pet." Leilani continues about how she confronted that girl and told her, "You stupid idiot. Don't you know never to bite the hand that feeds you?" From that day on, Leilani stopped feeding that girl.

"Just like that?" Materena asks. "No second chance?"

"You know me, Mamie. People are nice to me and I'm nice back. People are mean to me and I'm mean back . . . This soup is delicious! I'm going to have some more."

Materena watches her daughter help herself to some more soup and cackles at Leilani's declaration that she's feeling so much better now after that delicious soup. The period pain has definitely eased up.

As soon as Leilani is at the table, she asks her mother if she could ask her a question. "It's a bit private, though," she adds.

"Well, ask your question and I'll tell you if I can answer it or not."

"I'm just curious . . . I don't want you to think I'm being disrespectful."

What is her question? Materena asks herself. She is now very curious. "Come on, scientific mind." Materena smiles. "I'm waiting for your interrogation."

"Okay." Leilani puts the spoon down. "How was I conceived?" There. Leilani has asked her question and she can now continue to drink her soup, her eyes on her plate.

Materena can't believe Leilani's question. She's never asked her mother how she was conceived. Everybody knows that stories of conception belong to the mother and the mother only. The conception of a baby is a very private affair. Well, you have the right to know if you were conceived in a bed, on a rock, on the kitchen table, in the bathroom. But how? None of your business!

"Leilani, it's not the mouth that goes to the spoon," Materena says. "It's the spoon that goes to the mouth . . . and no slurping noise, please."

"I knew you'd be cranky."

"I'm not cranky! I'm just reminding you of the proper way to drink soups."

"It's fine if you don't feel comfortable telling me about my conception," Leilani says, making sure the spoon goes to the mouth and not the other way around. "I don't mind. Maybe it's too wild to be told." She chuckles.

"Leilani, the hormones have already started kicking, or what?"

"Oh, Mamie! You're the one always talking about the hormones!"

Materena shakes her head and laughs.

"Mamie, was I an accident?"

Materena stops laughing.

Was Leilani an accident? Well, most babies are accidents, aren't they? Materena asks herself. The only person Materena knows who fell pregnant because she decided to was Madame Colette. Twice Madame Colette said to her husband, "Jules, I'm ovulating, I'll see you in bed." But all the other women Materena knows (cousins, aunties, and herself) fell pregnant because they didn't think. Materena's three children were accidents. The first accident took place under a tree, the second in bed, and the third on the kitchen table. But the moment Materena discovered her children's existence, she welcomed them into her womb and into her life as if she had planned them.

"Mamie, it's fine if you can't tell me if I was an accident or not."

"You were not an accident," Materena says firmly.

"Was I a planned baby?" Leilani sounds like she doesn't believe this.

"You're here today, *non?* Doesn't this mean anything to you?"

"Oh." Leilani shrugs. "It's just that I always thought I was an accident." She now wants to keep talking about secrets — the ones she won't be taking to her grave.

"Don't tell me you have secrets to take to the grave," says Materena.

"Mamie, every woman in the world has secrets to take to the grave." Leilani says this with her very serious woman voice.

And now Materena is worried. Leilani is far too young to have secrets for the grave entrusted to her. Secrets for the grave usually come when you're much older, when you've earned the trust of people, when you've proved that simple secrets are safe with you, when you can live with the responsibility that comes with keeping secrets for the grave.

Because it is a huge responsibility, a heavy weight on the conscience. You've got to know how to switch off so that the secrets for the grave don't haunt you.

At fourteen years old Materena had no secrets for the grave to her name. She had to wait until she was twenty-nine to start collecting secrets for the grave, and she would have gladly waited twenty more years.

"How many secrets for the grave have you got so far?" Materena, even more worried, asks Leilani.

"Oh, about four."

"And who are they about?"

"I can't tell you."

"Are they about me?"

"I can't tell you."

"That means they're about me." Materena would give everything to be able to read Leilani's mind. "Are they about me?" But once again, Leilani refuses to divulge anything.

"Come on, girl," Materena pleads, smiling. "You know me. I'm very good at keeping secrets. I've got about two hundred and fifty secrets in my head . . . Come on, just tell me one."

"Who told everybody that I got my period?"

"Eh?" Materena didn't expect that question. Plus, it's not true at all that she told everyone. "Everyone?" she asks. "Who do you take me for? The coconut radio? I only told two people."

"Didn't I specifically ask you to keep the news of my period secret?"

"I only told two people!" Materena really can't understand why her daughter is making such a fuss.

"It doesn't matter if you've only told my secret to two people, Mamie." This time Leilani is cranky. "What is important is that you didn't respect my secret."

Materena is about to defend herself, to explain that when your daughter has her period for the first time, you, the mother, are *allowed* to share your joy, your emotions, the news with the family . . . But she doesn't want to get into an argument with Leilani about this. What Materena wants is for her daughter to reveal one of her secrets for the grave. The one that is about her.

But there's no way Leilani is spilling the bucket.

What else can you expect from someone who writes things in a diary?

Below the Knees

These days, when Materena talks to her daughter she's got to lift her head because Leilani's grown by at least two inches since her fifteenth birthday, that girl! It means Leilani's dresses, although still fine at the top, are far too short and need to be taken down. This is what Materena is planning to do today.

Materena carefully lays out Leilani's dresses (seven in total: five brown, one yellow, one white) on her bed. Now all Materena needs to begin is the mannequin.

"Leilani! I need you!"

"In a minute," Leilani calls. "I'm changing a lightbulb in my bedroom!"

"Make sure the light is switched off!"

"*Oui,* I know!"

All right, here's the mannequin now. With a long, resigned sigh, Leilani slips into one of her too-short dresses. This particular dress, brown with thick straps, a zipper at the back and pockets at the front, is way above Leilani's knees. Kneeling, and with one expert hand, Materena undoes the stitches at the bottom of the dress, lets the dress fall down below Leilani's knees, and marks the dress's new length with a pin.

"Everybody is going to know my dresses have been taken down," Leilani says.

"And so?" Materena doesn't see what the problem is. "At least you've got something to put on your body."

"Why do you keep buying brown dresses?"

"Because they're easy to wash."

Okay, next dress.

Still sighing, Leilani slips into another dress, this one white with thick straps, a zipper at the back, and pockets at the front. It doesn't need to be taken down too much. An inch should suffice.

"I look like a nun in this dress," Leilani points out.

"*Ah non,* not at all," says Materena. "You're very pretty in this dress, you look respectable."

Okay, next dress.

"Why can't I get a new dress?" Leilani asks, slipping into another brown dress with a zipper at the back but no pockets at the front.

"Leilani . . . you know about our finances." *Ouh,* Materena is having a bit of trouble undoing these stitches. She's going to need the scissors. "I'm still paying your encyclopedia off . . . and I'm also paying for that window your big brother broke at school, and plus, your little brother wants an electric mixer. All of this costs money."

Okay, next dress.

"Vahine got a new dress because she got ten out of twenty on the history test," Leilani says as she slips into another brown dress with thick straps but with huge yellow buttons at the front. "I got nineteen out of twenty . . ." Leilani's voice trails off. Materena lifts her eyes to look at her daughter for a second and shakes her head. She knows very well what Leilani is trying to say.

Now, it's not as if Leilani's excellent schoolwork is never rewarded. Materena often treats her daughter to an ice cream when they're in town or she buys the kids a family-size container of ice cream. There's always a reward. And yes, Materena was very proud when Leilani got nineteen out of twenty on her history test. It's not everybody who knows that Louis XIV, alias Roi Soleil, was vain. He liked to admire himself in the mirror, and everywhere he went a servant followed him with a pot in case the king of France had to relieve himself. The teacher wrote *Fantastique!* on Leilani's test sheet.

"Yesterday my math teacher told me I had a brain for mathematics," continues Leilani.

"I already know you've got a brain for mathematics," Materena says. "Your teacher told me at the last parents' interview. He said, 'Your daughter has got a brain for mathematics.'" Materena won't go into what else the teacher said. The only sentence she understood from that man was, "Your daughter has got a brain for mathematics."

"Yesterday, my French teacher told me I was very gifted with compositions."

"I already know this. Your teacher told me."

"My science teacher told me it's a pleasure to teach me."

"This was yesterday too?" Materena asks, suspecting that Leilani is starting to invent. At the last parents and teachers' interview, Madame Bellard complained to Materena about Leilani being a very challenging student to teach. According to Madame Bellard, Leilani is a typical scientist. She questions and questions and questions until everything makes sense, everything is proven. "I'm not a professor," Madame Bellard told Materena. "We are not at university here. This is a high school and I'm just a high school teacher."

So it's very unlikely for Madame Bellard to have told Leilani that she was such a pleasure to teach.

Okay, next dress.

"You know, the archbishop will be visiting our school next month, and do you know who will be reading him a passage from the Bible?" asks Leilani after a long silence.

Ah, now Leilani is going a bit too far, Materena tells herself. There's no need to bring the poor archbishop into the story.

"Leilani," she says, "that's enough *ha'avare,* don't you think?"

"I'm telling the truth! The archbishop will be visiting our school!" Leilani goes on about how preparations for his visit are already in place. Walls are getting painted. Flowers are getting planted. Students are rehearsing greeting the archbishop. You kneel and you kiss his ring.

Materena looks up at her daughter with tenderness in her eyes. Her story about the archbishop visiting sounds true and . . . *Aue . . .* Materena can't believe her daughter has been chosen to read the archbishop a passage from the Bible. What an honor!

"Vahine is so nervous," Leilani says.

"Oh . . . I don't see why she needs to be nervous. It's very easy to kneel and kiss a ring."

"She's not nervous about that . . . she's nervous to read for the archbishop."

"Ah," Materena says, a bit disappointed. "I thought it was you who was going to read for the archbishop."

"Me?" Leilani cackles. "Like . . ." One look from her mother and Leilani changes her tone. "Oh, *oui alors . . .* I wish I were reading for the archbishop . . . But I read in class yesterday . . . my English teacher said . . ."

"Don't move, I'm making a mistake here," Materena interrupts.

Okay, next dress.

"You know, Mamie . . . I won't be able to wear any of these dresses once I have breasts." This is Leilani's declaration and Materena bursts out laughing. That Leilani, she thinks. She will stop at nothing to get a new dress. She's so stubborn.

"Don't laugh," Leilani urges her mother. "This is serious." She explains that when you have breasts, you've got to wear dresses that can accommodate them. You can't wear dresses that are tight at the top.

Materena stops fussing over the stitches to meditate a little. But! It makes sense, what Leilani is saying. Once Leilani is going to start having breasts, she's not going to fit into any of her dresses. Materena can't believe she didn't think about that. She could be wasting her time taking down all these dresses today because Leilani's breasts are sure to be arriving very soon. They've already popped out a tiny bit. It's only a matter of time before they erupt.

Sitting in the back of Auntie Rita's car on the way to town the next day, Leilani can't stop grinning with delight. She's getting a new dress today and Rita, being an expert with fabric, is going to help her and Materena, who's not an expert with fabric.

"And what's the budget?" Leilani asks her mother, who is sitting in the front discussing fabric with Rita.

Materena, looking over her shoulder, replies, "The budget, the budget . . . there's no budget . . . If I have the money, I'll buy a nice dress, it's simple."

Then Materena goes back to discussing fabric with her cousin.

"And I get to choose the dress, okay?" Leilani says.

Materena glances at her daughter for a second and says nothing.

Back to discussing fabric with her cousin. "So, Rita? When is the sale at your shop?"

"I wouldn't mind a dress with thin straps," Leilani says. "I used to have dresses with thin straps when I was little." Leilani sighs with nostalgia.

Rita glances at her niece in the rear mirror and smiles. "Ah," she says, "I would give anything to be able to wear a dress with thin straps." Rita goes on about how much she envies women who can wear dresses with thin straps. Rita can't wear that kind of dress. Her arms are too fat. But to wear a dress with thin straps once in her life at least would make Rita so happy.

Materena puts a comforting arm on her cousin's shoulder. "Cousin, your beauty is on the inside and that's more important than the beauty on the outside."

"What do you mean to say here?" Rita asks. "That I'm not beautiful on the outside?"

"But *non!*" Materena exclaims in protest. "Rita . . ."

Rita chuckles.

Ouf . . . luckily Rita is in a good mood today.

Anyway, they're in town now and after driving around for twenty minutes looking for a free parking spot, Rita scores one at last. Rita can't stand paying for parking spots. She'd pay thousands of francs for an ornament, but there's no way she'd pay hundreds of francs for a parking spot. It's against her nature. That free parking spot puts her in an even better mood. Okay . . . all women out of the car. Let's go and get that dress.

First stop is a little shop where dresses don't cost the eyes of the head, dresses that are on sale all year round. Leilani drags her feet walking into the shop, which is crowded with mamas, young girls, and babies in carriages. Pop music is blasting out of wrecked *haut-parleurs.*

Ah! And what does Materena see hanging at the back of the shop? A dress that has not only been reduced by 50 percent but that is so beautiful. Feel the fabric! And check out the large pockets! Materena takes the dress off the rack and gives it to her daughter for her to go and try on, all the while praising large pockets. In Materena's opinion, women can always do with large pockets. You can put all sorts of things in large pockets: money for the truck, pens, sandwiches, bottles of lemonade.

Materena is still holding the dress, waiting for her daughter to grab it.

"So?" she says. "Go and try that dress on, girl. I can't wait to see you in it. You're going to look so beautiful." Then, looking at Rita, she adds. "Eh, Rita? What luck, eh?"

Rita looks at her niece and sees the desperation in her eyes. She smiles with compassion. Yes, she knows how it is when your mother chooses the dress you're going to wear.

"The pockets aren't ripped?" Rita asks Materena. She explains that when a dress is on sale it is usually because there's something wrong with it. Rita always pays full price for her dresses.

Materena checks the pockets. No, they're not ripped.

"And the zipper?" Rita asks. "It's not stuck?" Materena checks the zipper. *Non,* it's not stuck, it works perfectly. Rita feels the fabric and grimaces. "That's cheap fabric," she says, shaking her head with regret. "That dress is going to tear in the washing machine like that." She clicks her fingers.

"Ah, you think?" Materena asks. "And if I wash it by hand?"

Rita feels the fabric again and looks up to the ceiling for a moment, as if deep in thought. "Three washes. After that the fabric is going to tear. But you decide, it's your money."

Materena hangs the dress back on the rack.

Next shop.

Next dress . . . and Materena is so excited. She can't believe her luck today! She just loves the red dots on that dress, they really give it an air of gaiety.

Again, Auntie Rita steps in. "Cousin, the fabric . . ." But there's only so much Rita can say about fabric and she's running out of ideas. It's Leilani's turn now to tell Materena what's wrong with the dress she's just taken off the rack.

"I don't like that dress," Leilani says.

"What don't you like?" Materena asks.

"Everything, Mamie," Leilani says, trying to keep her sweet voice. "The shape, the size, the color."

"What's wrong with the color? Yellow is a beautiful color, what's wrong with yellow?"

"Mamie . . ."

"Oh," Materena says as she puts the dress back on the rack. "You're not going to wear brown for the rest of your life!"

Next shop.

Materena doesn't want to go into the next shop. She doesn't like the shopkeeper, who always looks at you like you're going to steal something.

Next shop.

No, clothes in that shop cost the eyes of the head.

Next shop.

No, that shop looks too high-class.

"Come on, let's go in," Rita says.

"*Ah non,* cousin," Materena says. "That shop is for rich people."

"Well, I'm going to look inside," Rita announces. "You can wait outside."

Rita and Leilani walk in while Materena stands outside. Every time Leilani waves her mother to come in, Materena waves her away.

Here's Leilani taking a lacy black dress off the rack. Facing her mother, she puts the lacy black dress in front of her and shakes her shoulders. Materena widens her eyes, meaning: Stop it, hurry up and put that dress back on the rack before the shopkeeper sees you!

Grinning, Leilani puts the dress back on the rack. Then she takes another one. This time it's a very long white dress with frills, which again Leilani puts in front of her, but this time she bows before her mother with her eyes closed.

But what's this? Materena asks herself. It's to try to get me into that shop? As Leilani puts the frilly dress back on the rack, Materena gets her purse from inside her pandanus bag, opens her purse (still in the pandanus bag) . . . Okay, there's five thousand-franc bills, one five-hundred-franc bill . . . lots of coins . . . total (approximate) is seven thousand francs.

Here's Rita at the door with her handbag casually resting over her shoulder. "And so?" she calls out. "You're coming in or not? You need an invitation?"

Materena looks down at her thongs, cursing herself for not wearing her shoes today. Her feet were hurting so much this morning. Well anyway, her thongs are clean, she scrubbed them last night. We're going to eat breadfruit today, tomorrow, and the day after, Materena tells herself as she walks into the shop, trying to muster all her dignity.

Ah, at least the music here is soft and relaxing. Here's Leilani holding a folded blue dress with thin straps, asking her mother if she can try it on.

"Why not?" Materena says, looking at the well-dressed women in the shop from the corner of her eyes. "But let me feel the fabric first."

Materena discreetly checks out the price tag as she feels the fabric. Oh, what a relief! The price is quite reasonable. There must be something wrong with it.

Materena asks Rita to feel the fabric.

"Top quality," Rita declares.

All right, then. Leilani hurries into the changing room, followed by her mother. She pulls the curtains closed and begins to undress. After a while Materena pokes her head in.

"Mamie! A bit of privacy here!"

"Oh," Materena whispers, half-cranky, half-laughing as she pulls the curtains closed. "Who do you think gave birth to you, you silly coconut."

Half a minute later and Materena is beginning to feel impatient. It doesn't take a century to slip into a dress, and plus, another girl accompanied by her mother is waiting to get into the dressing room. How come this shop has only one dressing room available? Materena asks herself. But there are some stupid people involved in commerce.

"So?" Materena discreetly calls out from behind the curtains.

"This is the dress I want, Mamie!" Leilani calls back.

"Can I look?"

Materena is just thinking of walking into the dressing room when Leilani pulls the curtains open in one theatrical movement, then rolls her derriere, one hand on her hip, before marching out of the room. You would think she was on the podium for the Miss Tahiti contest. The girl who'd been waiting for the dressing room to be free walks in with her mother following, and Materena calls out to Rita to come and see.

Rita appears in a flash.

Her face lights up, "*Aue!* Boys are going to fall on their knees for you."

But Materena is not sharing Rita's emotion. She had thought the length of the blue dress was just an illusion because the dress was folded. Frowning, Materena asks Leilani, "It's not a bit too short?"

"*Non,*" Leilani replies, "this is the normal length."

"Eh, stop . . . I wasn't born in the last rain . . . Bend over."

Leilani bends over.

"Eh here," Materena says, "I saw your underpants."

Rita, cackling, tells Leilani that she better make sure to always be wearing clean underpants then. She winks to Materena and since Materena is not winking back, Rita makes a serious face.

"That dress is just too short," Materena says. "It's shorter than all the dresses you have at home."

"No, it's not!" Then, pleading with Auntie Rita with her eyes, Leilani asks her what she thinks.

Aue, poor Auntie Rita, stuck between the tomato and the lettuce again, between the daughter and the mother. Is the dress a bit too short? she asks herself. Well, yes, but when you've got nice legs, you might as well show them off. If Rita had nice legs like Leilani's, she'd be wearing short dresses every day. But here, Rita doesn't have nice legs. When she sees Cousin Lily parading in her short dresses, making men of all ages trip over, Rita gets so envious. Some days, she feels like shaking Lily a little for her luck with those long brown muscular legs. So, is the dress a bit too short? No, not really, compared to what young girls wear these days.

"Not necessarily," she says.

"You see?" Leilani says. "This dress is fine . . . Please, Mamie."

Please, Mamie, Materena thinks. That girl only says please when she needs me to open my purse. She looks at her daughter and that dress — that dress is just too short. What a shame, because the fabric is top quality.

But what is a young clever girl going to get wearing a dress so short?

She's going to get a lot of attention from boys, boys who've only seen her in long dresses with thick straps, pockets, and huge buttons. Materena's cousin Tapeta never buys her daughter Rose short dresses. She always says, "I'm singing at the airport five mornings a week on top of my job at the hospital for Rose to go to private school to get her papers, and not for boys to give her interested looks."

Materena feels the same way. "I've taken my decision," she says. "And my decision is that the dress is too short." She goes on about how a dress like this is only going to cause trouble with boys.

"But I don't want to cause trouble!" Leilani's voice is no longer a whisper. "I just want to wear that dress for me!"

"I understand what you're saying." Materena turns to Rita and asks, "What do you think?"

And this is Rita's answer: "Even if your daughter wears a sack of potato, boys are going to look at her because she's got slim legs."

This answer comes out of Rita's mouth in one go. There was no need for five seconds of contemplation. But then again, she's not the mother of the young girl. She doesn't have to worry about certain things like Materena has to. And if Materena doesn't buy that dress, her daughter is going to do her long face. *Aue!* Imagine having the money to buy your daughter a new dress every week. What a nightmare!

"Mamie?" Leilani pleads. "You know me. Do I look at boys? *Non.* Never. I don't have the faintest interest in boys. I will go to university . . . I will become a professor . . ."

But she will stop at nothing, that one! Materena yells in her head. And she's going to be a professor now? Last month Leilani said she was going to be a social worker. She keeps changing her mind.

"You're going to be a professor now?" asks Materena. Leilani nods, her hands clasped in prayer, miming, Please, Mamie.

Eh, eh, Materena remembers back to when she was fifteen years old and the fashion was for shirtdresses with a picture of a fruit on the front. When you scratched the picture of the fruit you could smell its scent. There was a shirtdress with a picture of an apple, a shirtdress with a picture of a pineapple, there were many choices and everybody had a shirtdress like that except for Materena. Then one day, her mother said, "All right, let's go and get that shirtdress you've been talking about nonstop."

But when Loana saw the shirtdress in the shop, she looked at the price tag and did her horrified eyes. "This dress costs the eyes of the head!" she said. "What am I paying all that money for? The apple or the cheap fabric? You don't think we should buy ten pounds of apples instead of that apple here? And is this a dress or a shirt for when you sleep? It's way below the knees."

"It's a shirt!" Materena said with all her heart and soul.

Loana shook her head and mumbled, "All that money for you to look like an old woman."

Eh well, times sure have changed.

"All right, then," Materena sighs, smiling to her daughter. "Hurry up, go and put your dress on the counter before I change my mind."

We're a Different Generation

There's a *boum,* a party, this Saturday three houses away from where Leilani's best friend, Vahine, lives. Vahine has been invited and so has Leilani, and of course Leilani is expecting her mother to say, "Yes, of course you can go to the *boum.*"

Leilani has it all planned, so she tells her mother, who is hanging clothes. She'll be wearing her new blue dress (it has already made one of the nuns so cranky she sent Leilani home to get changed). She'll be picked up at around six thirty by Vahine's mother, she and Vahine will be picked up at around eleven o'clock from the *boum,* she'll sleep at Vahine's house, and then she will be dropped home on Sunday before nine o'clock, for Mass.

Materena, pegging a shirt, cackles. "For Mass? Why? Are you going to Mass this Sunday?"

Leilani has stopped going to Mass for months.

"Maybe," Leilani whispers sweetly. "So? Can I go to the *boum?* I'm nearly sixteen years old."

"Leilani, your birthday is in nine months."

"*Oui,* I know, but I'm already sixteen years old in the head."

Leilani goes on about how she's very mature for her age. She understands many things about life because she's part of such an extended family. Most of her friends at school wouldn't know what it means to share their last eggs.

"Ah." Materena chuckles. "Now I understand why you're so mature."

"Mamie . . . you're so *rigolote.*" Chuckling too, Leilani helps her mother peg a sock. "You know what I mean."

Well, that is the last piece of clothing to hang. Materena picks the clothes basket up and, walking toward the house, she says, "Girl, you've got plenty of time to go to *boums* when you're older."

"Mamie!" Leilani follows her mother, stomping her foot along the way. "You were young once, you used to go to *boums.*"

Materena informs her daughter that actually she didn't go to *boums* at Leilani's age. She went to baptisms, weddings, and funerals.

"Oh . . ." Leilani searches for the right word to say. "Oh . . ."

Leilani, elbows on the kitchen table, is openly admiring her mother sewing buttons on Tamatoa's shirt.

"Tamatoa always loses his buttons, doesn't he?" says Leilani.

Materena lifts her eyes and says nothing.

"You're such a good sewer." Leilani is still on her mission to persuade her mother to let her go to the *boum* this Saturday. She moans that she's so hopeless with sewing, she's not patient enough, she's not the kind to pay attention to the little details, whereas her mother is so talented with sewing — with everything she does, actually.

"*Merci, chérie,*" says Materena, smiling. She doesn't mind the compliment, even if there's an agenda behind it. However, Materena feels it's important to remind Leilani that she's offered to teach her to sew on several occasions.

"Oh." Leilani waves a hand. "Sewing is not really important for our new generation because we care about other things."

"What, for example?" Materena asks, very interested in what Leilani will say.

"Well . . ." Leilani looks into her mother's eyes. "The death penalty. The starving children in Africa. The laws. Empowering women. The alarming birthrate in Tahiti and in the world. Our generation has so many issues to worry about, Mamie. We need to loosen up, otherwise we'd go mad."

"Ah, I see." Materena nods knowingly. "And are you saying that the women of the old generation had nothing to worry about?"

"Of course I'm not!" Leilani exclaims, on the defensive. She explains that the women of Materena's generation paved the way for the women of her new generation. They said no to arranged marriages. They said no to work without pay. They said less sewing, please.

Materena bursts out laughing. And that is when Leilani attacks her mother with her request about the *boum.*

Materena stops laughing. "Girl . . . sometimes children have to accept their mother's decision." Then, smiling, Materena adds that she has her reasons for not letting Leilani go to the *boum.*

"What are they?"

Materena stops smiling and puts her sewing on the table. "Do I need to draw you a picture?" she asks.

"But what are your reasons?" Leilani insists.

Materena shakes her head with disbelief. She can't understand Leilani's generation. Her generation wouldn't dare ask their mother to justify her decision. What mamas said was the law, the final word. Well anyway, this is the new generation, and so Materena explains the situation, which has everything to do with danger.

"Danger?" The situation is still not clear for Leilani. "What do you mean? What's so dangerous about dancing?" Before

Materena has the chance to explain that the danger she's talking about has got nothing to do with dancing, Leilani is passionately defending the art of dancing, this wonderful art that is part of Tahitian culture. She's raving about the Arioi, the professional dancers from a long time ago, who traveled from one island to the next to entertain the people and bring peace.

How does my daughter know about the Arioi? Materena asks herself. I've never told her about the Arioi. Someone else must have told her. "The Arioi, eh?" Materena says. "And did the person who told you about them also mention how the Arioi were forbidden to have children, they had to kill their babies, all they were allowed to do was dance? Love was forbidden. Family was forbidden."

"All right, you win," Leilani says. "At least we both agree that dancing is not dangerous."

"Of course dancing is not dangerous! I've never said that! When I said danger I meant boys and girls, they drink, they do *conneries* . . ." Materena's voice trails off.

"Mamie, you know I'm allergic to alcohol." Leilani reminds her mother about the first and last time she had half a glass of beer, on her fifteenth birthday. She vomited. She was sick for three days. "Mamie, you know about the problem with my liver. It can't handle alcohol." Materena nods a vague nod and starts sewing again.

Materena keeps on nodding as Leilani talks about how young girls of today aren't interested in getting drunk, anyway. They're more interested in having fun, celebrating their youth with dancing, all the while exchanging ideas on the dance floor. "Please, Mamie," Leilani begs. "You can't keep me locked in a castle. I'm young. You always say life goes too fast . . . Please, Mamie. And plus, no boys will pay attention to me, I have a flat chest."

Aue, Materena thinks. If I say *oui* and something bad happens to my girl, I'm never going to forgive myself. If I say *non* . . . Ah, here's Pito coming home from his walkabout. He's jovial, of course. He's whistling a happy tune.

"Ask Papi," Materena says.

Materena usually doesn't consult Pito in decisions regarding the children, the house, the food, etc., but there's a first time for everything. Before Leilani has a chance to put her request forward, Tamatoa is in the kitchen.

"Papi!" Tamatoa asks, smiling. "Can I borrow your nice shirt for Saturday?"

"What's happening on Saturday?"

"I'm going to a *boum.*"

"Ah, and can I go with you?" Pito chuckles. "Yeah, all right, you can borrow my shirt, but you better bring it back with all the buttons."

"*Merci,* Papi!"

"Where's the *boum?*" Materena asks.

"It's near Vahine's house."

"Did she invite you too?" Leilani shrieks.

"*Oui,* and so?" Tamatoa doesn't see what the problem is.

"You've been invited to the *boum* too?" Pito asks Leilani, sounding very surprised about this.

"Well, *oui,* Papi. She's *my* friend."

"Ah, okay . . . you two have fun."

By the time Materena arrives home after Mass with her youngest son, her eldest son is on the sofa telling his father his exploits. He got lucky, and Pito is very delighted. Here he is, shaking his son's hand. Patting him on the shoulder. Welcoming him into manhood. Telling the new man that of course he doesn't mind that a girl ripped three buttons off this shirt to get to his son.

As for Leilani, she's in bed. She tells her mother the *boum* was so boring. The music was way too loud. She couldn't talk to anyone.

When Breasts Open the Eyes

To Materena's great relief, Leilani's growing breasts hasn't turned her into a boy admirer, contrary to what her cousin Tapeta told her to expect.

In Tapeta's experience, the day her daughter Rose started getting breasts, she turned into a boy admirer. These days, so Tapeta complained to Materena two months ago outside the Chinese store, Rose can't walk two steps without admiring a boy she likes the look of. These days, Rose is constantly smiling to boys, giving them the you're-a-nice-looking-boy-you look.

Tapeta is even more worried now that Rose got herself a weekend job at the Airport Café because, also in Tapeta's experience, the Airport Café is filled with boys who are after just one thing. If only Tapeta didn't need the extra money, she'd tie her daughter to a tree until she finished school.

Well, Materena is sure glad Leilani's getting breasts hasn't turned her into a boy admirer. They have just made her even more outspoken. She's never been afraid to speak her mind, and Materena doesn't see anything wrong with this. But she's even more outspoken now. For example, Leilani told her father that if he kept drinking the way he did, he was going to die of liver cancer. Pito shrugged and went on about how we're all going to die so we might as well die doing what we like. Leilani also told her father he was starting to look a bit yellow and that was because all his alcohol consumption was poisoning his blood. Pito laughed his head off, but then he went to check himself in front of the mirror. Materena had a good chuckle.

Then last week, Materena and Leilani were walking out of Euromarché when a toothless woman carrying a flour bag over her shoulder accosted them to sell them coconuts. The woman explained, with her sad voice, that her children had nothing to eat and that she was selling her coconuts real cheap. One thousand francs for a packet of three coconuts. Materena reached for her purse in her pandanus bag and saw that she had only one thousand-franc banknote left. She said, "Ah, it's your lucky day today, mama."

The woman dropped the bag on the floor and out came three coconuts, which she handed to Leilani, but Leilani, arms folded, didn't take them. She asked, "Are you sure the money is for the children?" The woman hurried to nod and went on about her children having nothing to eat. As she walked away, one thousand francs richer, Leilani called out, "Have a good drink!"

Now, Materena also suspected that woman was going to drink the money because she did look a bit . . . a bit like a woman who drank. But sometimes, so Materena explained to Leilani, who was criticizing her for having given that alcoholic money, sometimes you have to believe people are telling you the truth.

On the way home, a woman was smoking in the truck. People have been smoking in the truck for centuries and people who don't smoke just bear it. Nobody wants to have a fight in a truck because of a cigarette. That day, Leilani, looking at that woman (and she was not little), coughed and waved her hand in front of her face. Then she read (and not in a low voice) the announcement written next to the tariff. *It is forbidden to drink, smoke, and eat sandwiches in the truck.* Not only did she read the announcement written in French, she also read the one written in Tahitian. Then she went on again with her coughing. Materena discreetly tapped her daughter to be quiet. That woman was sure going to get annoyed very soon and start insulting Leilani, and then Materena would be forced to do something. It wasn't in Materena's plan to fight a big woman that day. It wasn't in Materena's plan to fight anyone, full stop. She tapped her daughter again to be quiet, but Leilani coughed even louder.

And the woman went on with smoking her cigarette, drawing on the butt several times before chucking her cigarette out the window.

Now, as far as Materena was concerned, Leilani had the right to let that big woman know of her discomfort, but . . .

Ah, one more example: yesterday, Materena and Leilani met Cousin Giselle at the Chinese store, where she told them about taking Isidore Louis junior to the doctor last week. He had a skin disease that looked like chicken pox, but it was something else Giselle couldn't remember the name of. Anyway, Giselle took her son to the doctor, who gave him some antibiotics and a cream. And now Giselle's three children have that skin disease!

Next thing, Leilani was asking her auntie why didn't she ask her doctor if her son's skin disease was contagious. In Leilani's mind, that should have been her auntie's first question to her doctor, and if she had done so, she might have been able to prevent the contagion. She would have made sure Isidore Louis junior didn't share his towel with his siblings. "Girl," Giselle said, not laughing anymore, "the doctor should have told me. It wasn't up to me to ask."

Materena dragged Leilani away before she started opening her mouth again and angered Giselle more.

But this didn't stop Leilani from talking about it later on at home. Leilani was so cranky with her auntie Giselle, her doctor, and everyone who doesn't think.

"Are we stupid or what?" Leilani exclaimed, putting the groceries away.

"Who's we?" Materena asked.

"We, us, Tahitian people." Leilani went on with her comments about how it's so stupid that a mother doesn't ask her doctor if her child's skin disease is contagious. It's so stupid that we let a stupid woman smoke in the truck when it is clearly forbidden. It's so stupid that we drink instead of feeding our children. It's so stupid that a priest can decide how many children we can have. It's so stupid that a woman covers her bruised eye with a bandage instead of leaving her husband. It's so stupid . . .

Materena went outside to water the plants. She needed time to think.

Anyway, Materena can do with a no-comment day today, and so she isn't going to ask Leilani to come with her to her favorite shop, Ah Kiong.

That Chinese store wouldn't survive without women like Materena, Tahitian women, Tahitian women without a husband, Tahitian women with too many children, Tahitian women who don't mind that their sunglasses don't protect their eyes, their towels don't dry the skin very well. Ah Kiong has been Materena's favorite place to spend her hard-earned money for five years now. Nothing there costs the eyes of the head.

The moment Materena announces that she's off to Ah Kiong, Tamatoa, doing sit-ups, says he wants coconut lollies.

"Where's your *please?*" Leilani, reading a book as thick as a Bible, asks. "That word doesn't exist in your vocabulary?" Of course Tamatoa tells his sister off, and of course Leilani tells her brother off. Materena grabs her bag.

Leilani, up and marching toward her room to get her shoes, tells her mother to wait. She's going to town too.

"Eh!" Materena calls out. "I'm going to that shop you don't like!"

"*Oui,* I know!" Leilani calls back. Leilani is ready and smiling, she nods to her mother the signal — Let's go. These days, Leilani smiles so rarely that Materena melts. Leilani is so pretty when she smiles. So, smiling back, Materena nods to her daughter the signal — Okay then, girlfriend, let's go.

They sit side by side in the truck, which is packed, as you would expect it to be on a Saturday morning. People always have a reason to go to town on a Saturday morning, even more so when it's the end of the month.

Facing Materena and Leilani is a very young woman with a newborn baby sucking on her breast. Materena gives her daughter the you-better-not-say-anything-about-this look. Saying something to a woman breast-feeding is asking for trouble, you're going to get your eyes scratched out. Plus, a woman breast-feeding is a beautiful thing to see. It's one of the many miracles in life. Materena has never stopped herself from breast-feeding her babies in public. When baby is hungry, you feed baby, and people who don't like it, well, look somewhere else, just as the American tourists are now doing.

Materena tenderly looks at that baby sucking at his mama's breast, and Leilani is doing the same, and Materena can't believe Leilani's eyes are full of adoration. Here she is staring at that baby with that beautiful smile that says, "Oh, but he's so beautiful, that baby." Leilani has always said that babies are ugly and that newborns remind her of little lizards. She must have changed her mind about this.

Materena goes on admiring the newborn falling asleep on his mother's breast and thinking how the father must be a *popa'a* because that is one very pink baby. Very soon, the young mother notices Materena's and Leilani's attention on her newborn. A smile follows, another smile, a word, and next minute she's pouring her heart out to Materena about how she's on her way to talk to her man, the father of that little one. She's going to tell him that the baby is his and that the reason he looks *popa'a* is because she's got an American ancestor. She's also going to warn her ex-boyfriend that if he doesn't recognize their baby, her grandmother is going to curse him. He's going to die of a horrible disease. His left leg is going to swell on him.

On and on the young girl goes about what her ex-boyfriend is going to get if he says again today that the baby she made with him on the sofa in the living room while his mama was at bingo is not his. He's going to get a horrible punishment if her son ends up having Father Unknown on his birth certificate.

Well, she's here at her ex-boyfriend's house now, she says as she presses the buzzer with one hand and takes her breast out of the baby's mouth with the other hand. But before she steps down from the truck, she wants to show Materena her baby's birthmark. Out come the baby's blanket, the baby's pants, the baby's diaper, revealing the baby's private part. Pointing to a tiny dot under one of the baby boy's balls, she informs Materena that his father has the same dot and at the same place.

So there. The young girl steps down from the truck with her head held up high.

Leilani, looking at her mother, shakes her head and asks, "Why do people always tell you their stories? It's amazing!" Materena tells her daughter that everyone is born with a gift and hers is to listen to people telling her stories. Leilani takes her mother's hand. Materena squeezes it with all her heart and soul. The last time Leilani held her mother's hand in public, she was ten years old.

They walk into Materena's favorite shop in a very good mood, making way for a dear old Tahitian woman. It's a real Ali Baba cave here, with every single shelf packed with cheap things, past-due-date packets of lollies included, and with cardboard boxes shoved in everywhere there's a space. And it's hot and stuffy.

Only a small price to pay. There's always a treasure to find here.

First, though, Materena leaves her pandanus bag at the counter (as always) and ignores Leilani's comment, "Mamie, stop acting like you're a thief." Materena has good reason to leave her bag at the counter. When you walk around the shop with a bag, you can be sure you're going to be followed by one of the shop assistants.

Ah, and what does Materena see out there? Stuffed on one of the shelves? Reduced by 50 percent? Towels!

Materena hurries to those towels reduced by 50 percent. Here, she's going to grab five. You can always do with extra towels when unexpected visitors decide to have a shower. Materena rubs a towel on her face — it's so soft. Is this silk, by any chance? Materena checks the label. Ah, she knew it. Polyester. Still, it's very soft. Here, she's going to buy three more. It's not every day that towels of this quality are reduced by 50 percent! They're almost giving them away. Here, let's grab two more towels.

Right then, Materena notices a young man in the corner, a young Tahitian man wearing a beanie with a ripped T-shirt and pants falling down his derriere. Looking like he's waiting for an opportunity to sneak the purse he's looking at under his shirt. The shop assistant, eyeing him with suspicious eyes, seems to be thinking the same. Materena turns to Leilani, who's staring at a young Frenchwoman wearing an immaculate office outfit with gold shoes and a silver handbag, admiring ornaments, and whispers, "Check that man there. He sure looks like he's waiting for an opportunity to sneak the purse under his shirt, eh?"

Leilani looks at the man and whispers back, "Here you go assuming again." In Leilani's mind, the Frenchwoman looks more like a suspect. She just doesn't fit the criteria of this shop's customers.

Materena tells Leilani that the Frenchwoman is buying her cleaner a gift.

"How do you know this?" asks Leilani. "That man may also be buying his cleaner a gift. Just because he's Tahitian doesn't mean he's a thief."

"Did I say he was a thief?" Materena grinds her teeth. "Stop putting words in my mouth."

"Mamie, these are your words."

"I didn't say he was a thief, I said he looked like a thief."

"Where's the difference?"

Aue . . . Materena is not interested in having an argument about thieves today. She goes on with her shopping, feeling . . . well, feeling a bit ashamed. She'd be the first to tell people, Don't judge an orange by its peel, and here she was judging an orange by its peel. *Pardon,* Materena says in her head.

She calls out to Leilani to ask her opinion about some ornaments to put in the garden. Materena doesn't know which one to choose.

Leilani comes over to give her opinion. "These gnomes look awful."

Materena is about to tell Leilani that, actually, she thinks the gnomes look really nice, when the shop owner yells, "Somebody stole all the sunglasses!" and runs over to lock the door.

She's onto the young Tahitian man real quick, who takes his shirt off at her request as she goes on about how she only took her eyes off him for ten seconds. The young man is not saying anything. He just does what he's told. He takes his beanie off. He takes his pants off. No sunglasses are found.

"Will you be checking that Frenchwoman too?" asks Leilani. But the Frenchwoman has already checked herself out.

Later, Materena and Leilani are walking to the snack not far from the trucks for Materena to buy Tamatoa his coconut lollies and Leilani a lemonade. Materena doesn't say a word, deep in her thought. Meanwhile, Leilani is going off at those French people giving Tahitian people a bad reputation, making them look stupid.

"We can't even look around in stores without being suspected of stealing! We have to sell coconuts to feed our children! French doctors don't tell us anything! French priests order us around! And look at . . . But do you see what I see?"

Materena looks to where Leilani is pointing. She can't believe her eyes! Sitting on a bench, the *popa'a* woman is taking a pair of sunglasses out of her silver bag and putting them on the Tahitian man's nose. And they're laughing their heads off, those two!

Unbelievable! I knew he wasn't innocent! Materena yells in her head. What an actor!

For the first time in weeks, Leilani, her eyes wide open, is speechless.

Sometimes the Fruit Does Fall Far from the Tree

Instead of catching the truck straight home from the market today on this beautiful afternoon, Materena walks to the cathedral in Papeete. She needs to talk to somebody.

And not to her mother, who's only going to say, "I don't understand, girl, you were not like that when you were Leilani's age. Don't worry, it's the new generation."

Not to Cousin Rita, who's only going to say, "She needs something, that girl . . . I don't know what, but she needs something. It's normal, it's the hormones."

Not to Pito, who's only going to say . . . who's going to say nothing. Materena has learned a long time ago that Pito is deaf when it suits him. He's definitely deaf when she talks to him about problems. Problems regarding his daughter? Let's not talk about it. She might as well be talking about the moon and the planets! As far as Pito is concerned, his daughter is fine. It's Materena who has got a problem. She takes things too seriously.

Materena walks into the cathedral, crosses herself, and looks around. She counts four women. Four women who, just like

Materena, need somebody to talk to, or perhaps they have something to ask. She's not surprised to find no men. The church for men is the bar.

There are women of all ages here today, one kneeling, another sitting with her head bowed, another standing up, her eyes staring at Jesus Christ on the cross, another hiding her face behind her hands. And Materena thinks, Well, I'm not the only woman with a heavy heart today. That's a bit of a comfort. Materena takes a seat right by the door opposite the statue of the Virgin Mary, Understanding Woman.

Materena looks at that woman, and just looking at her brings tears into Materena's eyes. Materena doesn't always cry when she looks at the Virgin Mary, but today she has to. Materena cries, all the while sighing.

It's okay, when you're in the church nobody judges you for crying on a beautiful afternoon. Nobody judges you for crying, full stop. In fact, only crying is allowed in the church. It's disrespectful to laugh your head off in the church, but you can cry as much as you want. Nobody is going to chuck you out of the church. So Materena cries her eyes out, all the while wiping her eyes with the back of her hand and pouring out her problem to the Virgin Mary, Understanding Woman, who understands all kinds of trouble.

Troubles between a man and a woman, sisters, brothers, cousins; between a mother and a daughter.

Aue, Virgin Mary, moans Materena in her head. Give me strength. Materena reminds the Virgin Mary how she's not the kind to annoy her about the littlest trouble and she's not the kind to make unreasonable demands, such as the winning *tombola* number. And she doesn't only speak to the Virgin Mary when she's got troubles. She also speaks to the Virgin Mary to thank her for all her love, guidance, help, everything. She's here today because . . .

She's here because she's *that* close to throwing her daughter into the street! That's the reason Materena is here. She knows she needs help; the way she sees things, it's not natural for a mother to want to throw her daughter into the street. It's more natural for a mother to love her daughter no matter what, to stand by her daughter no matter what because, once linked with the umbilical cord, we're linked for the eternity. But . . .

Aue, Virgin Mary, what is this challenge you're giving me? She's pushing me, that girl, she's doing everything for me to . . . to . . . want to shove her clothes and her books in plastic bags and kick her into the street. Then she's going to see where not respecting your mother takes you. It takes you into the street, that's where!

Well, Leilani is never really going to have to live in the street. A relative is bound to rescue her and then Materena is going to get a bad name. When you throw your children into the street, it means you're weak, you're a bad mother. "Shame on you," the relatives are going to say.

Oh, here's a well-dressed Chinese woman with very high-heeled shoes holding about ten shopping bags, walking into the cathedral. What has she got to ask the Virgin Mary? Materena wonders. The well-dressed Chinese woman sits in the front row. Drops her shopping bags on the seat. Rearranges her bun. She makes a fanning movement with the palm of her hand and Materena understands that the well-dressed Chinese woman is here because it's nice and cool.

But some people, Materena thinks.

You don't go into the church to cool down! Anyway, about Leilani, is she supposed to be my cross to bear in this life? she asks the Virgin Mary. Was she born to give me miseries? My boys don't give me half as much trouble.

These days, Materena can't say anything to Leilani without Leilani finding the little beast. For example, when Materena says that the reason Rita can't lose weight is because of her problems with hormones, Leilani says, "Auntie Rita eats too much."

When Materena complains of her hands being so used up because of all the cleaning they do, and dares tell Her Highness that she wouldn't mind another job because cleaning is so lonely sometimes, Her Highness says, "Get another job. Don't just complain about it. Make a change. Take control of your life!"

When Materena gives her last eggs to a relative because the Chinese store is closed, even though Materena needed those eggs to make a cake, Leilani reminds her that charity starts at home and that the relative is old enough to remember what time the store closes.

The more Materena tries to justify her actions, the more Leilani makes her feel like she's stupid.

Ah, the Chinese woman has had enough of cooling herself. She's up, and off she goes with her shopping bags, stopping by the door to face the Virgin Mary and do a quick movement with her head because it's disrespectful to walk out of the church without a little sign to the Virgin Mary or Jesus Christ.

Materena goes back to her misery.

Ah, what misery when your daughter thinks she knows better than you do. You're always on the defensive, on edge, and you can't relax. The problem with Leilani, so Materena analyzes, is that she's too much like her father. She's not diplomatic at all.

Materena smiles a faint smile to a middle-aged woman walking into the cathedral. The middle-aged woman also smiles a faint smile and sits right in front of Materena.

And now she's crying her heart out.

Fifteen minutes later she is still crying. Everyone else has left the cathedral except for Materena, who is asking herself if she should reach out to the woman. Because sometimes crying to the statue of the Virgin Mary, Understanding Woman, is not enough. You've got to cry to a woman in the flesh.

"Girlfriend?" Materena says quietly. "Can I help you?" The woman turns to Materena and holds on to Materena's hand. She tells Materena her name and how, ten minutes ago, she nearly died.

She was walking to the market when a concrete beam fell off a construction site and crashed onto the concrete path, missing Vairua by only half an inch. A woman on the other side of the road called out to Vairua, "Eh, girlfriend! You're okay?"

Vairua called back, "*Oui,* I'm fine! Thank you for asking!" But she was not fine at all. She was in shock. She stared at the concrete beam and saw herself crushed underneath it with blood dripping down her temples. She saw a crowd of people looking at her dead body. She heard them say, "Poor her, she's dead and she was just walking by."

Vairua stepped over the beam and kept on walking, all the while visualizing her wake. She saw herself in a coffin, dressed in a long white frilly robe, a thick wreath of tiare Tahiti flowers around her head, her hands resting on her chest, and she had no shoes. She's in her house, in the living room, and there's a crowd of people crying and shaking their head. In the far corner, an auntie is telling the kids to be quiet and to show some respect.

The moment has now come for the coffin to be nailed shut, and the mourners start to sing the Paea song to farewell this Catholic woman who belonged, who still belongs, here in Paea. One by one they kiss Vairua's cold forehead and tell her a few words.

Vairua's mother shoves her fist in her mouth for that daughter gone before her. Vairua's youngest son openly sobs on his mother's bare feet until his older brother pulls him away and says, "Mamie wouldn't want us to cry like babies."

As for the daughter . . . she is not here. That was when Vairua stopped visualizing her wake.

"My daughter was not at my wake." Vairua cries on Materena's hand. Materena doesn't know what to say, but she's thinking that perhaps Vairua's daughter lives in another country and couldn't get home in time because the planes were full. Or perhaps she had no money.

But the reason Vairua's daughter wasn't at her mother's wake, so Vairua tells Materena, was because Vairua kicked her out of the house six years ago. And the daughter never came back. Vairua just wouldn't accept her daughter becoming a Protestant. She wouldn't accept her daughter telling her that the Virgin Mary wasn't a virgin since Jesus had brothers and sisters.

Vairua expects her children, whom she raised in the Catholic faith, to remain Catholic till the day they die. Shaking her head with sorrow, she looks into Materena's eyes. "We used to be so close, my daughter and I," she says. "When she started crawling she'd always crawl to me, never away from me, and now she doesn't even come to my wake."

Vairua talks about the curse that makes all mothers believe that the fruit *has* to fall near the tree.

Catholic mothers must have Catholic children.

Hardworking mothers must have hardworking children.

Giving mothers must have giving children.

Tidy mothers must have tidy children.

Serious mothers must have serious children.

And on and on and on . . .

Smiling through her tears, Materena admits that it is a curse. "You know, girlfriend," she says, "when *pai* we think about it, it takes courage for a fruit to fall far from her tree."

"True," the woman who nearly died today replies, "but life is easier for everyone when we just fall back to our roots."

Nobody Is Getting Married These Days

It's quiet around here at the cemetery this morning. People haven't started visiting their loved ones, and Materena can sure do with a few moments on her own weeding her grandmother's grave, but she bumps into Mama Teta, on her way home from her husband's grave.

"Mama Teta, at what time did you arrive at the cemetery?"

Auntie and niece hug each other tight. "Are you all right, girl?" Mama Teta asks, looking into Materena's eyes.

"I'm fine, Mama Teta."

"You don't look fine to me. I've never seen you with *cernes* under your eyes before. What's going on?"

"Oh, I have problems with my daughter." Then, smiling, Materena adds, "Small ones."

"Better small problems than big problems," Mama Teta says, putting a comforting hand on her niece's shoulder.

"True."

"But better no problems full stop, eh?"

"*Aue,* Mama Teta, do you think this is possible?" Materena's eyes fill with tears. After meeting that woman in the cathedral last week, Materena has been very easygoing with Leilani. She stopped expecting her daughter to be like her. When Leilani didn't thank her mother for the cup of Milo she made her, Materena didn't say anything about it. When Materena complained about her sore belly (she was having her period) and Leilani rolled her eyes, Materena didn't say anything about it.

Anyway, lately Materena has been trying really hard to keep her cool, but last night she borrowed a pen from her daughter and said, "Thank you, girl," and Leilani got cranky. "Mamie," she said, "I don't care, it's only a pen!"

"So what if it's only a pen!" Materena shouted. "I can't say thank you? What? Do I have to be like you? Ungrateful?" And Leilani shouted again, "It's only a pen!"

Next minute, Materena and Leilani were shouting at each other, and Pito told them both to shut up. "You two are driving me crazy!" he shouted for the whole neighborhood to hear.

"Do you want to do a little *parau-parau,* girl?" Mama Teta asks. "I'm not in a hurry."

"I'm trying so hard to be a good mother, Mama Teta," says Materena, her voice trembling. "I don't know what to do anymore. I'm pulling my hair out. It doesn't matter what I do, it's always the wrong thing, you know. I'm going *taravana.*" Materena goes on about how she really can't wait for Leilani to get married and leave.

"Girl," says Mama Teta, "I've got bad news for you, nobody is getting married these days. Come, we sit in the shade and I'm going to tell you what happened to me last Saturday."

Saturday morning and what a beautiful morning it was. It's a good day to get married, and Mama Teta, yawning, forces herself to get out of bed. She starts the day with her usual *café,* makes herself a little something to eat, grabs her cosmetics bag out of the fridge, and heads for the bathroom.

The first thing she does is check in the mirror for the bits of gray hair that have grown during the past twenty-three days, since her last bridal driving job. No bride wants her chauffeur to look like she's on the age pension.

She plucks her eyebrows, blow-dries her hair, puts cream on the face, blue eye shadow, eyeliner, mascara, lipstick; the hair goes up in a neat chignon, and plastic white flowers go into the chignon. There, finished. Mama Teta is an expert at transformation after years dancing at the Pitate Club, where she'd go for a bit of fun to forget about her smelly sons for a few hours. Okay, now the suit, zipper, buttons, shoes. All right, time to go.

Mama Teta hops in the bridal car, all decorated with plastic red roses. She checks that the bride's gift is still in the glove box. Mama Teta is the only bridal-car driver on the whole island who gives brides a gift. She cares. It's only a little something, a little something for good luck with the marriage. She reverses out of the driveway and recites a little prayer for all the lunatic drivers not to be on the road at the same time as she is, and drivers without a driver's license, and drunk drivers, and drivers with poor eyesight, and stressed-out mothers, and cranky gendarmes.

Ouh, it's so dangerous on the roads.

No wonder Mama Teta hardly drives these days. She's glad today's bride doesn't live too far away.

Ah, here's the house of the bride's parents, right at the end of the dirt track. Yes, it's the only brick house around. Mama Teta parks the car and she can smell roasted pig, there's a party in the air. She slowly gets out of the car and waits for a family member to come and greet her. But nobody is coming out of the house, and so Mama Teta walks to the brick house, all the while calling out, "The chauffeur of the bride is here!"

There's still no response, and so she has to knock on the door. "*Ouh, ouh,* the chauffeur of the bride is here!" The door is opened but there's nobody at the door to greet the chauffeur of the bride, and so the chauffeur of the bride stays right where she is. Finally a middle-aged woman, all done up, comes to the door.

"*Aue . . . aue,*" she says, "there's a bit of a problem."

Mama Teta smiles. "There's always a bit of a problem at the last minute. I'll go and wait in the car, okay?"

The middle-aged woman, whom Mama Teta guesses to be the mama of the bride, or she could be an aunt, looks to the crowd outside, which has doubled in size in less than a minute. "Non, it's best you wait in the house, I don't want anybody to know there's a bit of a problem." And so Mama Teta walks into the house and is greeted by a crying bride in the living room. There's a man dressed in his funeral-and-wedding suit (the papi) standing by the crying bride and looking lost. From the living room, Mama Teta can see a whole lot of people in the backyard running around with family-size cooking pots and banana leaves and flower wreaths. She sits on the lounge next to a bunch of women of mixed ages. It seems to Mama Teta that the bride is getting cold feet.

And true, the bride is getting cold feet all right. She's going on and on about how she doesn't want to get married. And the middle-aged woman whom Mama Teta met at the door and who is definitely the mama is going on and on about all the food, and all the relatives, saying how so many caught the boat from Raiatea to Tahiti especially for the marriage.

"Think, girl," the mama says. "It's normal to be nervous, I was nervous when I married your papi."

"Ma," the bride says behind her tears, "I'm not nervous, okay, I just don't want to marry that *titoi . . .* that *con . . .* that . . ." And the bride bursts into tears. Mama Teta discreetly checks the time on her watch.

"Come on, girl," the mama says again. "I was so nervous at my wedding, I had to have a little drink to calm myself." Then, looking at the women sitting on the couch, the mama of the bride says, "We all got nervous on the day of our wedding, eh?"

Ten heads go on nodding.

"I'm not nervous!"

The poor mama doesn't know what else to do, and so she turns to the papi and pleads, "But say something to your daughter, you!" Then she falls on the couch next to Mama Teta.

"Daughters," she tells Mama Teta. "I'm sure you understand."

"I understand."

"How many daughters have you got?"

"I don't have daughters, I only have sons." But Mama Teta still understands the situation. She understands it from a bridal-car chauffeur's point of view.

"Ah, you're blessed not having daughters."

Mama Teta checks the time on her watch. The bride is now eight minutes late, and she's going to need at least ten minutes for her makeup to be redone and her hair too. The bride is always late, that's the tradition, but she can't be too late, otherwise the priest might get cranky and walk off.

The papi is standing beside his daughter, not saying anything, and so the mama is up again. "All right, I'm sick of the comedy, okay?" She marches to the bride. "You . . ." She pokes the bride's chest. "You're getting into that room." She points to a door. "And you're going to get fixed up and then you're going to get your behind into the bridal car." She points a finger at Mama Teta. "And then you're going to walk into the church and say 'I do'!"

"*Non!*"

"*Ah oui,* you are, my dear! I made a personal loan for your wedding." The mama points a finger at herself. "You hear? I signed some papers and your future mother-in-law gave me a carved wooden fruit bowl, and so you're going to get married!" The mama is now shouting at the top of her lungs.

The daughter looks into her mother's eyes. "You really want me to get married to somebody who's sleeping around, somebody who doesn't respect me? He's sleeping around, you hear? My future husband is a slut!"

Mama Teta looks at the ceiling. This has never happened in her bridal-car chauffeur's career. The living room is suddenly silent. It's hot and stuffy and Mama Teta is hungry and she thinks she should probably excuse herself now, as she's quite certain her services will not be required today.

Aue, she feels so sorry for the young woman.

As for the mama of the bride, she's lost for words and she must be feeling weak in the knees, because her husband has to support her. He says, "Listen, girl . . . What Teri'i has done doesn't mean he doesn't love you . . . All men do that . . . all men . . . it's just for fun, it's the heat, we forget ourselves, come on, let's go."

Oh my God, Mama Teta thinks, what a stupid man he is. What a fool!

"Excuse me? All men? We forget ourselves?" This is the wife talking and she's not leaning on her husband anymore.

The husband's face goes pale and he has to undo the top button on his shirt because the words he has just said are now choking him.

"All men? That means you too, then." His wife's voice is getting shriller. The husband wipes sweat off his forehead and coughs. He doesn't feel too well.

"All men, you say?" The wife looks at her husband like she's about to devour him raw. "I've had suspicions all my life, so tell me now, when you say all men, it means you too, eh?" She pushes him. "Eh?" She pushes him again. "Why are you pale, why are you sweating?"

"Angelica," he says.

"Don't 'Angelica' me, get out, get out, get out." She pushes him, but it's like trying to uproot a tree.

Mama Teta puts a hand over her mouth and shakes her head. What a situation!

"Get out, I say," the wife says to her soon-to-be-ex-husband. The daughter makes one desperate attempt to bring the attention back to her. She gets up and insists they all go to the church for her to get married. But her mother pins her back to the couch with the verdict: there is to be no wedding today.

"But what about the personal loan you made?" the daughter asks with big sorry eyes for all the drama.

"Everything is off — your marriage, my marriage — and we're going to celebrate our freedom." Then, looking at her ex-husband, the mama of the bride adds, "I had opportunities too, you know, it's not just you who had opportunities. I felt the heat too, but I resisted the temptations, I stayed a good wife to you even if you were a great big *zero* in bed. Get out of my house before I call my cousins."

Mama Teta is keeping her eyes on the dirt track as she drives the father of the bride to his cousin's house. The onlookers peer in, trying to see where the bride is. And she's thinking, Mama Teta, that she's definitely getting too old for this kind of business.

Anyway, this is what happened to Mama Teta last week.

"Ah, *non alors,*" Materena says, half-laughing, half-serious. "Does this mean my daughter is going to be living with me until she's thirty years old?"

"Why don't you stop trying so hard?" Mama Teta says. "Just give your daughter some space, that may be all she needs at the moment."

We Worry and We Expect

When a child is born in Tahiti, her placenta is buried under a tree and the child and the tree grow together. A healthy tree means a healthy child just as a sick tree means a sick child. When a child's tree is sick, the mother takes the sick child to the doctor.

But Tepua cannot do this. She gave her baby girl away for adoption to a French couple and she has no idea where her daughter lives except that she is somewhere in France. What irony too that after years of praying for children to stop coming her way, Tepua would get her wish after her sixth child was born, the one she'll never get to raise.

Relatives have told Tepua that her baby girl is not completely lost. One day she will return, they say, because the calling of a mother is louder than the calling of a land. This is a comfort to Tepua, but she would give anything to see her child grow right in front of her eyes, to give her cuddles when she's good and smack her with the wooden spoon when she's not *gentille.*

Tepua's sixth child is named Moea, and although that name is sure to have been changed to a *popa'a* name, she will always be Moea around here.

Moea is sick — her tree has spoken.

The news of this misfortune was on the coconut radio two days ago. And yesterday afternoon, Saturday, Tepua's ten-year-old son came to see Materena. He had a piece of paper with him and his mother's purse and he said, "Auntie Materena, Mamie wants to know if you can come to the house tomorrow at one o'clock for a little prayer for my sister Moea."

Materena immediately replied, "*Oui!* Tell your mama she can count on me."

The boy ticked his auntie Materena's name and said, "Now I'm going to call on Auntie Georgette." And off he went.

This morning, after Sunday Mass, Loma made a big song and dance because she's not one of the ten women requested for the prayer at Tepua's house when Georgette, who's not even a woman, is. Lily gave Loma a slap across the face and someone reminded Loma that until she starts saying good words about people instead of backstabbing them, she will never be invited to special occasions.

The ten very special women, holding hands, with their packets of tissues by their sides, are now sitting in a circle around the sick tree. Tepua, red-eyed and with swollen eyelids, thanks them all for coming. They all say that it is an honor to be present.

The prayer begins.

The women, eyes fervently closed, sing for the little girl and her tree. Every now and then someone half opens an eyelid to see if something is happening to the tree, something like a miracle. A few times, Materena's half-opened eye meets Rita's half-opened eye. Other times, the half-opened eye belongs to Lily, or Mama Teta. But Georgette's eyes are wide open. Materena thinks

Georgette looks strange, staring at the sick tree as if she's trying to hypnotize it.

The prayer goes on for an hour until Tepua calls for a break and the women go inside the house. It's a mess, but no one expects Tepua to have the energy to tidy up when her heart is a mess. No one pays attention to all the clothes lying around, the crushed plastic cups, and the dried grains of rice everywhere.

Materena and Rita, with slices of chocolate cake preciously wrapped in a tissue, go and stand in the kitchen by the louvers. As they look out to the tree through the four missing louvers, they eat and sigh and shake their head.

"I'm sure Moea is going to get better from today," Rita whispers.

"That is our hope, eh?" Materena replies.

Both women are whispering the whisper of respect.

"There's nothing like women's power," continues Rita. "There's eleven women here today and we're all giving that tree all the love and the power within us because . . ."

But here is Georgette now, running from her car to the tree with a bucket. Georgette, wearing her usual attire — baggy shorts, tight shirt, and tennis shoes, but this time with not one single piece of jewelry — pours the contents of the bucket on the ground. She's on her knees now, furiously spreading what looks like dirt around the tree.

Materena and Rita press their faces to the gap between the louvers.

"What is that Georgette doing?" asks Rita.

Georgette jumps to her feet, races back to her car, and comes back without the bucket to stand by the tree. She's looking down at the tree and scratching herself between the legs.

"But! Georgette is scratching her balls!"

"Shussh, Rita." Rita is all red in the face from trying to keep the laughter inside. She breathes in and out to calm herself down. But Georgette must have heard Rita's laughter, for she swings around. She sees Materena and Rita and waves, and then walking her feminine walk, Georgette walks to the house.

Minutes later, the prayers continue in the living room. The women sit on the ground, again in a circle, and again holding one another's hands, and all eyes are fixed on a newborn's name bracelet laid out on the cushion in the middle of the circle. The bracelet is closed and you can see how tiny the wrist of a newborn baby is. Smaller than a fifty-franc coin. Tepua explains how this bracelet was Moea's bracelet, but Moea wore it for only five hours because she left the hospital six hours after her birth with her new parents and without her bracelet.

Tepua wipes her eyes with her tissue and rests her head on her chest.

This bracelet, this tiny bracelet that we all wear after our hospital birth, is making the women cry out in pain, and not one single eye is opened as they fervently pray and beg the Virgin Mary, Understanding Woman, to take away whatever Moea's sickness is.

For two long hours.

Every now and then Materena stops thinking about her niece to think about her daughter. Following Mama Teta's advice at the cemetery four days ago, Materena has been giving her daughter space, but first Materena explained the situation, laid all her cards on the table. "Girl," she said to Leilani, at her desk doing her homework, "you've been very mean to me lately, it's like you hate me, but I'm not going to hate you back because I love you, so I'm just going to give you space, but if you need me, you know where I am." Leilani nodded a vague nod — yeah, whatever — and Materena left the room crying her eyes out. Since then, mother and daughter have been avoiding each other. Even

Pito noticed it. He said, "What is it now? *Aue,* you two are *fiu!*" Well, at least there hasn't been any shouting in the house.

When the ten women very special to Tepua leave, they are all red-eyed and exhausted. As they walk back to Rita's car, Rita says to Materena that praying with all your heart and soul is draining.

"When you cry a lot" — Materena sniffs into her tissue — "you get tired too. That saying — crying yourself to sleep — it's true."

"I gave all my love to that baby girl."

"Me too." Materena is aching all over. "I gave her all my love."

"And I gave her all the power within me." Rita gets into her car.

There's a bit of a traffic jam in Tepua's garden. Lily, who is riding her Vespa, has no trouble getting out. The same goes for the women who came barefoot. But no one waiting in their car is tutting the horn.

"Cousin, I'll walk," says Materena.

"*Non,* I'll drive you . . . I don't want you passing out on the highway."

The cousins remain silent except for frequent sighings of sadness, and they both jump with surprise when the back door opens and in sneaks Georgette.

"I have a confession to make."

"Ah, *oui alors,*" says Rita. "What were you doing with that bucket?"

Georgette confesses that all she did was put a bit of fertilizer around the tree. Materena and Rita, stunned, say in unison, "Fertilizer?"

Georgette hurries to explain that it's not that she doesn't believe in prayers, but she thought it could just be that the tree needed a bit of fertilizer. She's been thinking about this since yesterday.

"Jeez, Georgette," Rita says, "I hope you know about fertilizers! Too much fertilizer can be fatal! *Ah hia hia,* Georgette! What got into your head? I thought it was just dirt you put around the tree! Georgette, you stupid man!"

Materena tenderly reaches out for Georgette's hand. It must hurt Georgette when people refer to her as a man when she is, in her head, in her heart, in the way she dresses, a woman. A woman who is always so willing to help out because she was born with a big, giving heart. Georgette often says her penis has got nothing to do with her identity. She often adds, "I'm a woman through and through, even when I'm naked."

But Georgette shouldn't have tampered with Tepua's daughter's tree. All women have got to know their limit.

"Cousin," Materena says, worried, "do you know a bit about fertilizers?"

Georgette swears that she followed the instructions on the fertilizer packet religiously.

On the coconut-radio news three days later, it is confirmed that Tepua's sixth child, Moea, has been cured from her illness. Her tree is beautiful and healthy again. Some say this is the result of the fervent prayers to the Virgin Mary, Understanding Woman, at Tepua's house. Others say Madame Pietre took her adopted daughter to the doctor, because that is what mothers do. They worry and they expect.

A Long Time Ago

Materena fell in love with Pito a long time ago, but she still remembers those distant days when her mind would be all over the place.

She once forgot about a chicken cooking in the oven, despite her mother reminding her about it before leaving for a family meeting.

Loana came home to a burned chicken and a smoky kitchen. She yelled her head off, "Materena! Are you trying to burn the house down? I told you to take the chicken out of the oven at eleven o'clock! Do you think money grows on trees? Who's going to buy me another chicken, you? Do you think a chicken is cheap?"

Materena was in the clouds, she was in love with her secret boyfriend, Pito.

Now, almost twenty years later, she's in bed and Pito is snoring next to her.

Materena puts her head under her pillow, but she can still hear Pito's annoying snore.

"Pito!" Materena rolls him to his side, but Pito fights, he wants to stay on his back.

"Pito! I can't sleep!"

Growling, Pito rolls onto his side.

Materena closes her eyes, enjoying the silence. Then her mind starts ticking away about this and that: tomorrow night's dinner, Moana, who's just turned fifteen and who left school two months ago for an apprenticeship at the five-star international Beachcomber Hotel's restaurant as a chef, Tamatoa, enlisting for military service in France, how she needs to buy new thongs.

Suddenly a thought pops into her head. Is there a boy on her daughter's horizon? Lately Leilani has been so nice. (But *so* nice! Which makes a welcome change, Materena has to admit. Plus we've got singing love songs in the shower too!) And she's got that look, that special look girls get when there's a boy on the horizon.

Aue, girl, eh, Materena thinks, don't pay attention to boys, work hard at school, you're almost there. Get your degree and then you can look around as much as you like. Pick the best one of the lot.

The following morning, Saturday, Materena is on a mission.

"Girl?"

"*Oui,* Mamie?" Leilani is combing her hair in front of the mirror.

"Do you have a boyfriend?"

"*Non!*" Leilani laughs that little laugh that says yes.

"Girl," Materena says very seriously, "you can tell me if you have a boyfriend. I'm not going to get cranky, because it's normal."

"There's no boyfriend."

Okay then, since Leilani refuses to share the news, Materena is going to have to turn into a spy. The last time Materena peeped in her daughter's diary four years ago, she read that Leilani wanted to be a nun. But let's see now, eh? The hormones have arrived!

Here is that diary on the desk, wide open, that's a good sign. It must mean Leilani doesn't mind people reading it.

Materena, hands on her broom, ready to start brooming in case Leilani appears out of nowhere, begins to read.

"Eh?" she says out loud. "What's this? This is not writing!" There's a rectangle followed by a sun, another rectangle, a flower, a circle, a star, a square, and an exclamation mark. An exclamation mark means excitement, surprise, something you can't believe is true, thinks Materena, *non?*

Another way for a mother to find out secrets about her children is to listen to them talk to their friends. The trick is to listen while looking like you're not listening.

Materena, washing basket on her hip, strolls to the clothesline. Leilani and Vahine are lying on sarongs on the grass, but she doesn't say a word. She's so focused on her job. She puts the basket on the ground and, focusing, hangs the bedsheet first to hide behind it, all the while pretending she's looking for pegs.

"Girlfriend, you're sure we're not going to die with your invention?"

"*Non,* girlfriend, it's great for sweating."

What's going on? Materena asks herself. She peeps from behind the bedsheet. Leilani and Vahine are wrapping plastic sheets around their waists.

Aue! What is this? If Materena understands the situation correctly, the plastic sheets, combined with the heat of the sun, are supposed to make the girls melt. But what is there to melt? They're so skinny as they are.

Materena goes back to her job and waits for the girls to start talking about things.

"Mamie!" Leilani calls out sweetly. "Are you going to be long?"

Materena calls back that she's going to be as long as she has to because clothes should always be hung properly and not in a hurry.

"That's what Maman's personal assistant says too!" Vahine calls out.

Materena continues to explain the situation about hanging clothes. When you hang clothes properly, you don't need to iron them for too long, but when you don't hang clothes properly, you need to iron them for a while because the clothes are creased and . . .

After some time, the girls start talking, talking loud and clear, like they want the whole population to hear their conversation. They're talking in a foreign language that is definitely not English. Even if Materena doesn't understand that language apart from a few words of greeting, she can pick it up easily. When you have years of experience hearing the American tourists talk out loud in the middle of a street, in the middle of the market, in the truck, their language becomes familiar to your ears.

The language Leilani and Vahine are talking in sounds more like a made-up secret-code language. Every single word ends with *o*. And they're laughing their head off, those two silly girls.

Materena knows very well the girls are talking in a secret-code language because she's at the clothesline and they're automatically suspecting her to be listening — as if she's got nothing else better to do in her life. Materena hurries up with her job, shoving T-shirts and shorts onto the line. The secret-code language is getting on her system.

Every now and then she hears Vahine languidly pronounce the name of Materena's eldest son, Tamatoa. Vahine is in love with Tamatoa and the less he's interested in her, the more she wants him. It's complicated.

Well anyway, there are no more clothes to hang. Materena

marches back to the house, past the girls still going on in their *charabia* language.

"Eh," she says, "I'm not a spy, you know, and keep your laughter down, Moana is asleep. Some people work at night."

Later on Pito heads out of the house with his ukulele and his beer for a bit of practice under the sun, but at the sight of his daughter and her friend wrapped in plastic sheets, he quickly retreats back inside the house.

The girls are still outside hours later and Materena is getting worried. Sun goes to the head. Sweating too much is not good for the health.

"Eh, girls!" she calls out from the shutter. "You don't think you're brown enough? You don't think you've sweated enough?"

"We're nearly finished," the girls call back.

"You want something to eat?"

"Not now!"

"Something to drink?"

"Not now!"

All right, then, since nobody is hungry or thirsty, Materena gets the ironing board and the iron out to iron Moana's uniform. But first it's time to wake him up. It's twelve thirty.

The second Materena kisses her son on his forehead, he opens his beautiful green eyes, looks at his mama, and smiles.

"It's twelve thirty, *chéri,*" Materena says, caressing her son's hair.

Moana nods, sits on his bed, yawning, and stretches himself.

"When are you going to start having day shifts?" asks Materena. She feels so sorry for Moana. She doesn't know about that apprenticeship he's got, but it seems that an apprenticeship in a hotel means you're a slave all night long. You work ten hours a day, you work seven days a week, and then you get paid next to zero. "I'm going to complain to the hotel," Materena says.

"Mamie . . . I'm learning a lot of things at the hotel for when

I have my restaurant." After kissing his mother on her forehead, Moana goes and has his shower, while Materena finishes ironing his uniform.

"What are Leilani and Vahine doing?" Moana, out of the shower with his towel wrapped around his waist, asks.

"It's to lose weight," Materena says, shaking her head.

"Lose weight?" Moana asks, glancing at his mother. "They're perfect as they are, they're beautiful . . ." Moana's voice trails off and just looking at his eyes it seems to Materena that Moana is openly admiring his sister's best friend.

Materena says nothing. A long time later (more than one minute) Moana turns to his mother and takes his ironed uniform off her hands, all the while thanking her.

"No worries," says Materena. "You've got money for the truck?"

"*Oui.*"

"The boss is going to drive you home?"

"*Oui.*" Moana waits for another question, but Materena has no more questions to ask. She knows what she wanted to know, and so Moana goes and gets ready for work.

Ah, and here's her eldest son, all sweaty from his six-mile run and his workout at his friend's gym. He's in preparation for military service.

"Eh, Rambo," Materena says, "where's my kiss?"

"Mamie, I'm full of sweat," Tamatoa replies.

"I don't care!"

Tamatoa gives his mother a quick kiss on the forehead, looks out the shutter, shakes his head with disbelief, and asks, "What are these two crazy *nonnettes* doing?"

"It's to lose weight," Materena says, cackling. She adds with a wink how Vahine is so pretty, she's like a porcelain doll, and plus she's so nice. For a rich girl, Materena means. Looking at

Vahine you wouldn't know that her French father is a director of a company and that her mother was a former Miss Tahiti.

"*Bof.*" Tamatoa shrugs. "When I look at girls, I don't care if they're rich or if they're poor. I care more about what they look like, and that one is just too skinny." Then, doing his loud papa voice, Tamatoa calls out to his sister and her friend that boys don't like skinny girls, they like girls with flesh, girls they can hold on to, not bones that are going to break for a yes, for a no. Boys like strong girls with muscles on their belly and derriere . . . they like to throw a coin on a girl's derriere and watch the coin bounce back.

Vahine, sitting right up, turns to Tamatoa and listens attentively.

"Boys don't like skinny girls!" he shouts.

"Boys don't like skinny girls?" Materena asks.

Tamatoa gives his mother a strange look and heads for the bathroom to shower.

In the Confessional Box

Five days a week, here at the kitchen table, Mama George and Loma gossip about what they've seen with their own two eyes by the side of the road or outside the Chinese store or what they've heard with their own two ears, also by the side of the road or outside the Chinese store. But the weekend is different.

On Sundays, they gossip about what they've seen with their own two eyes and heard with their own two ears outside the church, after and before Mass.

And on Saturdays, confession day, Mama George and Loma talk about each relative who was in the confessional box for more than ten minutes.

And since only the priest can hear confessions, all Mama George and Loma can do is sit at the back of the church and time how long a relative has been in the confessional box. Loma is in charge of timing. The second the sinner walks into the confessional box she checks her watch, and the second that sinner walks out of the confessional box, she checks her watch again.

Then she leans over to her mother and whispers, "Seventeen minutes and forty-four seconds." Or, "Eleven minutes and fifty-two seconds." Or, "Two minutes and twenty-eight seconds."

The mother nods. She's in charge of checking how the relative walks into the confessional box and how the relative walks out of the confessional box. She looks at the body language and the facial expression, and when there are tears streaming down the sinner's face, Mama George shakes her head with disapproval.

Anyway, that is what Mama George and Loma do on Saturday mornings. They play detectives in the church, where nobody can tell them to go away. They'll be the first to admit that, unfortunately, their family is filled with sinners.

Now, when a woman is in the confessional box for more than ten minutes, Mama George and Loma declare she's been up to no good. If the woman has a man, she's seeing another man, and if she doesn't have a man she's seeing a married man.

And a young girl in the confessional box for more than ten minutes means there's a boy on the horizon. Mama George and Loma have the strong belief that it doesn't take ten minutes to confess you've talked bad about your mama, you gave her the evil look behind her back, you borrowed something from her without her permission. Sins like these are fine with the priest. He tells you, Don't do this again, that's not very nice, and sends you off with his absolution, his blessing, and a little smile.

Mortal sins, however, sins of the flesh, lust, young girls sneaking out of the shutter in the middle of the night to meet a lover, make the priest cranky like you wouldn't believe. His absolution comes at a price: a ten-minute sermon.

The mother of a young girl confessing sins of the flesh must be immediately informed of the situation. It's the rule and the regulation, according to Loma and Mama George.

* * *

Materena, about to cross the road on her way to visit her mother, has some information coming her way.

"Materena, Cousin! Materena, Cousin!"

This is the distinctive high-pitched voice of big-mouth Cousin Loma, and Materena hurries to cross the road.

Loma also hurries to cross the road. "Materena, Cousin!"

Materena quickens her steps, still pretending oblivion.

Loma starts to run. "Materena, Cousin!"

She's now in front of Materena.

"Eh, Loma!" Materena exclaims, surprised. "Where are you off to?"

"Didn't you hear me call out to you?" Loma asks, puffing.

"*Non,*" Materena replies innocently, "I was thinking about . . ."

But Loma is not interested in knowing what Materena was thinking about. She's more interested in delivering information about Leilani's recent fourteen-minute visit to the confessional box.

There, the information has been passed on to the mother of that naughty girl, who must be punished, and Loma waits for a reaction.

This is Materena's reaction from the inside: *What?* Fourteen minutes in the confessional box! My girl tells the priest everything and she tells me zero! Is my girl still a virgin? Who's the boy on the horizon?

This is Materena's reaction from the outside: she looks into Loma's eyes and sighs, all the while shaking her head. "Cousin." Materena places a hand on her chest like she feels so sorry. "You don't have *anything* better to do than time people in the confessional box?"

"Yes, I do!" Loma exclaims before stomping away.

Materena can now do one of two things. She can go home and question her daughter or she can go ahead and visit her mother.

Materena finds her mother in the garden pulling weeds.

"Eh, *chérie!*" Loana exclaims with joy. Loana is always happy when her daughter visits, even if the last time they saw each other was yesterday.

"How's the health, Mamie?" Materena asks.

"Oh, the health is very good," Loana answers, but she complains about her legs being a bit stiff when she gets up in the morning. Materena tells her mother that better the legs be stiff in the morning than something else more serious. The mother cackles, the daughter cackles, they look into each other's eyes with love, and that completes their greeting ritual.

"How's the house?" Materena asks.

"Oh, the house is fine, but it's falling apart."

"And the plants? How are they?"

"Oh, they're growing, but they could do with a bit of rain. And how are you, girl? Everything is all right?"

"*Oui,* everything is all right, let me help you weed."

"Oh *non!* The last time you helped me weed you pulled out my good grass. Just sit next to me and talk, my ears are opened."

"Leilani was in the confessional box for fourteen minutes," Materena says, making herself comfortable on the grass. "Loma told me."

"*Ah oui?*" Loana says, cackling. "Loma was in the confessional box too? She was hiding behind the priest and counting the minutes? She had a chronometer in her hand?" Loana tells her daughter that being in the confessional box for more than ten minutes doesn't necessarily mean there's a confession happening. Sometimes people just want to talk to the priest because he's got time to listen.

"I've got time to listen to my daughter!" Materena exclaims. "I always want to listen . . . You know me, Mamie, I love to listen to people . . . It's Leilani who doesn't want to tell me anything. I know we've had problems in the past, but we're friends again. She can tell me anything."

"Well," says Loana, "lie next to your daughter in her bed and patiently wait until she talks to you."

"Leilani?" Materena says absently as she's chopping onions later on. "Did you go to confession today?"

"What?" Leilani turns to face her mother. "Me in the confessional box?" She laughs. "Are you crazy?"

"Ah, you didn't confess?"

"I was with Rose," Leilani says. "*She* was in the confessional box. I was waiting for her outside. Father Arthur would be the last to know about my affairs!"

"Don't talk about Father Arthur like that!" Materena is cranky now. "He's a very nice priest even if his ideas are from the seventeenth century, he's interesting and . . ." All right, Materena thinks, that's enough talking about Father Arthur. But what about Rose, what was *she* doing in the confessional box for more than fourteen minutes? Should I tell Cousin Tapeta about this?

Eh, it's not my onions, Materena decides.

Much later, comfortable in her daughter's bed, Materena looks around.

Leilani's desk is a mess, there's paper everywhere (scrunched, torn, flat), pens, chewing-gum wrappers, and Materena wonders how her daughter does her homework in these conditions. Let's not talk about the bookcase. The encyclopedias are not in alphabetical order, books are standing on top of one another, and what is that glass doing in the bookcase? There's also a dirty spoon! And a packet of noodle soup! The map of the world on the wall is nice to look at — makes you realize the world is so big. That poster of rowers taken in a sunset is beautiful, it calms. Materena hasn't seen it before, it must be new. And what's with all these rocks everywhere? Is Leilani collecting them or what?

Aue, the poor plant in the corner is dying. When was the last time Leilani watered it? Materena makes a mental note to save it tomorrow.

Ah, Materena really loves Leilani's words of wisdom on the walls.

When you feel down, think of something that makes you happy.
To die with a clear conscience is the only way to leave this world.
Don't eat in front of people if you can't share.
Give because it makes you feel good. If you get something back, good. If you don't, it doesn't matter.
Don't visit people at eating times unless you've been invited.
Show respect to old people.
Show respect to all people.
KNOW WHAT YOU WANT AND MAKE IT HAPPEN.

Materena told Leilani all of these words of wisdom.

But the following words of wisdom come from the books Leilani has read or heard from other people (relatives and strangers).

Why worry about your beard when your head is about to be taken?

The truth is in the pudding.
Life passes by before we have the chance to understand it.
Make sacrifices that matter.
A man in love mistakes a harelip for a dimple.

Materena hasn't read that one before, it must be new . . .

Sex is the poor man's opera.

Materena hasn't read that one either. Materena, very interested, reads on.

Kisses are like almonds.
For news of the heart, ask the face.
Love makes all hard hearts gentle.
First prize is finding someone to be passionately in love with you for a lifetime.

Ah . . . here's Leilani.

"Oh," Leilani says, seeing her mother on the bed, "you're here." She ties the towel around her body tighter and walks to her wardrobe.

"I just felt like resting my legs on your bed. That's okay with you, *chérie?*" Materena hurries to add that her feet are clean.

"Of course it's okay, *mi casa es tu casa.*" Leilani is looking for something to wear tonight in bed, and meanwhile, water from her long wet hair is dripping on the floor. Materena tightens her lips before she starts going on about how hair must be dried in the bathroom and how hair shouldn't be washed at night.

Leilani has found her attire for tonight, an oversize T-shirt. She slips into it, dries her hair with the towel, drops the towel on the floor, wipes her feet on it.

Materena is looking but she's not saying anything, although

she really wants to. What's a towel, she thinks, compared to your daughter telling you secrets.

"You're all right, Mamie?" Leilani asks, walking to her desk.

"I'm fine, girl, no problems, and I'm not here to start a fight."

"You're worrying me."

"Why?"

"You're usually running around at this time of night."

"I know, well, tonight I'm on strike."

"Good for you." Leilani smiles as she sits at her desk. She grabs her schoolbag from under the desk, takes copybooks, books, and pencil case out, and attacks her homework. She begins to write, and furiously too. Materena has never seen anyone write so fast in her life.

But it's really unbelievable how fast Leilani can write!

The seconds turn into minutes.

Ten minutes later, "You're all right, Mamie?"

"I'm fine, *chérie.*"

Twenty minutes later, "Mamie? Is there anything you want to tell me?"

"*Non.*"

Patiently Materena waits for Leilani to start a conversation. It's quite boring lying in the horizontal position, staring at the ceiling and your daughter's back, waiting. Just as Materena is about to fall asleep, finally Leilani says the magic words.

"Mamie, can you help me?"

"Sure! No problems, tell me everything." Materena, excited, sits up.

Leilani needs help with the family genealogical tree.

"Ah," Materena says, disappointed. "I know my ancestors but only from my mother's side."

"That's all right, Mamie." Leilani passes a thick textbook for her mother to lean on, along with paper and a pen. "Thanks," she says. "I really appreciate you helping me with my school project."

Materena starts writing Leilani's name at the bottom of the page, links it to her own name alongside Pito's name, up to Loana's name, to the daughter of Kika Mahi née Raufaki from Rangiroa and of Apoto Mahi from Tahiti . . . on and on.

"Your great grandmother was born with twelve toes," Materena says.

"Ah really?" Leilani doesn't sound too interested.

But for Materena this is an interesting detail that she found out about through her godmother, the historian of the family. It's always more interesting for Materena to know more than just the date of birth and the date of death of her ancestors. Small details make them more real to her.

"You know what her nickname was?" Materena asks.

"Just write it down," Leilani says.

"*Ah oui?* So I just write that detail next to her name?"

"Hum."

Okay then, and so Materena writes her grandmother's nickname — Twelve Toes. Now, next ancestor.

"Your great great grandmother coughed nonstop."

"Just write it down."

"Your great great grandfather was the chief of Faa'a. He signed the Protectorate paper to France before the king of Tahiti. He gave Tahiti to the French people."

"Really!" Leilani exclaims.

"*Eh oui.*" It's not really something Materena is proud of but she understands her ancestor was under a lot of pressure, being a chief. "You want me to write this information?" she asks.

"Absolutely. Write everything."

Write, write, that's easy to say, Materena thinks. She much prefers to talk. "You don't want to write?" she asks. "And I'll just tell you the stories? All that I know?" Materena explains that she uses her hands enough during the day.

"Mamie," Leilani pleads, "just write slowly . . . I've got to finish my chemistry homework."

Aue, Materena thinks, it's like I'm Leilani's secretary, but it's good to help your kids with their school projects. So, applying herself by writing and reading out loud what she's writing, Materena resumes her task.

There was an ancestor who had a red beard.

Materena looks up. No reaction from Leilani.

An ancestor was who a Filipino sailor.

No reaction.

An ancestor who used to be a slave before she escaped and came to Tahiti. She was black, sixteen years old, and her name was Josephina.

"Josephina . . . what a beautiful name," Leilani says. "What a brave girl."

Then there were Leilani Lexter and Leilani Bodie from Hawaii, whom Leilani already knows about, an English ancestor by the name of Williams — he's the last ancestor on the list, and Materena's hand hurts.

"Finished! I'm not complaining, but my hand really hurts."

Materena gets up and gives her work to Leilani, who thanks her for all her help.

"Oh, for nothing," Materena says, kissing the top of her daughter's head. "Can I do anything else for you?"

"*Non,* it's okay."

All right, then . . . Materena might go and do some ironing, but first she's going to read more of Leilani's words of wisdom.

Forty muscles are needed to frown, only fifteen to smile.

Love is like the measles, we all have to go through it.

I have seen only you, I have admired only you, I desire only you.

"You know," Materena says, "when I was your age, I used to sneak out of the shutter in the middle of the night to go meet your father." Materena can't believe her ears. What on Earth made her confess this? It just spilled out of her mouth! Well, it's out, and Leilani might as well know today.

"Sneak out of the shutter!" Leilani shrieks, turning to her mother with a smirk on her face. "In the middle of the night!" She turns her chair around. "But I thought you and Papi met on Sundays, after Mass."

"After Mass? Who told you that?"

"Mama Roti."

Ah, that Mama Roti, thinks Materena. She's number one for inventing stories.

"So?" Leilani asks. "Where did you two naughties meet?"

Materena tells Leilani where and adds that Pito brought a quilt along and laid the quilt underneath the frangipani tree behind the bank. Leilani is getting very interested in the story. She particularly wants to know what her parents did on that quilt.

"Well," Materena says, "we talked, we did chitchat about the family, fishing, the weather."

"And what else did you do?"

"Well, we kissed . . ." Materena can feel the top of her head burning.

"And what else did you do?"

"We caressed . . . and there was the moon and the stars and the gentle breeze and the sweet perfume of the frangipani flowers and —"

Leilani bursts out laughing and Materena doesn't need to say more. It's clear what happened after the chitchat and the kisses and the caresses under the frangipani tree.

Sexy loving, that's what happened! Sexy loving always happens when there's chitchat, kisses, and caresses under the frangipani tree.

"Do your homework," Materena says, quietly leaving the room.

And now, in the kitchen drinking lemonade, Materena thinks about how she used to tell her mother everything: I saw a woman pick up a matchstick on the ground and she put it in her pocket. I saw an old woman with tattooed tears underneath her eyes, a girl and a boy kiss under a frangipani tree, a young man run with a bouquet of flowers, a woman walk with high-heeled shoes, holding a pack of taro.

And Loana would say, depending on the information: Oh, that's not good, that's so beautiful, that's disgusting, that's funny, that wasn't for your ears, you want me to wash your mouth with soap?

Materena also informed her mother of news regarding herself: my tooth hurts, my belly hurts, I feel constipated, I've got nits, my bum is itchy . . .

But by the time Materena was sixteen years old she was telling her mother nothing because . . . because there was a boy on the horizon, of course!

Loana didn't ask Materena why she'd stopped telling her everything until the day before Materena gave birth to her first child. "Why didn't you tell me you had a boyfriend?" Loana said. "You used to tell me everything. I would have told you about contraception. But now it's too late, you're about to give birth." When the mothers don't know what's going on, they can't help.

Materena walks back to Leilani's bedroom.

"You've got something else to confess?" Leilani asks, cackling.

"*Non,* it's not about that," Materena says. "It's about —"

"It's amazing how no one saw you walk to your nocturnal rendezvous. Did you wear a pillowcase over your head?"

"*Non,* I just ran fast."

"You ran fast, eh?"

"Leilani . . . ," Materena begins seriously, "I just want you to know that you can tell me anything, okay? Don't ever be afraid to tell me what you need, okay? I'm not going to ask you any questions. With whom, where, etc., okay?" Materena is a bit uncomfortable saying what she really means, but she's sure Leilani understands. She wishes Leilani would stop laughing. "Leilani! Stop laughing!"

"I just can't imagine you and Papi doing . . ." She can't say the word. "And are you still doing . . ." She still can't say that word.

"*Aue!*" Materena exclaims. "Do your homework."

And off she goes to iron. She switches the radio on to keep her company, tuning it to Radio Tefana to listen to Ati's love-songs program.

One Son Leaves, Another Son Arrives

Tamatoa is leaving next week, three months ahead of his scheduled departure date, and Materena is panicking — so much to do in such a short time!

Buy gifts to help her eldest son remember his island (coconut soaps, cans of corned beef, postcards, a bottle of blessed water). Organize a photo album of the family for Tamatoa to flick through whenever he feels homesick. A new suitcase! Pito's suitcase from military-service days was lent to a relative and never came back. Materena's suitcase from her hospital days giving birth is rusted and doesn't shut. Install the telephone, that's what you do when one of your children is on the other side of the planet.

After much running around, draining the emergency account, and borrowing a bit of money from her mother, Materena has everything under control. All she needs now is for her son to grant her a few minutes of his time in between training commitments and drinking with his mates.

"I need you. I have to tell you about the rules."

Tamatoa has just come home from training.

"Not now," he says.

"Now?" Materena says as Tamatoa walks out of the shower.

"I've got to get dressed first."

"Now?" Materena says as Tamatoa walks out of his bedroom. His hair is oiled and he reeks of perfume.

"Later," he says as he flees the house.

"What's with the perfume?" Materena calls out. "What time are you coming home? What are you going to eat tonight?"

Tamatoa doesn't come home that night, or the next day, or the day after. Materena starts to get really worried. People don't disappear for four days before they're about to do something they've always wanted to do in their life: catch a plane. Pito tells Materena not to worry, because it's the tradition to go out drinking with your *copains* before you leave for military service. You drink, you say good-bye, you have fun.

Materena is still worried. "I'm calling the gendarmes," she tells Pito, who is sitting in front of the TV, and she starts dialing.

Pito jumps to his feet and snatches the phone from Materena. "Relax, woman!"

Materena snatches the phone back from Pito. "I don't care what you think about the gendarmes! I'm calling the gendarmes!"

Pito pulls the cord out of its socket. "Tamatoa is just out drinking with his *copains!*"

"Oh, that's what you say." Materena plugs the cord back in. "It doesn't mean I have to believe you. What if my son is in danger? What if he's somewhere bleeding to death? Get out of my way, Pito. Get out of my way, I'm going to hit you with that telephone! It's my telephone, give me my telephone back! Pito, you *titoi,* you —"

"Are you two going to stop?" This is Leilani speaking. "He's with Vahine." Leilani explains how Vahine came to school this morning to give her medical certificate to the office and told her that . . . well . . . that all is great with Tamatoa.

"And her parents?" asks Materena. "They don't mind?"

"They're at a conference in Hawaii. Vahine's grandmother is looking after Vahine."

"But Vahine's parents are always away at conferences!" Materena exclaims.

"Ah, my boy is with a girl," cackles Pito, smiling away. He's all happy. It's like somebody has just told him that he's won the *tombola.*

Although Materena is very relieved to know her son is not in danger, it doesn't mean she's happy. What about the suitcase? When is Tamatoa going to pack it? And what is going to happen to Vahine when Tamatoa leaves? Materena knows how hard it is when the boy you love leaves on military service. Just thinking about it makes her even crankier with Pito.

Tamatoa comes home the morning before departure day and doesn't even tell his mother where he's been. He just comes home wearing the same clothes he wore when he disappeared four days ago, he comes home as if nothing was amiss. He kisses his younger brother, busy marinating chicken thighs, and he kisses his mother, also in the kitchen, helping out the cook.

Tamatoa looks at the bowls filled with food on the kitchen table. "What's with all the food?" he asks.

"But it's for your farewell party!" says Materena. "Your brother has been busy for two days for you."

"My brother, eh," Tamatoa says, giving him a little punch on the arm. "I hope you're going to cook my favorite dish, chicken curry."

"Of course I will," says Moana, grating coconut.

Materena looks at her youngest son and she is so touched by

all the cooking he's doing for his brother. She sure hopes Tamatoa doesn't forget to thank him properly later on. In the meantime, Materena would like Tamatoa to confess his whereabouts. "Where have you been?" she asks.

"Somewhere."

"You must like skinny girls now."

"Eh? What are you going on about?"

"Is she your girlfriend or just a body for your pleasure?"

"Mamie . . . it's not like in your days, okay?"

"*Aue,*" Materena sighs. "Sit down and eat while I tell you about the rules."

"The rules? What are you going on about?"

"The rules when you're a visitor! That's what I'm going on about, you big silly!" Materena doesn't want to tell Tamatoa about the rules on the telephone or in a letter.

"In a minute," Tamatoa says.

"In a minute" turns into many hours later . . .

The house is packed with relatives who have come for the farewell ritual, but right this moment, Materena has her son all to herself in his bedroom. The relatives are busy eating, anyway. It's not every day they get to eat Indonesian, Tahitian, and French dishes all at once. Materena hopes the relatives aren't going to eat everything. She hasn't eaten yet, and nor has Tamatoa.

Presently, he's crying silent tears, and just looking at him is breaking Materena's heart, but she's not going to tell her son not to cry, that he's a man. Crying is good for the soul, just as laughing is. You've got to release. If only Tamatoa also cried when he was not drunk.

Anyway, here are the rules that must be followed when you are on foreign soil and your family is on the other side of the planet.

First rule: no fighting with the locals, you don't want to upset the wrong family. What if it's the Mafia? And plus, it's not nice to fight.

Second rule: no rendezvous in a girl's bedroom, even if she tells you that her parents are fine with her having boys in their house. It's more likely that the girl's parents don't know anything about it, and all you're going to get is a gun pointed at your head, a thick piece of wood smashed across your back, or something equally horrible.

Third rule: never arrive with empty hands at a dinner even if your friend told you that his mother hates it when guests arrive with something. The reality is that hosts love surprises, and it doesn't have to be something to eat. Flowers are great. Perfumed soaps too. Show your gratitude for the invitation. The only people hosts never expect anything from, over and over again, are the relatives.

Tamatoa nods, meaning that he's registering the information, and Materena is very happy.

Fourth rule (still about being a guest at dinner): leave a bit of food on your plate to show the host you're too full to have another serving. If there's nothing left on your plate and the host can't serve you more food because there's no more food in the cooking pot, she's going to be very embarrassed. She's going to assume you're still hungry. Eat the food even if you don't like the taste of it, you don't know what it is, you've never eaten such a dish in your whole life and it looks bizarre.

"Don't you make anyone think I've been a bad mother to you," Materena says, "that I didn't raise you proper."

Another nod from Tamatoa as he puts his arms around his mother.

"You're a number-one mamie." He sniffs.

Aue, Materena thinks, it's so nice when the children make such confessions, even if they are drunk. She puts her arm around her son and is about to go on with the rules when the door of the bedroom swings open.

It's Pito, also drunk.

"Son," he says, jovial, "come outside with the men."

"Eh, I'm telling him about the rules," Materena says, holding her son tight.

"What rules? What are you going on about?"

"Well, the rules! The rules when you're a visitor, when you're in another country!"

"Materena, it's me who can talk about all that, okay?" With his hand, Pito summons his son to get up. "I've been in another country, I've traveled. You've never left Tahiti."

"Eh, I've been in more countries than you, I watch documentaries!"

Pito bursts out laughing. "Come on, son," he repeats.

And like he's done many times before, Tamatoa abandons his mother for his father's company.

The airport is packed. Tamatoa is the grandson of Loana, the relative who never says anything bad about anybody, and the son of Materena, the relative who is nice to everybody. By the time he's walking through customs, he has about one hundred shell necklaces around his neck, his shoulders, in his hands. He's less drunk than he was four hours ago (Materena made him stand under a cold shower for thirty minutes), but he still looks like he's falling asleep. According to Pito, speaking from experience, catching a plane drunk is better than catching a plane sober. First of all you don't get scared, and second, you sleep and so the time goes faster.

There's crying all over the place. The grandmothers are crying, the aunties and the cousins are crying, the sister is crying, the brother is crying. The sister's girlfriend (alias Tamatoa's secret lover) is wailing and digging her long fingernails into Moana's arm, scratching it too, and punching it, twisting it . . . Moana takes it all on. Anything to help his brother's ex-girlfriend.

But everybody knows that the woman suffering the most is the mother.

Aue, Materena needs to hold on to someone, her legs are weak, she's going to faint in a minute. Here's Ati on her left. No, not him, the relatives will gossip about how she held her husband's best mate instead of her husband, even if he was closer to her than her husband, who is hiding behind a pillar several yards away.

Here's Cousin Mori on her right. *Oui,* he'll do.

Mori puts an arm around Materena and says, "One son leaves, another son arrives, eh?"

Materena doesn't understand. She lifts her crying eyes to her cousin. "What are you saying?"

"One son leaves, another son arrives. Your son leaves, your daughter brings home a boyfriend," says Mori.

"What boyfriend?" asks Materena.

"But Leilani's boyfriend, the one with the motorbike."

"Boyfriend?" Materena says again. "Motorbike?"

"Ah," Mori says, realizing that once again in his life he didn't look where he was walking. He quickly moves back to the subject of Materena's son. What a fine man he's going to be, that one, Materena must be so proud . . .

There's a Boy on the Horizon

When you're angry and you ask questions all you do is shout and demand an answer there and then. Overreact.

Well, it's the same when you're sad.

Materena went so close to confronting her daughter at the airport about that boyfriend who has a motorbike, but she was too sad. It felt like her heart was being crucified.

In the days after Tamatoa left on military service, Materena moped around the house with her broom like a lost soul, brooming sad, long strokes here and there. She did feel a bit better when her son called to let her know that he had arrived in France and all was well, all was fantastic. He sounded so happy, and that was a real comfort to Materena. But it still felt like her heart was being crucified. She spent hours smelling the pillow of her son and the shirt he wore the day before he left. She inhaled the sweat, she flicked through the family album and caressed every single photo of her boy Tamatoa puffing his chest and flexing his arms, doing his big eyes and poking out his tongue, with his rooster, his kite, winking at the camera.

Cheeky boy, eh.

Aue . . . Materena could not stop the tears and she felt so guilty. How many times had she told Tamatoa, "I really can't wait for you to move out of the house!" after he'd made a mess of the house or come home drunk and woken her up. But she only meant next door, or the next suburb. She *never* meant the other side of the planet. *Aue,* the regrets, eh. What about that time Materena yelled at Tamatoa because he ate all the cookies? She yelled, "You think you're the only person in this house! You think you're the only person who likes cookies in this house! Bloody selfish!"

If Tamatoa were here today, Materena would go and buy him a packet of cookies. And not the plain, cheap cookies but his favorites. Delta Cream.

Aue, the agony, eh!

She got lots of embraces from Pito, Moana, and Leilani.

Pito's hug was a quick embrace. He tapped Materena on the shoulder and said, "Okay, mama, we stop crying."

Moana's embrace was tender and cuddly. Materena felt like a teddy bear in her son's arms. He said, "Mamie, we're all sad."

Leilani's embrace was strong and positive. She said, "Mamie . . . we're the strongest creatures on earth, don't forget." Materena laughed for two or three seconds and then she got sad again.

Nobody who saw Materena by the side of the road waiting for the truck to go to work dared call out a happy greeting to her, such as, "Eh! How are you today, Cousin? You're fine?" A nod is much more appropriate in such situations. A nod that is polite and full of compassion and that says, "I'm with you in your suffering, Cousin." Even Loma, the cousin voted most insensitive by the family, made sure to remain low-key.

Also, nobody has been visiting Materena except for Loana, herself the mother of a son who took off to the other side of the planet for military service and stayed there. Loana came by to hold her daughter's hands, caress her daughter's hair, cry along, and to say, "Girl, you've got other children to look after. Get up and walk." By this Loana meant: Stop the crying, full stop. It's time to cut the umbilical cord once more.

But Materena wasn't ready to do this yet. She had to cry for a little bit longer and remember those days when Tamatoa was a sweet little boy before he turned into a cheeky boy and, later on, a hoodlum.

It is only after a week that Materena starts to feel better. She realizes that military service is good for young men. It keeps them out of trouble. Okay then, time to cut the umbilical cord once more and get on with the day.

First on Materena's list is to find out about that boy who has a motorbike.

No more believing Leilani's stories that she spends two hours after school comforting Vahine because she still can't accept that Tamatoa has left to do his military service in France instead of doing his military service in Tahiti and marrying her.

Materena marches to her daughter's bedroom. After two knocks, she walks in just as Leilani is shoving something under her shirt.

"Mamie," she says, scribbling in a copybook, "I've got a lot of homework to do."

Okay then, Materena is not going to turn around the pot, beat around the bush. "I've heard you've got a boyfriend and that he's got a motorbike."

Leilani's response is an exclamation. "Who told you?"

Ah-ha, Materena thinks, now she tells me. Materena sits on her daughter's bed. "I just hope that you're protecting yourself. You don't want to fall pregnant with the wrong boy, a boy who's using you for his pleasure. Not counting the diseases and everything."

Leilani has stopped scribbling, and an angel must be passing through, because it's very quiet around here. Nobody is talking, nobody is moving.

"So?" Materena says to break the silence. "Who's the boy on the horizon?"

The silence continues until Leilani turns to her mother, who is patiently waiting. She confirms that there is a boy on the horizon and he does have a motorbike, but she can't really call him a boyfriend.

"*Ah oui?*" And why not? Materena asks herself. He's a married man? He's, like, thirty? "And how come you can't really call him a boyfriend?"

Leilani informs her mother that she doesn't really want to be his girlfriend and she's trying very hard to resist him, but it's so difficult.

"*Ah oui?*" And now Materena is really worried. And why does Leilani have to resist that boy? He's a cousin, that boy? He's a foreigner? He's a Protestant? "And why do you have to resist him?"

Leilani sighs a long, resigned sigh. "I know I shouldn't," she says. "I mean, resist him . . ." She looks to the wall, her eyes squinting like she's trying to look at something in the distance, far away. "He's got everything on my list."

List? Materena is intrigued. She doesn't know anyone in the family who has lists. The only person she knows who has lists is her boss.

Madame Colette has lists for everything: appointments with her doctor, her dentist, the headmistress, her husband, people's birthdays, her exercises, her son's school marks, and her dinners. Madame Colette is constantly writing lists. She's got notepads all over the place, and she's always stressing out because of them.

Materena never writes lists. All she knows is that . . . sometimes you remember and sometimes you forget and you decide what you're going to eat ten minutes before the Chinese store closes. You ask around, "Hey, Cousin! What are you eating tonight?" And then you run to the Chinese store to buy the ingredients. If, for example, a cousin calls back, "We're eating a baked chicken," and you don't have enough money to buy a whole chicken but suddenly the desire to eat chicken comes to you, well, you buy chicken wings. Materena has never, ever heard the relatives say, "We're eating this because it's on my list!"

But imagine writing a list for a boyfriend. Materena has never heard of such a thing! "List?" she asks. "What list? What's this?"

Leilani puts a hand under her shirt, fumbles for a few seconds with her bra, and now she's holding a folded piece of paper. Hesitating, she passes it to her mother. "Here. Read."

"You keep pieces of paper in your bra these days?" Materena asks with a cackle. She just wants to lighten up the vibes a bit. "I thought only old women kept papers in their bra. Money, most of the time," Materena continues as she unfolds the mysterious piece of paper. "Money and handkerchiefs."

And with that, Materena begins to read.

My boyfriend must be a reader like me.

Materena glances at her daughter for a quick second.

My boyfriend must not be an alcoholic. One beer or two per day is fine, but not ten.

Materena smiles. That boy on the horizon sounds like a very good catch.

My boyfriend must be a nice person.

Materena nods. She agrees. One hundred percent.

Being handsome is definitely optional.

Materena reads on, agreeing over and over again. And she thinks, Who would have thought of a list like this but my own daughter, eh? It's very clever. But it's a bit unrealistic. When you're in love, you're in love, you don't see properly. Everybody could be telling you that he's not for you, but you believe that he is and so he is. "That boy," Materena asks just to make sure, "he's like on your list?"

Leilani nods, her eyes twinkling with delight. "He's got the most beautiful body." She sighs. "He rows three days a week."

Oh, it's very easy to have a beautiful body when you're young, Materena thinks. But what is there to resist? Materena asks in her head. Whoever that boy is must be Monsieur Perfect. Too good to be true.

"Where does he live?" Materena asks out of interest.

Leilani casually replies that the boy she's trying to resist lives in Punaauia PK 18.

"Punaauia PK 18!" Materena is exclaiming, because it costs millions to live there. The houses have electrical gates and access to the white-sanded beach. Then, at PK 21, where Pito's family is from, you've got the fibro shacks.

"Oh, Mamie, you're impossible. So what if he lives in Punaauia PK 18? He's not a king."

"I know that . . . but tell me, why do you have to resist that boy?" As far as Materena is concerned, there's some news coming, some news that is going to make her go silent. Some news like, The boy is a Casanova, a heartbreaker.

But the news is that he's too nice.

"Eh? What?" Materena asks, confused. "That's the reason you have to resist him?"

Leilani confirms this with a slow nod. "Sometimes I wonder if it's just an act to get into my pants," she continues.

Materena bursts out laughing. "One minute you're telling me nothing and next minute you're telling me everything!"

"But what do you think, Mamie?" Leilani asks. "How can I tell if he's being nice because he is nice or if he's being nice because he wants to get into my pants?"

Materena looks up to the ceiling. "Let me think a little."

"Was Papi really nice to you at the beginning?" Leilani asks.

"*Non,* he was like he is today."

"And you still went with him?" Leilani sounds like she can't believe her ears.

"What do you want," says Materena, shrugging. "Love is like that. You can't explain. What's the boy's name?"

"Hotu Viriatu."

And before Materena can say anything about this piece of information, Leilani advises her mother that he's Catholic, he's not from an enemy family, and he's not a cousin.

He's just Hotu Viriatu: twenty-two, handsome, smart, and nice.

"You're nice too," says Materena. "Nice people sometimes attract each other."

"He's had five girlfriends."

"Five," calmly repeats Materena. Five! she yells in her head. But he's worse than Ati, that one! At least Ati had had only two girlfriends by the time he was Hotu's age.

"Is this a lot?" asks Leilani.

"Oh . . . it depends." These days Materena is very careful with what she says to Leilani. Leilani goes on about Hotu's ex-girlfriends. The first one was when he was seven years old, and the next four were from when he was eighteen years old to twenty-one. As she names those four girlfriends, Materena exclaims.

Hotu was the boyfriend of last year's Miss Tahiti!

And before her there was the champion rower from Hawaii! And before her there was one of the nieces of the president of Tahiti! And before her there was the daughter of the man who owns the Vaima building!

Each time Leilani confirms with a nod, and before Materena

has the chance to say that Hotu might have exaggerated a little bit, Leilani informs her mother that she didn't find out about these women from Hotu but from his mother.

"Ah, because you met the mama?" Materena is so surprised. It is unusual for the mama to want to meet her son's girlfriend so soon! Materena met her mother-in-law when she was pregnant with her first child with Pito. Materena's cousin Giselle met her mother-in-law the day after she gave birth to her first child. On the whole, in Tahiti anyway, mothers are pretty selective when it comes to meeting their son's girlfriends. The romance must be over a year, at least. "Hotu's mama invited you to her house to talk?" Materena asks.

"*Non,* she just walked past the restaurant and saw us." Leilani adds that Hotu ducked under the table, but it was too late. His mother had seen him. So she came in and made herself comfortable at the table. She looked Leilani up and down. She talked about the weather and this and that, Hotu's famous girlfriends, whose photos are hung in the living room.

Now, Materena understands that when a girlfriend becomes an ex-girlfriend it doesn't mean you put all her photos in the trash. No, you put her photos in an album. The only girlfriend who gets to be in a frame and on the wall is the current girlfriend. That is what Mama Teta does with her youngest son's girlfriends. When the girlfriend is current, she's in a frame on the wall, and when she ceases to be current, she gets transferred into the album.

And the girlfriends Mama Teta was very fond of and is still very fond of get their pictures downsized so that they fit in Mama Teta's purse.

But it's one thing doing this and it's another framing your son's ex-girlfriends and putting them up in your living room.

"Hotu's mother sounds like a bizarre woman," Materena says, getting up. "What does she look like?"

"A Christmas tree," laughs Leilani. "Mamie, she's got so much jewelry, it's ridiculous."

"Hum." Materena nods.

"And you know what they say about people who wear a lot of jewelry," Leilani goes on.

"*Non.*" Materena wouldn't know this. She doesn't know anyone who wears a lot of jewelry.

"They have a low self-esteem," Leilani informs her mother. "They're not confident. That's why you are confident, because you don't wear any jewelry except for your wedding ring."

"Ah." Materena agrees with a nod, although she's not really following her daughter's explanation. In her mind, the reason some people wear a lot of jewelry is because they can afford to buy a lot of jewelry.

"She's Tahitian, she's brown as, but she speaks like she was born into the French aristocracy," says Leilani. "She has a French accent, Mamie! She does the *reuh-reuh!*"

"Ah." Anyway, let's go back to Hotu's ex-girlfriends, Materena would like to know who broke up with whom. She's not particularly interested in Hotu's mother right now.

"He did."

"He did, eh?" Materena says, shaking her head. Now she can see the type. He sounds like Monsieur Casanova, that one.

"Mamie, he had to go back to France, you know," explains Leilani. "To finish his studies."

"What does he do?" Materena can't believe she forgot to ask this very important question. What the boyfriend does is always the first question mothers are supposed to ask.

Well, he's a dentist. Leilani explains that at the moment he's working with a dentist in town, but he will be opening his own practice soon.

"A dentist!" exclaims Materena. "How old was he when he finished school? Twelve?"

"Seventeen, like I will be when I finish school." Leilani goes on about how it's the normal age to finish school when you don't repeat classes. "And Hotu didn't become a dentist for the money," stresses Leilani.

"*Ah oui?*" Materena can't help being a bit skeptical. Everybody knows that people become dentists (and doctors) for the money. Anyway, that's the general belief.

Leilani continues about Hotu's mission as a dentist: to educate people on the importance of looking after their teeth (because bad teeth affect health), and to donate several hours of his time each month to poor people who can't afford a dentist and who badly need one. That's why Hotu is taking lessons to perfect his Tahitian. He wants to be able to speak to people who can't express themselves in the French language.

"Ah, his Tahitian is not really good?" Materena asks.

"Oh, he's like me, you know. He gets by . . . he's like many of us."

Materena nods in agreement.

"He's so wonderful." Leilani sighs. "He really wants to give something back to the world, having had such a fortunate childhood. But I don't think it's the right time for me to be with him."

"All right, then." Materena gives her daughter a long kiss on her forehead. She's had enough of hearing about the dentist, since Leilani's plan is to resist him. "Listen, girl," says Materena, "forget about that boy, okay? Work hard at school. Get your degrees and a good job. Then, if the dentist is still free and you still feel strongly about him, don't resist him anymore. But he sounds to me like a real nice person."

Now, Materena can say in all honesty that she has experience in a lot of departments. She knows, for example, how it feels to have Father Unknown written on a birth certificate. To be alone most of the nights, cook dinner for six in less than ten minutes, greet relatives so that they feel welcome, get rid of relatives so that their feelings don't get hurt. Materena knows a lot of things about the everyday life, but she has no idea how it feels to love someone you have to resist. She's never had to resist physical attraction.

When she met Pito and fell head over heels in love with him, she didn't stop to think if he was a good catch or if there was another, better specimen waiting for her on the horizon. She just ran to Pito with open arms and with 100 percent passion. Since then, she's never looked at another man.

Oh, Materena is not saying that when a good-looking man walks her way she closes her eyes, *non.* She looks, she admires the body and she admires the face, but that's it.

Materena has resisted a lot of things in her life, like she's resisted telling her mother-in-law off to her face, hitting Pito on the head with the steel frying pan he gave her for one of her birthdays, slapping her big-mouth cousin Loma across the face . . . Let's just say that Materena knows very well how hard resisting can be, and resisting physical attraction must be even harder. If Materena was in such a situation she'd avoid being in the whereabouts of the man she wants so bad but has to resist because he's married, he's a cousin, it's not the right time.

But her daughter's plan of action is very different. In fact, Materena doesn't really believe that Leilani is doing much resisting these days.

Leilani is coming home later and later, and since Materena knows that the reason for her daughter's lateness has got nothing to do with Leilani comforting her crying friend, she doesn't need to ask all kinds of questions. She doesn't need to ask, "How's Vahine? Is she still crying over Tamatoa? Is she still going to send him a framed photograph of herself? Is she still thinking of tattooing Tamatoa's initials on her hand?"

Materena has to ask only one question, a very specific question, a question that requires a very specific answer — a yes or a no. And the question is, Did you resist today? That is the question Materena asks the very next day, the question she asks every day from then on.

Did you resist today?

And these are the answers Materena gets.

"We just talked."

"I wasn't with him, I was with Vahine."

"I wasn't with him, I was with Rose."

"The truck ran out of petrol."

Ah, here's Leilani coming home now, five minutes later than yesterday.

"So, girl?" Materena asks. "Did you resist today?"

"Stop asking me that question!" Leilani exclaims with a faint smirk.

And Materena understands all that there is to understand.

Hotu Viriatu

If your daughter is thirty years old when she first gets a boyfriend, the relatives say, "Ah, finally! About time! It's a miracle!" If your daughter is in her twenties, the relatives don't say much. But when she's not even seventeen years old, the relatives talk about it for days and days. They say somebody has got fire up her arse!

Oh, they don't say these very words to the mother. Say these very words to any mother and you'll get a slap across the face, so the relatives just interrogate the mother. "I heard your beautiful daughter has got a boyfriend. And who is he? And where did your daughter meet him? And who's the family? How old is he? Has he got a job?"

Materena, about to go to the Chinese store, braces herself for the upcoming interrogation. She can't hide forever. Plus, she much prefers to be interrogated on her way to the Chinese store, outside the Chinese store, inside the Chinese store, anywhere but in the whereabouts of her house. Because when the relatives are in the whereabouts of your house, they trick you. Before you know it, they're inside your house. And before you know it, they're sitting on the sofa in your living room.

Now, Materena could just ignore the questions fired at her. She could say, "It's none of your onions. Mind your own onions." But the trouble with relatives, some of them, most of them, all of them, is that if they don't get informed, they invent. They believe every word the big-mouth relative of the family — Cousin Loma, the one and only — says.

If you want the truth to be known you've got to speak.

Aue . . . might as well give the population what the population wants. Following is the information Materena is prepared to share today.

Yes, her daughter has a boyfriend, and Materena much prefers this situation to another situation, like her daughter being at the mercy of different boys who are after only one thing. True, her daughter's boyfriend is older than Leilani, but we're talking about just six years here, not twenty.

Leilani's boyfriend's name is Hotu Viriatu (he's Catholic, he's not from an enemy family, and he's not a cousin). He's very charming. He won Materena over in one second with that beautiful smile of his. His teeth are so white! What about the body! *Ouf!* What a fine specimen, that's all Materena can say.

He came to visit last night, but at least he called first to warn of his arrival, unlike many people Materena knows. Materena had plenty of time to hide the parts of the walls that had a bit of paint peeling off. She ignored Leilani and Pito making fun of her. Monsieur Dentist arrived not on his motorbike but in the silver BMW his father bought him when he came home with his degree. After the greetings, Pito asked Hotu to take him for a drive in his BMW. "Eh," Pito said, "take the old man for a drive, okay?"

"Pito!" Materena said under her breath. She was so embarrassed!

"Sure," Hotu said, "I'll take you for a drive."

"You can fix my teeth too, eh?" Pito said, walking out of the house, winking at Materena just to annoy her more.

Nevertheless, despite the embarrassing situation with Pito asking Hotu to fix all his teeth (free of charge, of course), it was fun last night. After the drive, Hotu talked to Materena about what a fine girl Leilani is. "She is so smart," he said, "and I know where she gets her beauty from." Immediately after this lovely compliment, Pito decided to challenge Hotu to an arm-wrestling competition.

Pito won.

He's all muscles, Leilani's boyfriend, from all the rowing he does. Pito hasn't done any exercise in twenty years. So don't go looking from midday to fourteen hours to put two and two together.

Of course Hotu let Pito win, and he did this because he knows it's a good idea to let the father of the house win. When the father of the house wins, he's very happy. He's not stupid, Leilani's boyfriend.

When he left, Pito tapped Leilani on the shoulder and said, "Eh, your boyfriend is too skinny. Tell him to eat a bit more."

As for Materena, she said, "What a nice boy!"

Okay, who's going to be the first relative to be asking Materena about her daughter's boyfriend? The first relative who says something nasty is going to get it!

Ah, here's Cousin Mori sitting under the mango tree next to the petrol station, as per usual. But today, for some reason, Cousin Mori is not drinking, and he's not playing his eternal accordion.

"*Iaorana,* Cousin!" Materena calls out.

Mori, waving and smiling, calls back, "*Iaorana,* Cousin!"

Materena stops in front of Mori and waits for Mori to start questioning, but all she gets from him today is a perplexed look. Yes, Mori's eyes are definitely saying, "*Oui?* And? Have you got something to say to me?" So Materena wishes her cousin a good day, he does the same, and off she goes.

Ah, and who does Materena see in the distance, running toward her? Cousin Loma in flesh and bones, the relative who saw Leilani waiting at the petrol station for Hotu to arrive one night, and who in just one minute found out there was a boyfriend on the horizon. The relative who no doubt has been running all over the neighborhood informing the population and the coconut radio.

"Cousin!" Loma's smile is full of morbid curiosity. Her eyes are also full of morbid curiosity.

"All is fine?" Materena casually asks as she greets Cousin Loma with light kisses on the cheeks.

"*Oui! Oui! Oui!* All is fine!" Loma is so excited today. "So! Leilani has a boyfriend! I saw them yesterday, and he's got a BMW? So Leilani has a boyfriend?"

"Well, you saw him, so you know," Materena says.

"I can't believe he's a *popa'a!*"

"Eh what?" Materena says. "What are you going on about?"

"Ah, he's not a *popa'a?*" Loma asks, confused. "It's just that . . . he's so white."

"Lots of Tahitians are white!"

Loma does her I'm-not-so-sure-about-that look. When you're a Tahitian, you're brown, you're not white. "Maybe there's a white ancestor in his family," Loma goes on.

"Eh, Loma. We all have white ancestors, okay. If you want to see pure Tahitians, go back to the first century." She can't believe Loma mistook Hotu for a *popa'a.*

Materena didn't even see that Hotu was white. When he walked into the house all she saw was a good-looking young man with combed hair and cut fingernails. She also saw his crisp ironed pants and shirt and the white shoes he didn't take off before walking into the house.

She didn't see that he was white.

How could Hotu be white, anyway? He's always in the sun! That Loma, Materena thinks. She needs glasses.

"His name is Hotu Viriatu, does that name sound *popa'a* to you?" Materena asks.

"*Ah non,* that name sounds very Tahitian . . . And how many sisters and brothers has he got?"

"One sister."

"He's not Tahitian." Loma does her I'm-not-impressed look.

"Eh, Loma," Materena snaps, "must we have ten children to be Tahitian these days? I have three children, does this mean I'm not Tahitian? Or does this mean I know when to stop?"

"He's got a job, at least?" asks Loma the detective.

Ah, here's Cousin Giselle. Materena can sure do with a break from Cousin Loma's stupid questions, and presently Cousin Giselle, with her big pregnant belly and her tribe of three children, is hurrying over.

"Cousin Materena!"

"Cousin Giselle!"

The two cousins give each other big hugs and kisses.

"You're fine?"

"I'm fine, Cousin," Materena replies as one by one she kisses her cousin's children, aged two to six.

"So Leilani has a boyfriend?" Giselle asks.

"*Eh oui,* what do you want, that's life."

"Eh, eh," Giselle says. Then, getting more teary by the second, she goes on about how it was like only yesterday that

Leilani was born, and now she's nearly seventeen years old, she's a woman and she has a boyfriend.

"*Aue,* love, eh," she sighs. "It's so wonderful, especially at the beginning . . . If only it stayed that way . . . the first kiss . . ." She stops to flick her two-year-old boy's hand pulling at her dress.

"Love?" Materena cackles. "You mean to say passion, Cousin." Materena tells Giselle about that kiss Leilani and Hotu gave each other outside the house before he left. Materena didn't mean to look, of course, she was just putting rubbish in the trash can, and she saw the lovers kiss as if one of them was about to leave for war and never return. That kiss just went on and on and on and on.

"*Oh, la-la!*" Giselle exclaims. "Somebody has got fire up her . . . And he's a *popa'a?*" Again, Materena rectifies the situation to Giselle. Then it's Auntie Stella's turn to be enlightened, and another auntie, and another cousin, and another cousin, and another cousin, and three mamas.

Well, they're all very pleased that Leilani's boyfriend is a local and not a foreigner, like Rose's Australian boyfriend, because foreigners always go back to their country and they don't necessarily ask the woman to follow. Sometimes, of course, this is not a bad thing.

Anyway, he's a local, that's one bit of information out of the way. What is his family name? His family name is Viriatu, he's Catholic, he's not from an enemy family, and there's no connection whatsoever.

And . . . has he got a job?

He's a dentist.

"*Ouh!*" The relatives are so happy for Leilani. "Lucky girl," they say.

"Lucky us!" they shout. "He can fix our teeth for free!"

And where did they meet, the relatives want to know.

Ah, that's another story altogether. They met in the truck, and usually Hotu never catches the truck since he has a motorbike and a car. But one particular morning he was driving his motorbike to work and it broke down. And so, for the first time in his life, Hotu Viriatu caught the truck.

He stood by the side of the road and waved to the first truck that came his way. It was Papa Lucky-Luke's truck, the truck locals never catch because Papa Lucky-Luke's such a slow driver and he doesn't play music in his truck.

That's the truck Leilani always catches, that way she can read on her way to school or write things down in her little notebook and she doesn't have to listen to music she doesn't like. She loves it that Papa Lucky-Luke's truck is always empty.

So anyway, Papa Lucky-Luke's truck stopped and Hotu hopped in with his backpack, holding on to his helmet. Leilani didn't even look up, she was so busy writing. This went on for minutes until Hotu, who'd been staring at Leilani, felt it was the right moment to say something.

And so he said, "Are you writing your memoirs?"

Leilani looked up. "Pardon?"

"Are you writing your memoirs?"

She laughed, he laughed, they looked into each other's eyes, and as we say, the rest is History with a capital *H.*

The relatives agree that it's an unusual way for two people to meet. There's no story like that in the family. In the family people meet at the Chinese store, the snack, the church, the nightclub, they meet at the airport, as it happened with Rose and Matt. Matt was ordering a coffee at the Airport Café while waiting for the check-in line for the plane to Australia to be less busy. He'd been on a three-week visit to Tahiti, surfing. At the Airport Café, Matt and Rose met, and Matt didn't catch his plane.

All right, then, now that the population has been informed

about Leilani's boyfriend, the population can go on with their chores. But there's one more thing Materena has to say.

"Hotu is allergic to alcohol!" Materena is all smiles. She expects the relatives to share her delight. A Tahitian man who doesn't drink? Are you crazy?

But the relatives aren't sharing Materena's delight. Nobody is jumping up and down with joy and everybody has got a story about how when they met their man, he said he was allergic to alcohol. Apparently this is a very popular pick-up line.

"*Iaorana,* princess . . . my name is . . . and I'm allergic to alcohol." The relatives can't believe Materena didn't know about it.

Getting Serious

What can a mother do, Materena says to Cousin Rita, when her daughter is in love and all is new and wonderful? She can't compare, she can't preach, especially when she had a baby at nineteen years old.

She just has to accept the situation.

Like Vahine's mother did when one of her relatives visited to say, "Eh, Cousin, do you know your daughter has joined a dancing group and that she's leaving for France next week to pursue that boy she loves?"

"What boy?" Vahine's mother replied.

"But Tamatoa Tehana! Don't you know anything? Where have you been? At a conference again?"

Like Tapeta did when an Australian surfer knocked on her door one sunny day holding his surfboard and said, in his broken French, "Is this the house of Rose?"

Materena will just have to accept that her daughter wants to live with her boyfriend because she wants to be with him twenty-four hours a day, seven days a week. *Oui,* it's the big love between those two, they want to be an official couple. It's not enough that they see each other every day, eh? They talk for hours about electrons and protons, chemistry and other complicated words, and Leilani does whatever Hotu says.

Materena dropped her broom when Leilani said, "Guess what we did this weekend?" Materena thought Leilani and Hotu were spending the weekend at Hotu's parents' weekender in Vairao. Instead they rowed from Tahiti to Moorea together.

Materena dropped her broom when Leilani told her, "Guess where Hotu and I slept in Moorea?" Materena guessed that Leilani and Hotu stayed at the Club Med. But Leilani and Hotu slept on the beach under the stars, like in the old days.

And what's with the massages?

Last time Materena stood behind the closed door to Leilani's bedroom to catch a tiny bit of the "biology tuition," she heard Leilani say, "What am I massaging now? Quick, give me the medical word or I'm stopping! All right, here's an easy one for you. What am I massaging now?" When Hotu cackled, "My reproductive organ?" Materena hurried away.

Another time, Moana knocked on Leilani's bedroom door to offer the lovebirds some almond cookies he'd just baked, and Hotu opened the door wearing Leilani's underpants around his head.

Plus, those two are always laughing their heads off.

Two weeks ago (Leilani's bedroom was half-open) Materena saw Leilani and Hotu sitting on the floor, holding each other by the chin and singing, "I hold you, you hold me by the goatee beard, the first one who laughs gets a slap."

This is an old Tahitian nursery rhyme. Materena went on spying to see who would be the first one to laugh. After half a minute, Hotu burst out laughing and said, "You're crazy, I'm marrying you."

But last week, in the middle of the night, Leilani shouted, "Not until I have a job!" Pito, watching TV, and Materena, ironing sheets, looked up and waited for the continuation. But there was no continuation, just a complete silence followed by Hotu's faint cackle. So Pito and Materena went back to what they were doing.

Then, three days ago, Materena was putting something in Tamatoa and Moana's bedroom when she heard Leilani shriek, "I can't go on, it's hurting me!" And then Materena heard Hotu say, "Just a little bit more . . . come on, you can do it." Poor Leilani was moaning like she was in real pain! Moaning like she was giving birth, actually. What is going on in that room? Materena asked herself. Some kind of torture? After two seconds of reflection, Materena's mind was made up. She stomped over and put her hand on the doorknob, took a big breath, then changed her mind when she heard Leilani tell Hotu that she had no idea how weak her belly muscles were, and how she'll definitely aim to do fifty sit-ups every day from now on. Ah, Materena thought, relieved.

And last time . . . Well anyway, what can a mother do when her daughter wants to be with her boyfriend twenty-four hours a day?

She can tell her daughter to wait a little, have fun, go to the cinema, plan your future, finish school, you only have three months left. But the daughter is most likely to say, "It's my life, you had a baby at nineteen years old. And it's not as if I'm leaving school."

Aue. Materena sighs. She's sure all of this is Hotu's idea. He thinks he owns Leilani just because she tattooed his initials on her hand two days ago. When Materena saw that tattoo, she went mad. She yelled at Leilani, who yelled back, and they had their first big argument in two years. Pito, who was watching a kung-fu movie, told them both to shut up.

Aue. Materena sighs again. Here, she's going to have another Coca-Cola that Cousin Rita has brought along with her today. And here, she's going to have some chips Cousin Rita has also brought along with her today. She's feeling so sad. Just thinking about Leilani not living here in this house anymore is terrible. But then, thinks Materena, the house will definitely be more relaxed. Materena won't be on edge whenever Leilani drops her study to follow Hotu and his plans to rediscover their island, which he missed for five years when he was stuck in France.

Aue, children, eh . . . they give you tears.

One son leaves for another country, another son says he's going to Bora-Bora to be chef at a hotel there, and now it's the daughter's turn to leave. What do I do to my children? Materena asks herself. They can't wait to leave me, or what?

Aue, Materena is so sad, but she can't go on doing her long face with her cousin visiting and sitting right next to her at the kitchen table.

"So, Cousin?" Materena says. "Work is fine?"

"Cousin," Rita replies, "you can be sad. I understand. I'm not here for you to make me laugh." She puts a hand over Materena's hand. "It's a shock when the daughter leaves the house." Rita knows what's she's talking about. When she left her mama's house at the age of thirty-one, her mama was inconsolable for three whole weeks. It didn't matter that the relatives said to her, "About time! Alleluia!" Auntie Antoinette cried nonstop.

"Has Leilani packed her bags yet?" Rita asks.

"*Non,* not yet, they're going to find the house first."

"Ah." Rita caresses her cousin's hand. "Be strong, eh, Cousin?"

Aue . . . the packing of bags . . . it's very sad for the mama. In Rita's opinion, it's best that Materena doesn't watch, because if she watches her daughter pack those bags real fast, like she can't wait to get out of there, well, she might get a bit hurt.

That happened with Rita's mama. Rita was stuffing her

clothes in her suitcase (because she couldn't wait to get out of the house and live her own life with her boyfriend) and her mama was standing by the door, crying her eyes out, moaning, "The way you're stuffing those clothes in that suitcase, it's like you've been living in a prison here."

"Don't watch the packing of bags," Rita says. "Go in the kitchen and do something, okay?"

"*Oui,*" Materena says, wiping her eyes with the back of her hands. "I just hope Leilani is going to choose the house she's going to live in. She's the one who's going to be in that house most of the time . . ."

"True." Rita nods in agreement. "I hope too that there aren't too many doors in the house. I should have told Leilani about the doors, doors are bad. Doors suck energy. It's true," she says to Materena's skeptical look. "Lately I've been having zero energy, but really zero, even with all the vitamins I take."

"Ah, because you take vitamins?" Materena didn't know this.

"When you're past thirty and you're a woman, you've got to take vitamins," Rita says, and goes on about doors again. Doors make it impossible for love to grow because people are always on edge. It's true, Rita swears, because lately she's been so edgy with Coco.

"Doors . . . ," Materena says vaguely. "What kind of doors? Opened doors, closed doors, doors that keep banging shut and you get cranky?"

"Doors, full stop!" Rita shouts crankily. "It's not complicated! I told you before! I explained to you!" Then, quickly remembering the situation, Rita goes back to doing her air of compassion and speaking softly. "Be strong, Cousin. At least Leilani is not moving to another country."

"Well, I just hope Leilani isn't going to let Hotu take her to the other side of the island." Materena shakes her head with resignation. "It's a very long way when you want to see the family."

"Cousin," Rita says, cackling, "have you seen Tahiti on a map of the world? It's a dot . . . to go around the island takes less than an hour."

Materena gives her cousin an angry look. "In a car, Rita, *oui,* but I don't have a car . . . If I want to see my daughter for five minutes, I have to be in a truck for two hours."

"Oh," Rita hurries to say, "I'm sure Leilani is not going to go and live on the other side of the island. She doesn't need to hide."

Aue eh, Materena thinks. Here, she's going to have a bit more Coca-Cola.

"You know what Pito said when Leilani told him she was moving out with Hotu?" Materena asks.

Before Rita has time to guess, Materena tells her what Pito said. He said that he's going to put the TV in Leilani's room because he wants to watch the TV in peace without Materena brooming in the living room or ironing in the living room. But there's no way Materena is going to let Pito lock himself in Leilani's room with his TV and his beer. As far as she's concerned, her daughter's bedroom is going to stay just as it is. Pito wanted to put the TV in his sons' bedroom too when Moana left, but Materena told him no way.

"My children's bedrooms are not for TV," Materena says to Rita. "Leilani wants to come home, no problem, her bedroom is here waiting for her."

Rita nods. She understands what Materena is saying. Her mother did the same. When Rita moved out, her mother said, "You want to come home, no problem, your bedroom is here waiting for you." But Rita can't see herself ever living with her mother again. They would be fighting every day. Still, it's a nice thought, knowing your bedroom hasn't been turned into the family TV room or the storage room in your absence.

Rita's bedroom is still as she left it years ago. Materena's bedroom is also still as she left it years ago and her daughter's bedroom is going to share the same fate. And talking about Materena's daughter, here's the girl in question coming through the door, all smiling and happy, and announcing that she and Hotu have found the perfect house! And plus, the rent is cheap!

"Oh, when the rent is cheap," Materena snarls, "there's something wrong."

"And how do you know this?" Leilani laughs. "You've never rented a house in your whole life, Mamie." Then, sitting next to her auntie Rita, she asks, "Auntie Rita, tell me, you who've got so much experience in renting houses . . . When the rent is cheap, does it mean there's something wrong?"

Oh, la-la . . . poor Auntie Rita. Stuck between the lettuce and the tomato yet again. When the rent is cheap . . . does it mean there's something wrong? Well yes, of course! When the rent is cheap it means the house is run-down, that's what it means. The house is run-down, there are missing louvers, and there are holes in the walls, or somebody died in that house. Then again, sometimes the rent is cheap because the owner of the house just wants someone in the house to look after the garden, but there are usually conditions, like no children in the house and no animals in the house. But then again, sometimes the rent is cheap because you get lucky, you were at the right place at the right time.

So . . . when the rent is cheap does it mean there's something wrong?

"Not necessarily," Rita says.

"I hope there's not a hacked tree in the garden," Materena says, looking into her daughter's sparkling eyes. And before the daughter gets the chance to inform her mother, the auntie asks if the house faces north, because the house has got to face north, you've got to have the morning rays of sunshine filtering into the house through the louvers.

"*Ah oui,* Auntie!" Leilani exclaims. "The house faces north all right!" And here she is demonstrating with her hands which part of the house faces where, and Materena, who still doesn't know where north is, shakes her head, thinking, Here's Leilani going on again with her geography.

Like it's more important than to know that when there's a hacked tree in the garden, it means something bad has happened. Someone fell off that tree and died.

Like it's more important than to know that the house is not built on top of a sacred site. There's a story about Tahitian builders who stumbled upon a sacred site in the middle of digging the foundations of a hotel, and they were horrified, the poor men. The priest was quickly called to the site, along with the Tahua priest and professional bone removers. It was a whole ceremony. The priests recited prayers, the professional bone removers counted the bones, the journalists took pictures of the ceremony, the TV people filmed the ceremony, and everyone from the neighborhood watched. It was quite a big ceremony. But the hotel went on being built despite protest marches. And even today, bizarre things are always happening in that hotel.

Nobody in their right mind is going to build a house or a hotel on top of a sacred site. "Your house?" Materena asks Leilani, who's still going on about north and all that. "It's not built on top of a sacred site?"

Leilani stops talking to give her mother a funny look, then looks back to her auntie Rita, who says, "I hope there's not too many doors, girl, doors are bad, they suck the energy out."

"There's no doors," Leilani says.

"No doors?" Materena and Rita say together. "What do you mean, there's no doors? You can't have a house with no doors!"

Well, there are no doors in Leilani and Hotu's house.

"How do you lock the house?" Rita asks. She's wondering about that house. No doors? What is this house? A cave?

Well, there is a door, the door to get in and out of the house, but then once you're in the house itself there's no doors.

"So what do you have?" Materena asks. "Curtains?"

"*Non,*" Leilani replies, "just empty space. You walk in the house and there's the living room, the bathroom, the kitchen, and the bedroom."

Materena and Rita look at each other.

"Then," Leilani continues, "you go outside and there's the veranda with the table to eat and there's the view right in front of your eyes. The view of the ocean."

"You can see the ocean from your house?" Rita exclaims, all excited. "You can see the sun rise in the morning?"

Rita is so excited she hugs her niece and congratulates her. She's been trying to get a house with ocean views for years, but once people move into a house with ocean views, they stay in that house. They don't move. All Rita can say now is that today must be her niece's lucky day. How many times does a house facing north with ocean views and no doors come up for rent? Ah, Rita is feeling a bit envious.

"You're so lucky, girl," she says.

But Materena is not sharing her cousin's opinion. When a house has got views it means the house is on the top of a hill, and you know what that means, eh? When a house is on top of a hill, true, you're going to have a view, and it's not bad to have a view, you can admire the view, the magnificent ocean, and all that. But you've got to get the telephone connected because the relatives aren't going to walk all the way up the hill only to find out that there's nobody home. They're going to want to go to the telephone booth and ring to make sure someone is going to be in the house by the time they climb that hill. You're never going to have unexpected relatives visiting.

Now, sometimes that is not a bad thing. But don't forget that when a house is on top of a hill, it also means it's a long way from the main road . . . from the Chinese store. You're not going to be able to decide at six o'clock what you're going to cook and then stroll to the Chinese store, minutes before it closes, to get the ingredients. You're going to have to run. And if you're pregnant, you're still going to have to run. And if you have a baby in the carriage, you're still going to have to run.

Good luck to you on your way back to your house with all the shopping bags.

Materena tells all of this to her daughter.

"*Oh, la-la,*" Leilani says. "I'm going to have my driver's license next year. And so what if I have to run down the hill and up the hill with the shopping bags? It's good exercise."

"There's a breadfruit tree in the garden, at least?" Materena asks.

This is a question Tahitian mothers often ask their daughters when they are moving out to be in their own house, to live by their own rules and regulations. You can have hibiscuses and lemon trees and pawpaws and palm trees, but if you ain't got a breadfruit tree . . . poor you.

With a breadfruit tree nearby, when there's no money in the bank and no money in the can, no worries. Just climb that tree and get a breadfruit and eat it barbecued, baked, in the stew, fried, with butter and jam.

So, there's a breadfruit in the garden, at least?

Non, there's no breadfruit, and this doesn't bother Leilani at all because she doesn't really like breadfruit and Hotu doesn't really like breadfruit either and so . . .

Materena cackles. "Ah, that's what you say now, but wait

until you have a couple of children, you're going to love breadfruit." Well anyway, Materena stands up and asks if it's possible to see that house on top of a hill which has a view but not one single breadfruit tree.

Within minutes, the three women are on their way, with Leilani in the front of the car to give Rita directions.

"Turn left here." Rita turns left and they're now heading for the RDO, the road that takes you to the top of the mountain. Materena, looking out the window, shakes her head with disbelief. It's one thing to be living on top of a hill, but it's another thing altogether to be living on top of a mountain.

"Turn right," Leilani says.

Rita turns right and glances to Materena through the rearview mirror. They haven't even done one mile, so it means . . .

"Keep going . . . keep going . . . turn left . . . and here's the house . . . my castle."

Rita switches the engine off and comments on the house. "The house is very small and looks a bit abandoned," she says, "but it's very cute. All it needs is a good coat of paint. But look at that frangipani tree growing next to the veranda! It's so beautiful! It must be over one hundred years old! What do you think, Cousin?" Rita asks. "The house is cute, eh? And look at that frangipani!" Materena admits that the house is very cute and that the frangipani is very beautiful, and she's now looking at the view. This is a very beautiful view, she thinks, it's a shame the airport is in the way, but still, you can see the island of Moorea. And there's the green house on the corner before you get to the airport and a bit further, the Chinese store, and a bit further, the petrol station.

Well, she didn't go too far, that one. Materena smiles with relief and thinks, She's not silly. "How much is it going to cost Hotu for you two to live here?" she calls.

"I'm paying the rent, Mamie."

Materena turns around. "But how are you going to pay the rent? I hope you're not saying that I'm —"

"But *non,* Mamie! I'm not like that!" Leilani explains that she's got everything figured out in her budget book.

"Ah, because you've got a budget book?" Well, Materena is very impressed.

"*Oui,* I've got a budget book and a job," a proud Leilani announces.

"A job? Where?"

Leilani informs her mother and auntie that she had a very successful interview today with a very nice old Chinese man who owns the pet shop in Papeete. And she will be working every afternoon after school from four to six. She will also be working two Saturdays a month. This job will give her enough money to cover the very cheap rent and a few necessities on top, such as rice and toilet paper.

Now, when a woman and a man move in together, when they share the roof, the bed, and the kitchen table, it means they're getting serious. Only time can tell how long these two will last — how long their respective families will be using the term *in-law* when referring to the lovebirds since they're now an official couple, as good as being married — but it doesn't mean the family can't guess, the family can't bet. "Who's saying six months? Four months? Two months?"

Sometimes the family is right and sometimes the family is wrong. People they thought would pack up their bags and go back to the mama after three months of cohabitation sometimes stay together for two years. Others who the family thought were so perfect for each other have packed their bags and gone back to the mama after two weeks.

You can never tell with these things.

The word in Materena's neighborhood is that Hotu will pack his bags in three weeks because his girlfriend can't cook or iron, she can't do many things that make a man happy. Her mother deliberately never taught her these things.

But when you are the daughter of a professional cleaner, you're ahead of everyone else in the cleaning department. And when you've seen your mother cook over a thousand meals, cooking isn't witchcraft. And when you're a man who's lived five years away from home, you're ahead of all the men who've never left a home run by a woman (first the mother, then the woman).

Okay, Leilani and Hotu's house is not as clean and tidy as it should be and the meals aren't as delectable as they could be, but when passion is new, who cares about such things?

Ah true, according to Leilani and Hotu's neighbor, it's the big love between Leilani and Hotu. Apparently, when the neighbor sees the young couple chase each other in the garden and they fall on the grass and embrace, when she sees the young lovebirds sleep on the roof for a bit of romance under the stars and the moon . . . *eh hia,* she gets nostalgic. She remembers the days when she was young, when her man was hooked on her real bad. When she sees Leilani running up that hill with her boyfriend following on his motorbike and driving very slowly, taking a good look, whistling one whistle of admiration after another, the neighbor wishes she weren't fifty-two years old.

But don't think everything is always rosy out there on top of the hill, though, there have been some arguments, and big ones too. Ah yes, the neighbor confirmed to Materena that objects have occasionally been flying out of the house through the door. Here, one morning, so the neighbor dutifully repeats to Materena, Hotu and Leilani had a fight outside, right next to the motorbike. It was about his mother having a key to their house, or something like that. The neighbor was at her sink doing the dishes.

And another time, it was in the afternoon, so the neighbor also dutifully repeats to Materena, Hotu and Leilani were outside on the mat reading. One minute they were hugging and next minute they were yelling at each other, but the neighbor didn't understand what they were yelling about. There were too many complicated words, but the neighbor was sure they were arguing about the death penalty.

And another time, it was about six o'clock at night, Leilani and Hotu were on the veranda yelling at each other, but the neighbor, unfortunately, had to race to the Chinese store to get some cooking oil, so she never found out why.

Well, all that yelling is reassuring Materena. When a woman yells, it means she's not lying low taking shit. And Materena is relieved her daughter is the one paying the rent. When a woman pays, she has rights.

Still, Materena feels so lonely these days with Leilani no longer living at home. She spends her nights cleaning, going through the photo albums, listening to the radio, and getting cranky at that talk-back DJ who, really, has zero listening skills. He sure loves the sound of his own voice, that one.

That Name Duke

Tapeta's grandchild is definitely a boy. The sex of Rose's baby wasn't revealed using the needle test because Rose doesn't believe that a needle hanging over a woman's navel can predict what the sex of the baby is.

"Come on," Rose said to her mother, "what's this? Witchcraft? If the needle swings left to right, the baby is a boy, if the needle moves in a circle, the baby is a girl?" *Non,* Rose wasn't interested in doing the needle test, but she's 100 percent sure that her baby is a boy. She saw him in her dream. She saw her son.

In the dream, Rose was paddling a surfboard, paddling through a rough current, it was very dangerous, and she turned to tell her son, "Faster, my son!" The boy was about six years old, and he replied, "I'm doing what I can, Mamie!"

What a strange dream, Tapeta thought when her daughter told her about it. Rose has never paddled a surfboard in her life.

Anyway, that dream when Rose was paddling a surfboard with her son was, as far as Rose is concerned, a sign that the baby inside her is a boy. She doesn't want to do the needle test to confirm this, she already knows she's going to have a boy. She knows because of the dream, and she knows because she just knows.

And Rose's son is going to be called Duke because his father, who called yesterday from Australia, wants his son to be named after Duke Kahanamoku.

That's why Tapeta is going to town today to buy a book about that man Duke Kahanamoku. And it just happens that Materena and Leilani are also going to the bookshop in Papeete. The three meet by the side of the road to wait for the truck, and that is how Materena and Leilani get to hear about the story of Rose's baby being a boy and his name being Duke.

"Duke?" Materena asks. "Who's that man? He's a singer?"

"*Aue non!*" Tapeta says. "He was a surfer."

"Was? He's dead, this Duke?"

"*Oui,* he's dead."

"Ah, that's sad."

"Oh, he died an old man, he didn't die young."

"Ah, that's good."

"He was a Hawaiian."

"*Ah oui?*"

"*Oui,* and . . ." Tapeta waves distantly to a relative walking on the other side of the road, and passes Materena all the information she got from Rose about that Duke Kahanamoku. He was a Hawaiian. He was a Hawaiian surfer. But he was not just any kind of surfer. He was a legendary surfer. He was the best. Well, that's all the information, and it's not much.

"Ah, here's a truck." The three women hop in and there's no need to squeeze too much today. The truck is empty apart from a couple at the far end talking to each other in English. American tourists. They're all red from the sun. They turn to the three Tahitian women and smile. The women return their smile.

"I thought Rose was going to call the baby Manutahi," Leilani says. "That's what she told me last week. Manutahi for a boy and Taina for a daughter."

"Well, now it's Duke," Tapeta says, a little annoyed. She would have much preferred that name Manutahi. He's an ancestor and we know who that man was. We know that he was the chief of Faa'a, he was the greatest orator of all, but he was Protestant. And he also signed the French Protectorate, and this before the king Pomare. He gave Tahiti to the French. But, as far as Tapeta is concerned, that name Manutahi is better than that name Duke. At least it's a Tahitian name. At least we know that Manutahi wasn't a horrible man.

Aue . . . and what is this stealing names from the Hawaiian people?

"My name is Hawaiian, Auntie," Leilani says, cackling.

Auntie Tapeta has no comment, and just then, the truck stops unexpectedly, sending the passengers to their left, and in hops Mori.

"Eh, Cousins!" he shouts. "Eh, Niece!" Mori makes himself comfortable in between his two cousins. The American tourists aren't talking anymore and Materena guesses that they're just like all the people who don't know Mori. They're intimidated by the way he looks. They're taking him for a dangerous criminal on the run.

"And where are you three off to?" Mori asks, used to having people who don't know him go silent as soon as he appears.

"To town," Materena says. "And you?"

"To town too." Mori explains that his car is getting a tune-up and that's why he's catching the truck today. "And why are you going to town?"

Materena lets Tapeta answer Mori's question. Her reason for going to town is more interesting than Materena's.

Tapeta tells Mori about the situation with Duke.

"Ah, I see," Mori says. He goes on about how he fully understands Tapeta's concerns because names aren't just names. They're very important. It's like that man he knew, his name was Adolph, but everybody called him Hitler and one day that man confided in Mori. He said that he was going to be cranky at his mama for the rest of his life for giving him that name Adolph.

"His mama didn't know about that name?" Materena asks, shocked.

"Well, it seems not," Mori says. "Mamas, sometimes . . . nothing in the head."

"*Aue!*" Tapeta laments about how none of this would have happened if Rose had married a local. She goes on, blaming herself for Rose falling in love with a foreigner. Rose has always had boys chasing her, and Tapeta always had something to say.

"Henri who? Henri Whistler? The son of Robert Whistler? Have you seen that sumo? He walks ten steps, he can't breathe. Ah, that Henri may be slim now, but in a couple of years he's going to be a sumo. All the Whistlers are big, they eat a lot in that family."

"Richard who? Richard Matete? They're from Huahine, the Matetes, *non? Ouh,* they're violent, these people. Go check the prison, it's full of Matetes. There's a lot of Mahis in prison, you say? You mean six, and excuse me, but we only steal hi-fi systems and cars in my family. We don't kill people."

"Robert Tehototo? He's a cousin, girl! You better take that boy out of your mind! Do you want deformed children? Stop looking at boys, Rose! You've got fire up your arse or what?"

Aue, Tapeta laments . . . She blames herself for Rose marrying an Australian but she doesn't blame herself for Rose getting married instead of finishing school. Rose got married in Australia while visiting her boyfriend, who had been kicked out of Tahiti for having an expired visa. Rose and her boyfriend drove from one registry office to the next until a civil-marriage celebrant in Bowral said, "Come back tomorrow with sixty bucks." The other marriage celebrants said, "We can't do that. It's illegal." Then they asked the Australian, "Mate, is she marrying you to stay in our country?" And the Australian barked, "We're in love!"

"*Aue,*" Tapeta says, brushing her niece's fingers, "don't you leave school for a boyfriend." Tapeta explains how it's okay to leave school to look after your sick mother, but it's stupid to leave school for a husband.

"Don't you leave school," Tapeta repeats.

"I won't, Auntie."

"And what are you going to do when you finish?" Tapeta asks. "I hope you're going to go to university. Your mamie will be very proud. So? What's your plan? Why don't you become a schoolteacher? They earn a lot of money."

"Auntie!" Leilani exclaims. "I'm not just interested in the money, you know!" Leilani stresses that her plan is to get a job she's passionate about even if it pays little money. As long as it helps her make a difference in this world. But she doesn't know what that job is yet, she's still searching. Until then, she plans to take on any job to cover the rent and bits and pieces.

Auntie Tapeta slowly nods. "Well," she sighs, "as long as you have your baccalaureate you're going to be fine. It's one big key in your pocket already."

"That's what I've told her," Materena says.

"I'm so cranky with Rose . . ." Tapeta's voice trails off.

She's about to add something else when the truck stops unexpectedly, sending the passengers to their left, and in hop four young men with surfboards. They're brown and they've got long Rasta hair and they look tough, and they look like Tahitians but they could be something else. They could be Maoris. It's very hard to know sometimes.

The American tourists stop talking.

"Eh," Materena discreetly says to her cousin Mori, "your cousins."

Mori looks at his cousins and nods.

They nod back and start talking to one another in English.

Materena glances at those Maori surfers. She sees the muscular arms, she sees a few scars, and she sees that name Duke tattooed on one of the surfers' ankles. She sees that name again on another of the young surfers, but this time it is tattooed on the palm of his left hand. And here it is again on a leg. And here it is on a jaw. And Materena guesses that for these young men, Duke is a hero, Duke is a loved one. Or perhaps Duke is a relative.

"Eh," Tapeta whispers to Leilani as she brushes her dress, "you saw the name? You know what name I'm talking about."

"*Oui,* I saw," Leilani says. "I like the boy on the left . . . he's so cute."

"Ask him about the name," Tapeta says.

"Auntie," Leilani says between her teeth.

"Come on, ask! Do it for your auntie."

After a bit more persuasion from her auntie, mother, and uncle, Leilani has to embark on an interrogation. Her first question to the surfer sitting on the left is, "Is that name Duke tattooed on your jaw Duke Kahanamoku?"

It is, and the surfer looks very pleased that Leilani knew Duke's last name. He smiles and would probably have done more if it wasn't for big, scary Uncle Mori.

Well anyway, for the record these surfers aren't Maoris, they are Hawaiians. Also for the record, Duke Kahanamoku was the greatest Hawaiian surfer of all time. He survived the legendary monster swells in Waikiki called Bluebirds. On location for a film, he also saved ten people from drowning at a beach and was presented with a gold medal for his bravery.

He was himself a Man of Gold. He had a heart big like this.

The four Hawaiians demonstrate.

He was and still is an inspiration for all of us Hawaiians.

Tapeta's mind is now at peace, so she tells her relatives, but she still feels sorry for her grandson. It's for sure he's going to be teased at school nonstop in Tahiti with that noble name.

Words That Cut

Materena is watering the garden when she notices that Leilani's birth tree, her frangipani, has brown leaves and its flowers are on the ground.

Aue! Virgin Mary, Understanding Woman! Have pity on me! Materena drops the hose and runs inside her house to call . . . call who? The emergency ward at the hospital? Hotu's mother? She has no idea where Leilani is. She could be at her house studying for the exam on Monday. She could be at the beach. She could be anywhere!

It's Sunday morning, six o'clock. For all Materena knows, Leilani could be lost in the middle of the Pacific in a canoe.

All right, then, Materena is going to run up that hill. She quickly gathers her things and rushes out the front door, falling on her daughter just as she steps out of the house.

"You're here!" Materena exclaims, squeezing her daughter tight. "*Aue,* I got so scared, I thought . . ." Materena stops talking. Something is not right. What's all this trembling Leilani is doing? Materena looks up and sees that Leilani's lips are quivering. "Girl? What happened? What's going on? Come inside the house before the relatives start peeping from behind the curtains."

Once inside the house Leilani bursts into tears on her mother, and all Materena can do is hold her daughter tighter and repeat, "It's all right, girl, cry . . . You want Mamie to make you a Milo?"

They go into the kitchen and Materena is anxious to make her daughter a Milo, but *nom d'une merde!* Just when you desperately need milk, there's an empty milk container in the fridge.

"There's no more milk," Materena says. "You want a cordial?"

"*Oui.*" Leilani hiccups.

Materena makes the cordial and sits next to her daughter, putting a loving arm around her.

"What happened, girl?"

"Mamie" — Leilani sniffs, a hand gripping her glass — "my heart feels like it's being crucified." Then, laughing, Leilani adds, "Sorry for laughing at you when you used to say this to me."

"It's okay, I don't mind if you think I'm funny." Materena knows this isn't the end of the tears, though. When you laugh in the middle of crying, it means you're going to burst into tears not long after.

"My heart really feels like it's being crucified."

And here, Materena was right. "Cry, girl," she says. "Crying is good, let it all out. Cry."

As Leilani lets it all out, Materena, crying silent tears, thinks: Hotu? You just wait, you. You hurt the wrong girl, boyfriend. But just a minute, Leilani could be crying because of something else, something more serious.

"Girl," Materena says, anxious now, "did somebody die?"

"Me." Crying even more, Leilani buries her head in her hands.

Ah, Materena is relieved. It's only a story about love. And she patiently waits for Leilani to start talking.

Minutes pass.

Okay, Leilani drinks her cordial, good. More minutes pass.

Leilani wipes her eyes with the back of her hands, good. She runs her hands through her hair, very good. She starts talking.

And here's the story.

Yesterday afternoon at four o'clock, Leilani wanted to have Hotu's baby.

By four twenty p.m. the same day, Leilani wanted to kill Hotu.

They were at his parents' house so Hotu could replace two lightbulbs because Hotu's father is away and Hotu's mother can't change lightbulbs.

As Hotu was unscrewing the lightbulbs, Leilani was standing near him, thinking, I love him so much I want to have his baby. Mamie can change lightbulbs by herself. What's wrong with Constance?

As Hotu was screwing the new lightbulbs in, his mother said, "Why don't you two stay for dinner? I'm all alone tonight."

Hotu looked at Leilani, who said, "Sure," thinking, I hope she cooks better than the last time we ate here. Mamie is a better cook than Constance. Hey, I'm a better cook than Constance!

But first Constance wanted to have a scotch on ice on the veranda.

So they all went to sit on the veranda overlooking the white-sanded beach, and Constance sighed, "What a beautiful day!" She went on talking about how she felt like having her garden landscaped, she wanted new plants, she wanted a couple of rocks here and there and she wanted a fountain. She spoke, staring at the ocean, about how her plants always died, and all the while Leilani was winking at Hotu and he was winking back at her. They didn't have Constance's dying plants in their mind, that was for sure.

Then Constance moved to the subject of her cleaner, whom she suspected of stealing food out of the freezer. "Chicken breasts just keep on disappearing," she said. Anyway, Constance counted the chicken breasts today and so her cleaner was going to be in for a big surprise on Monday.

"Nobody steals from me," Constance spat, "especially not a cleaner."

At that precise moment, Leilani excused herself to go to the bathroom. She can't stand Constance's stories about her cleaner being a thief, her cleaner not putting things back where they belong. Constance insists on everything being in the same spot in her house in case she goes blind one day. For example, the salt shaker is on the left side of the pepper shaker and not the other way around. My cleaner did this, my cleaner did that, Constance went on. Every time Leilani is here, all Constance wants to do is put her cleaner down. And, of course, this really annoys Leilani, knowing many cleaners, including her own mother.

The bathroom is located at the front of the mansion, but Leilani didn't get to the bathroom, she stopped instead in the living room to look at those damned enlarged and framed photos of Hotu with his famous ex-girlfriends.

She looked at these photos and thought, Why is Constance keeping them? What is she trying to tell me? This is the last time I'm coming here.

At that precise moment, Leilani heard Constance tell her son, "I've never said anything to you about your choice of girlfriends . . ."

Walking on tiptoes, Leilani moved closer to the veranda and hid behind the curtains. She listened even though her mother had told her many times never to listen to people talk when they don't know you're listening. It's not proper, Materena has always said, it's not proper and you might hear words that are going to cut you.

But Leilani just couldn't help herself listening.

"You are a fool." (Constance speaking.)

"Maman, that's enough." (Hotu speaking.)

"Do you realize what you are doing?" (Constance speaking.) "That girl already has your initials tattooed on her hand. Next, she'll get herself pregnant. You're blind. Look at all that you own. She has nothing. She is a nothing, her family lives in a fibro shack."

"It's a house." (Hotu speaking.)

"It's a fibro shack" (Constance correcting) "with potted plants to hide holes in the walls."

Hotu cackled.

"Already she has her whole family getting you to fix their teeth for free!" (Constance exclaiming.)

What? (Leilani exclaiming in her head.) Hotu didn't tell me any of this!

"What?" (Hotu laughing.) "Her whole family? Are you drunk already? I've only seen her grandmother, Mama Roti."

Mama Roti! (Leilani exclaiming in her head.) How could you do this to me?

"When you marry the poor" (Constance sniggering) "you don't go anywhere. The rich marry the rich, and the poor marry the poor. You're a fool. Who is she? The daughter of a cleaner. Oh, I'm sorry, a *professional* cleaner. Because there *is* a big difference." (Constance being sarcastic.)

Hotu laughed.

His mother joined in.

"Stop talking about that." (Hotu speaking.) "Leilani will be here soon."

Leilani tiptoed to the other side of the living room, crouching down and feeling like vomiting. Her vision was blurred and the thought that came into her mind right that moment was to go into the kitchen and get a big knife to stab mother and son. But she appealed to God instead to give her strength: God? I know I haven't been to Mass lately, but watch me, feel my pain, give me a hand. In case you've forgotten me, I'm Materena's daughter, she's the relative who is nice to everybody. She's a professional cleaner.

Soon after, Leilani felt much better. She stood up straight, smiled a big bright smile, and sang, "I'm back!"

Hotu was talking about plants by the time Leilani sat down next to him.

"Those ones will never pick up, Maman," Hotu said, stroking Leilani on the arm. "You need plants that tolerate salt."

This was what Leilani wanted to do to Hotu: bite his arm off and punch him in the face.

But instead she turned to him, winked, and leaned over to whisper in his ear, "I need my ration. I want to be on top of you." Hotu turned to Leilani and showed her his beautiful white teeth.

Five minutes later they were riding home, having declined Constance's invitation for dinner.

Fifteen minutes later, Leilani was on top of Hotu.

By ten o'clock that night, Leilani had done this three times, and Hotu collapsed in bed before having anything to eat.

This morning, Leilani got up at five thirty and wrote Hotu the following very short letter.

I don't love you anymore. When I look at you it's like I'm looking at a tree. My uncle Mori will get all my stuff this afternoon.

Then she sneaked out of the house and walked down the hill, stopping several times to ask herself, Am I overreacting? But how dare he let his mother mock my mother! Leilani kept on walking.

And now she's here.

* * *

"I can't believe that Mama Roti!" Materena exclaims. "What a nerve!" Materena goes on about how she made it clear to Pito and their relatives that they were not, under any circumstance, to ask Hotu to fix their teeth for free. "You want new teeth," she told them all, "you pay, all right? Don't you dare embarrass me."

"Mamie?" says Leilani, cranky now. "Have you been listening to me?"

"*Oui,* of course," Materena hurries to say, thinking, That Mama Roti! What a nerve! "Girl," Materena continues, "people have been making fun of professional cleaners for centuries, I'm used to it, you know."

"Well" — Leilani grinds her teeth — "I don't like it."

"Sure, I see what you're saying, but people always mock mothers-in-law, you know, like I mock Mama Roti and Papi mocks my mother."

"*Oui,* but there's mocking and there's mocking!" Leilani explains that it's okay for her mother to mock Mama Roti about being so rude because she *is* so rude. It's okay for her father to mock Mamie Loana for being a bit of a martyr because she *is* a bit of a martyr.

"Eh, oh," Materena interrupts, "be careful what you say. My mother is not a martyr."

"She is, Mamie, she's always going on about how she can't get white sand for her mother's grave and if only she had a bit more money she'd go back to Rangiroa to get the sand herself. I've been hearing this ever since I was a child."

"That's not being a martyr! You can't talk. Your mother didn't die when you were fourteen years old. You . . ." Materena stops talking. She's not in the mood to fight about her mother today. "*Chérie,*" she continues tenderly, "don't leave Hotu just because he laughed about me, okay? I don't want to have this on my conscience. Leave him because you don't want to settle down too young or because he's too demanding, but don't leave because he mocked me behind my back. You know . . . I can tell you now. It really annoyed me to see Hotu walk into my house with his shoes on."

"Lots of people do that when they're wearing shoes and not thongs." Leilani gives her mother a cranky look.

"He chews his food for such a long time."

"That's the proper way to eat."

The proper way, Materena thinks. Well, maybe it is, but it's still very annoying for her to watch Hotu eat. So many times she nearly shouted to him, "But swallow!" Well anyway, it's obvious to Materena that now is not the right moment to criticize Hotu, because Leilani is still in love with him. The mama can only criticize her daughter's boyfriend or husband when he's completely out of the picture. As far as Materena is concerned, Hotu is not completely out of the picture yet. There could be a reconciliation.

Ah, a motorbike is arriving right now, and there's only one person Materena knows who owns a motorbike. Leilani springs to her feet and instructs her mother to tell Hotu that she's not here.

"Girl, he knows you're here. Where else could you have gone? Children always run back to their parents when they're sad."

"I don't want to see him."

"But you've got to explain the situation!"

"Why?"

"Why? So he knows never to make fun of cleaners ever again, that's why . . . Stay right where you are, I'm going to tell him to come inside the house." Materena opens the door.

Here's Hotu without his helmet, without his shoes, and with so much suffering and anger in his eyes. *Aue,* Materena thinks. She hopes he's not here to make a scene. She hopes she's not going to have to call out to a cousin to get Hotu off the property. She hopes she's not going to have to use the 100 percent steel frying pan to put some sense into Hotu's head.

"Eh, Hotu!" Materena says. For the moment, she's just going to act surprised.

She leans over to greet him as she always does, with a kiss on each cheek. But he puts his arms around her and squeezes her tight. She pats him affectionately on his back, hoping he's not going to burst into tears on her.

After a while Hotu gently pulls away and asks to speak to Leilani.

"Come inside," Materena says.

Non, he prefers to stay outside. Okay then, and so Materena goes and gets Leilani, in her bedroom now, on her bed. But Leilani is not coming out.

"Leilani, get up, hurry up, it's an order." Although Materena is semihappy that it's over between Leilani and Hotu (if it is really over), she feels Hotu needs to know what he's done. "When I look at you it's like I'm looking at a tree" is, in Materena's opinion, not a proper separation line. It's too cruel.

"Get up."

"Fine." Leilani gets out of bed, stomps to the door with Materena following just in case Hotu decides to do something horrible, like put his big strong hands around Leilani's small neck.

Leilani, facing Hotu and with her arms folded, asks him what he's doing here.

"Are you out of your fucking mind?" says Hotu.

"What do you mean, am I out of my fucking mind? It's you who's out of your fucking mind!"

"What the fuck did I *do?* What's this note?" Hotu fumbles in the pocket of his jeans and reads it to Leilani. "Is this a game?" On and on the two of them go, and Materena can't believe the language! She had no idea Leilani knew so many swear words. Plus, their voices are rising by the second and very soon there's going to be a crowd.

"Children," Materena says softly, "come inside the house."

But Hotu is too busy screaming about how much effort he's put into chasing Leilani. With all the other girls, they chased him. One even sent her father to him and he said, the father, "My daughter wants you. You're taking her out to the restaurant tonight." Another girl swam to the pontoon in front of his house and cried out for help, he was in the garden watering the plants. "Doesn't this show you anything?" he screams.

A crowd is rapidly forming around the lovers. There's nothing like a bit of cinema before breakfast and Mass. Meanwhile Hotu is still going on about how much he loves Leilani, how he was going to tattoo her initials on his hand, propose marriage . . .

Heads are shaking with disbelief in the crowd, meaning, Leilani, you're such a coconut-head, breaking up with someone like him. Plus, he's a dentist!

"Are you finished with your monologue?" Leilani interrupts.

"*Just tell me what I've done! Tell me anything! But don't lie to me that I'm a tree, because I don't believe you!*"

All eyes are now on Leilani. The truth is about to come out, like in detective movies when the mystery is revealed.

So here it is, for Hotu's ears, for the crowd's ears, for the whole world to hear.

"*You mocked my mother!*"

"Excuse me?" Hotu sounds very surprised to hear this.

Is this the reason? relatives gathered in the crowd ask each other. Everyone was expecting something bad, something cruel, like, Hotu slept with another woman.

"I mocked your mother?" Hotu asks, his eyes on Materena. And for the first time since knowing Hotu, Materena can now see that he *is* white.

Actually, he's quite pale. It must be the shock.

"I mocked your mother?" Hotu asks again. "You've mocked my mother ever since you met her. It's almost a full-time job for you."

Hotu repeats (word for word) all the things Leilani has said to him about his mother. He even assumes Leilani's facial mannerisms and gestures perfectly as he says:

"I'm sorry, but your mother really looks like a Christmas tree with all that jewelry she wears. She's obviously not allergic to gold. She's only allergic to work. She's never worked in her whole life! What's wrong with the woman?

"Your mother can't change lightbulbs! I don't believe this. What *can* she do?

"There's something wrong with people who are always looking at themselves in the mirror. Your mother even looks at herself when she walks past shop windows! She's a narcissist, all right.

"Why does your mother speak as if she was French? Is she ashamed to be Tahitian? But she looks so Tahitian, that's what I don't understand! Is she having an identity crisis?

"Has anyone ever told your mother that the reason plants die is because they never get watered? Your mother is buying plants every week! Hasn't she cracked the code yet?

"Oh, your mother's cleaner resigned? Well, I'm not surprised! Who wants to work for a woman like your mother? I'm sorry, but there's something wrong with people who put other people down to get a kick. Your mother puts her cleaner down, she puts bank tellers down, salespeople, and she even puts nice old women selling flowers down. Your mother really needs to see a psychiatrist. Who will be carrying her coffin when she dies?

"Your mother only likes people if they've got a lot of money, even if she was a pauper herself until she caught your father. I'm not surprised she closes her eyes on your father's infidelities. As long as she has his checkbook she doesn't care."

Eyes are popping out of people's heads, and everyone is waiting for Hotu to go on with all that Leilani has said about his mother (especially the bit about her being a wronged woman), but he stops talking to look at Leilani, now very pale herself.

"Well," she says after a while, and clearly embarrassed, "you mocked my mother too, so we're equal."

Leilani repeats (word for word) all the things Hotu has said (to her) about her mother:

"Your mother is constantly sweeping. I feel sorry for the broom! It never gets a minute of rest in that house." Then Leilani looks at Hotu fiercely in the eye.

He cracks up laughing.

She cracks up laughing too.

"Come on," Hotu says, "let's have a coffee at home and talk about things."

Leilani doesn't need to be persuaded, though she says, "All right, but only to talk." After a quick kiss for her mother, she's on that bike holding her boyfriend tight.

And nobody is surprised.

Every day there's a couple separating in the neighborhood, there's a woman throwing all of her man's clothes out the window with the words, "It's finished! Go back to your mother!"

Then a few hours later, that same woman is picking clothes off the ground and calling out, "*Chéri!*" And life continues, eh?

Well, it's the same with Hotu and Leilani. Life continues. Hotu is extra nice to Materena, and Leilani does not speak to Hotu's mother.

Leilani is so in love with her man that the day after finding out she's passed her baccalaureate exam, she walked across the road from Hotu's surgery to Dr. Bernard's surgery to convince the sixty-five-year-old doctor, looking for an assistant/receptionist, that she was fit to carry out such duties. Leilani passionately sang her assistant/receptionist attributes. "I can write very fast, I have an excellent memory, and I never assume anything. I can take secrets to the grave and I scored twenty out of twenty on biology and chemistry tests in my baccalaureate. I'm ready to start on Monday."

Dr. Bernard must have been impressed with Leilani's speech, because he just said, "Well, I'll see you on Monday, then."

So now Leilani and Hotu work across the road from each other. They can wave to each other ten times a day.

They can go to work together on the motorbike, have lunch together on a bench in the park in Papeete, swim a few laps at the swimming pool after work . . . love each other till death do them part.

This morning, on her way home from the frame shop with Leilani's baccalaureate certificate (enlarged and mounted in a gold frame), Materena stops outside Dr. Bernard's surgery to look at her daughter.

Just now Leilani is hanging on to every word Dr. Bernard — tall and gray, with his arm around a young woman holding a newborn — is telling her. She's smiling and nodding in agreement in between scribbling Dr. Bernard's words. Just being a perfect assistant/receptionist, and an overqualified one at that.

And Materena cannot help feeling a twinge of disappointment, but then she reminds herself that Leilani only intends to be an overqualified assistant/receptionist for one year.

Sighing, she keeps on walking, with her daughter's well-earned degree facing the public for anyone interested to see.

At the Drive-in Cinema

The movie tonight at the drive-in cinema is a love movie, and Materena loves movies about love. But the love movie tonight is not the reason why Materena is here at the drive-in cinema. She's here to help Mama Teta raise money for the church, and they're going to do this selling *mape.*

Tonight is not the first time Materena has helped raise money for the church, but tonight is her first time selling *mape* at the drive-in cinema. It's against the law to sell things to eat at the drive-in cinema. There's a snack for the customers to buy popcorn, packets of chips, Coca-Cola. But as Mama Teta said to Materena this morning, it's for the church they're going to sell *mape,* so it's fine. With the church in a story there's no law, because when the church needs money, it's to do good deeds, and when you help the church do good deeds you get help from above.

Mama Teta's car is now three cars away from the ticket office. She leans over to the glove box to get her rosary beads, which she then hangs on the rearview mirror. And Materena, half-laughing, says, "And what's this for, Mama Teta? So they don't suspect we've got about sixty bags of *mape* in the pandanus bag hidden underneath the blanket at the back of the car?"

"*Shussssh!*" That is all Mama Teta replies.

And to the young man at the ticket office, she says, smiling a friendly smile, "I hope the movie is good!" Then Mama Teta drives away. But unlike the other cars circling around the parking lot looking for the best parking spot, she parks at the first spot she sees. The parking is not an issue since Mama Teta won't be watching the movie, being too busy selling *mape,* hopefully the whole lot. That is the goal tonight. The car is parked next to the headphones, and Materena reaches for her pandanus bag out of the back.

Mama Teta snatches Materena's hands off the bag. "You can't go selling the *mape* right now, girl!" She explains that they have to wait for the movie to start, for the lights to be switched off. The selling can only take place in the dark.

"Mama Teta," Materena says, "when people are watching a movie, they don't want somebody annoying them with *mape.* Now is the best time."

But Mama Teta insists that the operation be carried out in darkness. Well, not really in total darkness, since there will be a little bit of light coming from the screen, but it won't be as bright as it is now.

"There's a security guard, girl," Mama Teta says. "He's mean, he patrols with a flashlight and a baton. He used to be in the army." Then, almost whispering, she continues, "If he catches you . . ."

A story follows, a story about the mean security guard catching a woman, a good, innocent woman selling *mape* to the people inside the cars watching the movie, because she was poor and she needed the money to feed her children. And the good woman begged the security guard to close his eyes on her illegal act, but he took her with his baton and his flashlight into his office for interrogation. He interrogated her, although she had already confessed, then he called the gendarmerie and two gendarmes arrived in their police car with the siren and took the good, innocent woman into their office for interrogation. They interrogated her, then they took her fingerprints, and that meant she got a criminal record.

Materena sighs. She's getting Mama Teta's message, all right, which is: You don't think you could, by any chance, sell the *mape,* all the *mape,* by yourself? The fact is that Mama Teta is afraid of gendarmes, everybody in the Mahi family knows this.

"Mama Teta, I'm going to do the selling, you just stay in the car," Materena says.

"*Non,* I'm going to do the selling too . . . but my legs . . . *aue,* they hurt a little tonight, I don't know why." Mama Teta puts a hand on Materena's hand. "It's okay with you if you sell the *mape . . .* all the *mape?* I'm not forcing you."

"Of course it's okay," Materena replies. "I'm not really here to watch the movie."

As soon as the movie begins, Materena is off on her mission to sell sixty packets of *mape.*

Materena walks past the cars, her eyes looking for people of her age because, in her opinion, people of her age have a conscience about the church. Well, she doesn't see many young people at the church on Sundays, but people of her age, ah yes, lots. Materena looks for those people and at the same time follows the movie — without sound. The actor is so handsome and the actress is so beautiful. Right now, the actor and the actress don't know that they're going to fall in love with each other. They're too busy arguing. Materena can't hear what they're saying but she can see by their faces that they don't like each other and that they're arguing. But soon, they're not going to want to argue. Soon, they're going to want to be in love.

Okay, time to sell some *mape.*

She stops at a car to ask an old woman if she would like some *mape.* "It's to raise money for the St. Joseph Church," she explains. The old woman wants to see the official paper signed by the priest, and the church's official church stamp must be on that official paper. "How do I know you're not lying?" she asks.

"Pardon?" Materena says. But some people! she thinks.

The old woman goes on about how she's had lots of people asking her for money for the church and the money is not even for the church, it's for them.

"Well, the priest didn't give me any papers," Materena says.

Well, no official paper means no *mape.*

"Okay, thank you," Materena says.

In the movie, the actor and the actress are now smiling at each other. Eh, eh, Materena thinks, they're falling in love!

"*Mape?* Delicious *mape* cooked today."

Materena sells two packets and moves on to other people of her age. "*Mape?* Delicious *mape* cooked today."

Materena sells one packet.

"*Mape?* Delicious *mape* cooked today."

The woman in the car asks if the *mape* are hard, she says that she likes her *mape* hard and not soggy, she can't eat soggy *mape.*

"The *mape* are very hard," Materena says. "We don't sell soggy *mape.*" She sells five packets.

One packet.

Two packets.

A young Frenchwoman is now asking Materena what *mape* is.

"It's very delicious," Materena says.

"But what is it?" The Frenchwoman turns the light in the car on and asks to see the *mape.* Materena passes her a packet and glances at the man sitting in the driver's seat looking bored. The Frenchwoman looks at the *mape,* then she prods the *mape,* then she tries to squash it.

"Is it a vegetable? A fruit?" she asks.

"The *mape* tree is very tall, it takes years to grow," Materena says.

"Oh, that's very interesting, but is it a vegetable or a fruit?"

"It's a fruit."

"And is it in its natural state?" the Frenchwoman asks.

"Eh?"

"Did you pick the fruit off the tree and put it straight in a packet?"

"You have to cook it."

"How long did the process of cooking take?"

"Natalie!" This is her man speaking. "Just give that woman her money and get a packet of whatever it is called." But the woman says that she wants to know what she is eating because she's wary of food poisoning.

"You must always know what you are eating, Louis," she says. "Do you recall our holiday in Germany when you were ill? Do you recall the mushrooms? One can never be too cautious about poisonous —"

"Our *mape* is not poisonous," Materena interrupts. "We've been eating *mape* for hundreds of years. If *mape* were poisonous, there'd be no Tahitians left in Tahiti today and I wouldn't be selling you *mape* right this moment to raise money for the church."

"Oh, it's for the church, I'm sorry." The Frenchwoman hurries to get a banknote from her bag. "I admire you."

She gives Materena the money and Materena gives the woman the packet of *mape* she prodded and tried to squash minutes before. And after saying, "Thank you very much for helping the St. Joseph Church," Materena goes on with her mission.

She has a lot of luck tonight selling *mape.* It seems everybody wants to eat *mape.* Nobody wants to get out of the car and walk to the snack. If only she'd brought along some drinks to sell too. But suddenly, a flashlight illuminates Materena and a man is walking toward her.

Hei! It's the bloody security guard! Materena shrieks to herself. She runs this way and she runs that way, she runs in front of Mama Teta's car and sees Mama Teta watching the movie and enjoying her popcorn. That Mama Teta! Materena thinks. Her legs must have got miraculously better in the last twenty minutes for her to run to the snack!

The security guard is getting closer and closer, and poor Materena has got a stitch. Her legs can't take it anymore. She's slowing down, actually, she's going to have to stop and give herself up.

"Halt!" The security guard yells.

Materena has got to do something about the evidence real quick because when there's no evidence, there's no crime. She's learned that rule watching a detective movie once.

Okay, the *mape* have been discarded under a truck and now Materena can start running again. But here, she recognizes Hotu's car five spaces up. Saved!

She didn't know Leilani and Hotu watched movies at the drive-in cinema. She thought they only watched movies at the Cinéma Concorde in town. Well anyway, they're here tonight.

Ah hia, here's the security guard! Better start running!

Materena starts to run toward the BMW with the intention to sneak in and hide, but . . . just a minute . . . Yes, that's Hotu at the wheel, and he's kissing the woman sitting on the other seat. But that woman Hotu is kissing has got very, very short hair. Materena's daughter has very, very long hair. What's going on around here? Materena is so shocked she stops running. Her heart is going *boum, boum, boum.* She can't believe her eyes.

Aue . . .

But what should Materena do now? Should she go and tell Hotu off? It's not really her onions what Hotu does when he's not with Leilani . . . or is it? Like father, like son! Eh, eh, my Leilani, eh, Materena thinks. They're still kissing, Hotu and that woman, and now he's taking her top off and now he's licking that woman's breasts!

Aue! Is this what happens when a couple spends too much time together? Materena wonders. The man gets bored? He needs a change? Since they've met, Hotu can't go anywhere without Leilani following, and vice versa. They're always in each other's shadow, those two, and Rose is always telling her cousin how lucky she is to be with the man she loves, unlike Rose, who hasn't seen her Australian husband, also the father of the baby inside her belly, for five months.

And here is Hotu now in *flagrant délit.* Materena is so confused. The last time she spoke to Leilani and Hotu's neighbor (alias Materena's spy), she said it was still the big love on top of the hill.

Last time she spoke to Leilani on the telephone, which was yesterday, Leilani talked about her new favorite subject: Dr. Bernard (Hotu often jokes that luckily Dr. Bernard is sixty-five years old, otherwise he'd be jealous). "Dr. Bernard is my hero," Leilani said yesterday. There was not a word about Hotu playing around, but then again Leilani wouldn't know . . .

A hand grabs Materena's wrist, making her stop thinking and jump with fright. Ah, it's only the security guard. He's saying how he's seen Materena selling *mape* and how it's against the law to sell anything at the drive-in cinema. There's a snack for people when they want to eat. The security guard wants Materena to follow him into the office, but Materena is not going anywhere and right now she really doesn't care that she broke

the law, right now she's more concerned about what her son-in-law is doing behind her daughter's back.

"Eh," Materena says to the security guard, "let go of my wrist . . . See that couple there? In the BMW? Switch your flashlight off." The security guard, still holding Materena by the wrist, looks up, and now he's chuckling away. He lets go of Materena's wrist and switches his flashlight off. And now both Materena and the security guard are watching the couple half-illuminated by the light from the screen. And what are they up to, Hotu and his mistress?

Ah . . . the mistress has flattened her seat and Hotu is . . . well, he gets on top of his mistress and . . . one of the mistress's legs is out of the window and . . . the other leg goes on top of the wheel . . . and . . . well, now the mistress's legs are around Hotu, and her arms are around Hotu too . . . and Materena glances at the security guard and it looks to her as if he's getting a bit too close. She takes a step to the side.

The security guard also takes a step to the side.

Meanwhile, in the BMW . . . *Oh, la-la,* it's the full passion. Hotu and his mistress are kissing as if tonight was their last night together. Now what is that security guard trying to do? Materena just felt his hand on her back. Is he *crazy?* She takes another step to the side.

The security guard also takes another step to the side.

Meanwhile, in the BMW . . . Ah, finished already? That didn't take long . . . The mistress is now putting her top back on and Hotu is doing his pants up.

And what is that security guard doing?

Well, he's trying to kiss Materena on the cheek. "Eh!" She shrieks. "Are you crazy?"

She takes another step to the side, and the security guard follows, all the while going on about how Materena has lured him here to watch that couple and so it must mean she's interested.

What? Materena can't believe her ears. But! Is this all men think about? And he's getting a bit desperate, the security guard. He wants his kiss. Materena has to slap him across the face to bring him back to reality. She also has to make a quick dash to the BMW, and before you know it, she's in the car on the backseat, surprising Hotu and that woman, who turns around.

"*Chérie!*" Materena exclaims, all happy and relieved to see her darling sweet daughter. "You had a haircut today?"

"Mamie!" the daughter also exclaims, hurrying to grab her deodorant out of her bag. "What are you doing here?" Leilani goes on madly spraying her deodorant around. "What are you doing here at the drive-in cinema?"

Eyeing the security guard, who's looking a bit stunned now, Materena explains the situation, that she was helping Mama Teta sell *mape* to raise money for the church.

"Ah," Leilani says seriously, "that's very nice of you to do that."

"*Ah oui,*" Hotu confirms, cackling, "that's really nice of you."

There's an awkward silence now in the BMW and Materena guesses that her daughter and the boyfriend are thinking, Did she see us? Materena understands. It's embarrassing being caught doing sexy loving by your mother. Materena was caught by Loana twice in her life with Pito. She didn't know what else to say but, "Eh, Mamie!"

"Eh, Mamie," Leilani says, pinching Hotu's leg to make him stop cackling, "otherwise, did you sell a lot of *mape* tonight?"

Rose's Baby

The story on the coconut radio is that it's so nice Rose's Australian husband stays at the house to look after the baby because some men, even if they don't have a job, you're not going to see them at the house looking after the baby. You're going to see them by the side of the road looking after their drink and their mates. Ah, true, many relatives are saying. It's so nice for Rose's daughter she is in the hands of her father, who can't get a work visa, and not in the hands of the *nounou. Eh hia,* what a lucky baby girl Taina-Duke Johnson is, even if her father lets her cry for hours.

That's why Tapeta visits her granddaughter every day straight after work. She visits to see that all is fine, that her granddaughter has got diapers and that there's milk powder left in the can and that she's not crying her eyes out.

Rose's Australian husband never minds Tapeta visiting. The moment he sees Tapeta arrive he smiles. He kisses Tapeta on the cheeks, he asks her if she's fine, he asks her if she'd like a coffee, a cookie, and then he asks her if she's staying for a while. If she's staying for a while, like a couple of hours, he asks her if she could look after the baby while he goes for a quick surf. And Tapeta always says, "Of course I don't mind. Go." Tapeta much prefers to be alone with her granddaughter anyway. That way she can carry her like she wants.

Tapeta is visiting now, expecting to find Matt reading his English books in the living room with the baby locked in the bedroom, crying her eyes out. But the front door is closed.

"Matt, *iti e!*" Tapeta calls out. "Are you in the house?"

No answer.

Tapeta calls out again until the neighbor appears. Some people came in a Toyota, she informs Tapeta, and there were surfboards on the roof of the car and they tooted the horn, they shouted out the window. They shouted in English, so the neighbor can't say what these people shouted. But Rose's husband came out of the house running, and then he talked to the people in the car for three seconds, and then he ran back inside the house and then he ran back outside with his surfboard, and then he put his surfboard on the roof.

"And the baby?" Tapeta interrupts. "My granddaughter?"

"Ah, the baby? Yes, the baby went in the car too with her papi. And yes, the baby was crying her eyes out."

Tapeta thanks the neighbor and walks home, thinking. Thinking that Matt is going to leave the baby in the car because he's a man and he's got nothing in the coconut and he wants to please himself.

Thinking that he's going to ask a woman sunbaking on the beach to mind his daughter and the woman is going to say okay because she's going to succumb to Matt's spell — the blond hair, the American face. Or maybe the woman is going to say yes because she's a very nice woman, but what if she says yes because she's got plans to steal that baby because she can't have a baby and that baby is so cute?

Tapeta thinks about ringing Rose at the airport to inform her of the situation. But if Rose yells at her husband, he's never going to speak to Tapeta again. Then, when she visits, he's going to quickly grab baby Taina and refuse to let Tapeta hold her.

Aue! Tapeta chases the negative thoughts out of her head and reminds herself that Matt is very intelligent and intelligent people just don't do stupid things. After all, that Australian has spent four years at university.

Tapeta is still walking when Cousin Mori appears in his car and toots the horn. Tapeta waves a distant wave meaning: Yes, I saw you, but don't stop to talk to me. But Mori stops his car and gets out in a flash with the words, "Cousin! Rose's baby is in the car!"

"What?" *Aue,* here's Taina, wrapped in the beautiful quilt her grandmother has made for her, sound asleep in her cane basket, her *biberon* by her side. Ah well, Tapeta thinks, Matt must have bumped into Mori and asked him to look after the baby for a couple of hours.

But this is not how Mori got possession of the baby.

Mori tells Tapeta he was driving his car to Taapuna for a drink at the bar there. He was a little bit thirsty, he got a craving for a beer. He parked his car next to a secondhand Toyota with racks on the roof because it was in a very good spot, it was in the shade of a tree.

For a while, Mori looked at the people surfing Taapuna Break, thinking how crazy these people were. Taapuna Break is renowned for being very dangerous. You fall and you crack your skull open on the reef.

When Mori finally got out of his car, he looked at that Toyota and saw that the window of the backseat was wound down and there was a quilt hanging down from the roof rack. Mori looked around and, since there were no witnesses, he peeped inside the car. He just had to know what was behind the quilt. It wasn't to steal or anything like that, Mori stresses to Tapeta, he was just being curious. And so he peeped inside the car, saw a baby, and there and then he said to himself, But! This is Rose's baby girl!

Mori opened the door, grabbed the cane basket, and put it in his car, thinking that way he could keep an eye on the baby. He was going to wait for that Australian surfer, Mori guessed him to be surfing with all those crazy people out there, to tell him off for leaving his daughter in a car, but then Mori remembered he had something else to do. So he drove off with Taina in the car to give her to Tapeta.

Tapeta looks at her cousin with affection. "Eh, eh, *merci,* Cousin." But here, she gets thinking. She knows the baby in the cane basket is her granddaughter. She's seen her granddaughter over one hundred times and she can recognize her granddaughter with her eyes closed, but Mori has only ever seen Rose's daughter three times. And he was drunk all those three times and not just a little. Mori could have taken a baby that wasn't Rose's baby at all but another woman's baby, and Mori could have found himself in very serious trouble. Prison, for example? Mori's police record wouldn't have helped. Caught stealing six times?

"Mori," Tapeta asks, "how did you know the baby was Rose's baby?"

"Because I knew, that's all," Mori says.

"You've only seen Taina three times and each time you were drunk, and not a little."

That's true, Mori admits, but the second he saw that baby, he repeats, the words "But! This is Rose's baby girl!" came into his mind.

Tapeta decides that Mori had spiritual guidance. The Virgin Mary, Understanding Woman, herself was right behind Mori as he fulfilled his very important mission. Perhaps it was because the Virgin Mary was pleased with Mori getting a painting of her image spray painted on the hood of his car. Or perhaps the Virgin Mary was honored with the way Rose's husband had so beautifully painted her image on the hood of Mori's car and so she saved his daughter, with Mori as her helper. Yes, Mori's saving Taina had to have something to do with the Virgin Mary, and the Virgin Mary even made the little girl quiet because her cries could have attracted the attention of a mean person.

Tapeta thanks the Virgin Mary, Understanding Woman, with all her heart.

Meanwhile, back in Taapuna, Rose's husband is paddling back to the shore as fast as he can, then he runs to the car and is about five yards away when he senses something is wrong. There is no quilt hanging from the roof rack. He runs faster, his heart beating with anxiety, he opens the door, sees that the cane basket along with the baby has disappeared, and, shouting, he runs to the other side of the car. He runs to all the other cars parked nearby and looks inside every single car. He pushes a big woman out of his way. He runs this way and he runs that way, all the while crying his eyes out. People start to think he's a mad person. He falls down to his knees, puts his head in his hands, and cries out, "Oh God! Oh God!" Then he stands up, looks around to the people staring at him, and goes on running again. He runs and he runs, and eventually he runs into a police station.

There, crying half in his language and half in French, he reports his daughter missing.

This is the incredible story. And this is the reason Rose's husband has decided to go back to his country, taking his wife and his daughter along with him.

He said that he wants to go back to work, but all the relatives present here tonight to farewell Rose and Taina know Matt just can't face another day being asked, "What on earth made you leave your six-week-old baby girl in a car? What have you got in your head? Rocks?"

Right now, Rose's beautiful daughter is in her auntie Leilani's arms, with Uncle Hotu nearby, openly admiring his niece and his woman.

On the other side of the room, Materena, listening to her cousin Tapeta's moans, watches her son-in-law.

She chuckles in her head and thinks, Here's one who's getting clucky.

Leilani herself also looks like she's getting clucky. Here she is, lovingly rubbing her nose against the baby's nose . . .

If someone had told Materena three years ago that her daughter was going to meet a really nice boy, marry him, and have children, she would have said, "I sure hope not! My daughter is going to go to university!"

But we don't own our children's lives.

At the airport the following day it's crowded, of course. Sometimes you wonder if the airport is big enough to cater to the growing flow of people leaving and coming home. Tahitians have always been keen travelers. In the old days, they traveled in canoes, these days they travel in planes.

The crowd at the departure gate is crying tears of sorrow and the crowd at the arrival gate is crying tears of joy. More than half of the crying crowd belongs to the Mahi family of Faa'a, mourning yet another child leaving the nest, another *vahine* following her man back to his country.

But no child has ever left with a baby before, so the sorrow on this hot morning is tripled. The poor grandmother, Tapeta, is . . . there are no words to describe. It's one thing to farewell a daughter you've raised, another to farewell a granddaughter you might never see again.

"*Aue,* my heart is breaking," Tapeta moans, bending down to inhale the sweet scent of her granddaughter's feet. The baby girl is sound asleep in her mother's arms.

On the other side of the airport people are welcoming loved ones home.

"*Maeva, bienvenue!*" they shout with arms outstretched, and Materena thinks about how she'll be back at the airport next week for her daughter's best friend, Vahine, who's finally coming home thanks to Leilani and Moana paying her fare.

Women Have Better Ears

Ati is here to pick up Pito for a bit of fishing, but Pito is not home.

"He's out," Materena informs Ati.

"Where?" asks Ati.

"Where? I don't know, he's gone walkabout." Pito might have gone to visit his brother Tama, Materena thinks, because Pito said something last night about Tama having a bit of difficulty with their brother Frank at the moment . . . but she can't be sure. All she knows is that Pito is not at home. He left about half an hour ago.

"Ah," says Ati, still standing at the door, looking like he wants to come inside the house, but Materena is not inviting him in. She doesn't need the whole neighborhood to start gossiping. There are enough stories of wives getting on with their husband's best friend going around. Not only that, but Materena really has nothing to say to Ati. They have nothing in common. They can't talk about children, since Ati has none. They can't talk about plants, since Ati has none. But Ati just won't go away.

"How's your speedboat?" asks Materena finally. Ati's speedboat just popped into her mind.

"Looking good, I'm thinking of having it painted blue."

"Ah . . . blue is a nice color . . . And your mama? How is she?"

"She's fine, she plays bingo these days."

"*Ah oui?*"

What now, Materena wonders, but to look into Ati's brown eyes and feel a bit strange. Ati's brown eyes are always getting him into trouble with women . . . And anyway, it's not really wise to look into your husband's best friend's eyes for too long.

Just as Materena is about to tell Ati that she was actually on her way to her mother's house, Leilani appears. "*Ouh ouh!*"

"Eh, Leilani!" Materena calls out, glad her daughter is visiting.

Ati will simply have to leave now, but Leilani tells her uncle how happy she is to see him because there's something she'd like to talk to him about — something really important.

"Come in the house, Ati," says Materena. What else can she do? Let Ati and Leilani talk outside? *Non,* it's not done, so here's some nice freshly squeezed lemonade.

"Tonton," Leilani fires away as soon as she's at the kitchen table, "I'm really annoyed with that DJ you work with at Radio Tefana." To prove her point Leilani does her little cranky eyes at her uncle.

He takes a sip of his lemonade.

"I'm actually thinking of lodging a complaint."

Ati takes another sip of his lemonade as Leilani talks about Radio Tefana, the radio that supports Independence, and also the radio that hires stupid people.

"I'm not talking about you," Leilani says, "I'm talking about the other DJ. He's so . . ." Leilani shakes her head with anger.

"I'm not a DJ," says Ati. "I just play love songs. Tihoti is the DJ."

"Tihoti, *oui,* I'm talking about him, what is his last name?"

"Why?"

"Because I'm serious about lodging a complaint, and I'm also thinking of sending an article to *Les Nouvelles.* That big-mouth has got to be stopped!"

"Since when do you listen to Radio Tefana?" Materena asks. This is news to her. Leilani's first experience with Radio Tefana was four years ago. She'd called to give her opinion about all those people who call Radio Tefana to moan about the past, those acres of land Tahitian people have lost over gallons of wine, those days when they were called uneducated, ignorant savages. "Moan, moan, moan," Leilani said. "Let's move forward!" In Leilani's world, people would light a candle instead of cursing the darkness. Anyway, Leilani called the radio and was cut off halfway through her passionate speech to make way for a Bob Marley song. Since then she's vowed to have nothing to do with that radio — ever, until she dies. She must have changed her mind about that.

But, so Leilani reminds her mother, she doesn't want anything to do with that radio — ever, until she dies — however, she hears a lot about that stupid *titoi* in the waiting room at the surgery. She hears the shocking, degrading things he says on air about women.

"What does he say?" Materena and Ati ask.

What does this stupid man say on air, laughing his head off? Well, this:

He says that he met a woman at a nightclub and went back to her house because she needed to be calmed down. The next morning, when the DJ woke up, he saw, among other ugly things men only see sober (so the DJ professed), that his lover had varicose veins on both her legs. He chewed his arm off and flew out the window.

He says that when he's stuck in the traffic in Papeete, he doesn't curse the mayor, he doesn't swear, he doesn't beep his horn in frustration, *non.* He just looks at women and rates them from one to ten beers. A no-beer woman means that she's very beautiful and that he could sleep with her sober. A ten-beer woman means that she's one ugly woman and that he could sleep with her only if he was very drunk.

He says that after a woman has a couple of kids, she's ruined. A woman with something in her head is dangerous. A woman who talks too much is a bore. A woman with cracked hands is a turn-off. A woman with saggy *titis* reminds him of a cow.

Materena's jaw drops. "I'm going to punch that man in the face if he continues to talk like that about us!"

"You're not the only one who feels that way," Leilani says, "but we need to do more than that, we must get him off the air."

She goes on about how talk-back radio DJs have certain responsibilities to abide by. They are in a powerful situation and should do something constructive with it, such as uplift people, educate them, reassure, entertain, but stupid jokes are really not necessary. Actually, it should be stipulated somewhere in DJs' contracts that jokes must be funny, and only at the expense of the DJs themselves, not their listeners.

"My role at the surgery," Leilani continues, "is also about giving people, women especially, hope, to let them know that they're still beautiful women even with distorted varicose veins or cracked hands or a breast lost to cancer. I can't have someone like that *titoi* ruin all my good work. Is he actually aware that more women listen to the radio than men?"

"Really?" Materena asks, interested.

"Absolutely, ask Tonton."

"Really?" Materena asks, looking at Ati.

The love-song DJ nods in agreement. "It's true, the people who call me to request a love song are mostly women."

"But of course!" Leilani exclaims. "It's proven that men watch TV and women listen to the radio."

"How come?" Materena is getting very interested in the discussion.

"Well, because men sit on the couch, whereas women are busy running around cleaning or ironing or whatever, and they need music to make those chores less boring."

And with this statement Leilani bangs her fist on the table. "Tonton, do you know what your radio needs?"

Before Ati has the chance to reply, Leilani shouts, "A woman!"

"A woman," Ati repeats.

"What's wrong with my idea?" Leilani snaps, her eyes firing bullets at her poor uncle.

"*Rien,*" he hurries to say, "it's just I never thought about that before."

"Well, start thinking, Tonton. I'm surprised that idiot is still alive, even more surprised that he still has a job. Who is he? The son of the boss? It's not acceptable anymore, Tonton, to say degrading words about women, you know. Imagine that the stuff that idiot says *on air* is about your mother? Or your sister, Mamie, me, your goddaughter!"

Silence falls as Ati, deep in thought, nods a slow nod, the nod that says, "I hear you."

"So?" Materena tells Ati, half-serious, half-laughing. "When are we going to hear a woman's voice on your radio, eh? What are you all waiting for?"

"Women have better ears anyway," Leilani says.

"Ah, true, women have better ears," Materena confirms.

"Women DJs would bring so much to Radio Tefana," Leilani continues.

"*Ah oui,* true."

"You've got to do something, Tonton."

"You've got to do something, Ati."

Poor Tonton Ati . . . he looks like he's having trouble swallowing his spit.

He must be regretting setting a foot in this house today, in which live two women rebelling for the same cause.

Mama Teta's New Business

The whole population is talking about Mama Teta's new business. Well, all the relatives, at least. Ninety-nine percent of them are saying, "That one, when is she going to stop thinking about businesses? When you're her age you're supposed to just grow old peacefully!"

But Materena believes in dreams. "*Bon courage,*" she tells Mama Teta outside the church.

"*Maururu,* girl," Mama Teta says, affectionately tapping her niece's hand. "Luckily, we women know that word, courage."

"And what is your new business going to be?" Materena asks with interest. Nobody has bothered asking Mama Teta this. As soon as the relatives heard the words *new business* they shrieked, "What? A new business at your age?" And so Mama Teta told them nothing.

"You're not too busy?" Mama Teta asks. Auntie and niece sit on the church steps, where Mama Teta's future business is revealed.

"A nursing home." Materena nods several times, meaning, Ah . . . I see. "And it's going to be at your house?"

"*Oui,* at my house," Mama Teta confirms. "Oh, I know that my house isn't a four-star hotel, but it's a house. There's a roof." Her nursing home, she insists, is not going to be like the CAPA nursing home, where the old people sit on their bed waiting for the night to come because they've got nothing to do. Her nursing home (Mama Teta's voice rises with excitement) is going to be a place for friendship and fun. Her old people will play cards, grow their own vegetables, bake their own bread, do talk-talk, laugh, and share experiences.

"Mama Teta," Materena exclaims, "your nursing home sounds like a good place!"

Cackling, Mama Teta thanks her for the kind words about her new business but admits that selling it to her son Johno was another story.

"Ah, he didn't like that business?" Materena asks.

"Well, let's just say that he wasn't too enchanted at first." Mama Teta advises her niece that she did not ask Johno to come over to discuss her new business idea. He just turned up without any warning — which was nice, says Mama Teta, at least one of her sons remembered he's got a mama. And she was glad it was Johno because Johno works at the Socredo Bank, he knows a bit about finance and everything. Mama Teta thought she wouldn't mind his opinion.

But first Johno gave his mama the latest news about his kids; all is fine and how this happened and that happened. Mama Teta was enjoying hearing about her grandkids, but Johno diverted the conversation to a weird dream he had the night before about his mama falling off a cliff. "So, is everything okay with you, Ma?" he asked.

"But of course!" Ah, Mama Teta likes it when her kids are

worried about her. "You know, sometimes," she confides to Materena, "I wish I could be dead for one day just to give those kids a kick, make them realize I'm not immortal."

Materena, who has not had a phone call from Tamatoa for nearly three weeks, gives a snort. "And so, about Johno's dream?"

"Well, he said I was walking and next minute I was falling, and then he opened his eyes. He says to me, 'Is everything okay with you, Ma? Have you had a checkup recently?' and I told him, 'Your dream has got nothing to do with my health, it's got to do with my future, because I have a business idea.'"

"A business idea?" Johno looked a bit perplexed by this, reports Mama Teta. "A business idea," she confirmed, offering her son a beer. "And it's a good business idea, let me tell you about it."

She did, and for Materena's information here's what Johno said. Mama Teta uses her fingers to tick them off:

(1) "But you've already got a business, Ma."

"You mean my bridal-car driving business?" Mama Teta asked. "*Bof,* I'm going to stop that business. Nobody is getting married anymore, that kind of business is way too slow; plus, my eyes are going a bit funny on me and you need good eyes to be a driver."

"Just get glasses and advertise some more," Johno replied.

(2) "Your house is not a good location for a nursing home. You can see the cemetery."

"And so?" Mama Teta didn't see where the problem was.

"Ma, think a little, eh? Think about the cemetery."

"What about the cemetery? It's not like my old people are going to sit and admire the cemetery, they're going to be too busy playing cards, planting vegetables, and enjoying themselves."

"Ma . . . do you think your old people are going to be happy with a cemetery next to them?" He went on about how the cemetery was going to make the old people sad because the cemetery was going to remind them of their death. In his opinion, the old people will be waking up happy, and then one look at that cemetery and they will be sad. They will think, One day it's going to be me in that cemetery.

Mama Teta shrugged. "Eh, Johno, how many old people do you know? Old people don't go around thinking they're immortal, it's up to the young people to think that."

(3) "Do you want my honest opinion?" Johno asked before he left.

"Oh, you know, give me your opinion, don't give me your opinion, I'm still going to do my new business."

"Well, if it's what you want" — Johno said this like he didn't believe his mama's new business idea was going to become a reality — "but you know, it's hard work looking after old people."

He went on about other unimportant things meant to discourage Mama Teta, but what happened was the opposite. Mama Teta was even more excited about her idea. As far as she's concerned, this is her life, she says to Materena, and she believes in herself. After all, she passed her driver's license at the age of fifty-six years old, when most women think their life is over.

She overcame her fear of running a child over and learned not to worry so much about all the gendarmes roaming around the island. She passed her driving test with flying colors and became a bridal-car driver.

But Mama Teta is now ready for a change. "Looking after old people is less stressing than driving on the road, especially these days," she tells Materena. Before Materena can agree or disagree with this statement, Mama Teta informs her that she feels very positive about her new business idea. She feels positive because whenever she thinks about it, she gets all happy inside. And this means she's on the right track. "I used to be very happy driving brides around," she adds, "but I'm not anymore. Eh, things change, girl, and life is short. We've got to do what we love."

That's what Mama Teta told Johno too, and this is what Johno said before he left: "You're going to have a lot to do in the house."

Mama Teta asked, "Are you telling me that your bank is going to lend me the money?"

"It's not my bank, it's not my decision."

"Well, see what you can do, okay?" Nodding vaguely, Johno walked to his car, and after a quick wave to his mama, smiling from ear to ear, he drove off, shaking his head.

But last week, Johno was pleased to advise his mother that he'd throw a couple hundred thousand francs into her venture, enough to repaint the house and fix it up a little. "I can get the rest of the money from the government," Mama Teta tells Materena. "Johno already went with me to fill out the papers."

Two days later, the whole population is talking about how Mama Teta changed all the curtains in her house and even bought two new single beds. "But, she's serious, that one," the relatives say. "And at her age! It certainly makes you think."

Materena agrees with this 100 percent. Right now, Mama Teta is an inspiration for Materena.

At the Zizou Bar

Tonight Materena feels like going out, and why not? She'll be forty years old next Wednesday. Isn't it about time she experiences dancing in a nightclub?

How about at the famous Zizou Bar?

The house is clean and tidy, she doesn't feel tired, and all her children are away. Tamatoa is in France, Leilani is with her boyfriend in Moorea for a romantic weekend, and even Moana is doing a bit of romance tonight after work with a mystery girl.

So Materena is going out to the Zizou Bar, where her mother and father met.

Materena has always wanted to have a quick look inside that bar but she's never had the courage. The same as she's never had the courage to search for her father. She didn't have the courage because . . . well, because she didn't have the courage. She thought, He's not going to want to know me. I'm just a cleaner. Well anyway, that's an old story and Materena isn't interested in dwelling on it. She just wants to go to the Zizou Bar.

At the Zizou Bar, French *militaires* and local girls meet and dance, and when they get hungry from all the dancing they walk across the road to the quay for a little conversation and something to eat at the *roulotte.*

People say that the girls who dance the night away at the Zizou Bar wouldn't be dancing one single dance at the local bar because they're not good-looking enough for the local men. At the Zizou Bar, those girls are queens because the *militaires* are prepared to dance with anyone as long as it is a woman and she's Tahitian. Well, that's what people say today and that's what people said in Loana's day, when she used to be a regular at the Zizou Bar.

Tonight Materena is going to see all of this for herself, and she's expecting Pito to escort her.

"I'm not putting my feet in that bloody bar." Pito doesn't even take his eyes away from the TV.

"And why not?" asks Materena.

Pito's answer is a mumble. He's not putting his feet in that bloody bar because . . .

Materena immediately guesses the reason. She gives Pito the death look. "Ah, it's okay for you to have a wife who has a *popa'a* father and it's okay for you to have children who have a *popa'a* grandfather, but it's not okay for you to put your feet in the Zizou Bar!" Pito lifts his eyes to Materena for a second and says nothing.

Materena furiously rearranges things around the living room and goes on about how she will just have to go to the Zizou Bar by herself since her husband thinks that the beer they serve at the Zizou Bar is poison.

Pito sighs.

"Go on, sigh," says Materena. "Why did I ask you, anyway? You wouldn't even help your mate Ati when he had trouble with the *militaires* because you didn't want to be seen near the Zizou Bar. What has the Zizou Bar ever done to you?"

"Eh!" Pito is cranky now. "Leave me alone with that Zizou Bar story, okay? I don't force you to come to my bar, so don't force me to go to your bar!"

"Of course you don't force me to go to your bar," says Materena. "You don't want me at your bar, full stop. You want to be with your *copains* and . . ." Okay, that's enough about Pito and bars, thinks Materena. "Well, I'm going to go out with Cousin Lily," she says. "Cousin Lily knows about bars and everything."

Pito tells Materena that it is a very bad idea to go out with Lily because Lily is trouble. It's best to go out with Rita instead.

Materena immediately gets the picture. "You know, lots of men wink at Rita when she's walking around in Papeete, it's not just Lily who can be trouble."

Pito nods distantly, concentrating on the TV screen again. Materena is going to ask Rita to escort her, but just as she's about to dial Rita's number, something occurs to her and she marches back to the sofa, where Pito is sitting still like a statue. "What's this about Lily being trouble, eh? And me? You don't think I can be trouble?" Before Pito has the chance to comment, Materena is dialing Rita's number again.

But Rita is not picking up the phone, not even with Materena calling with her code: three rings, hang up . . . three times. She must be out. "*Ah hia hia,*" Materena says to herself. "Eh well, maybe it was a silly idea for me to go to that bar."

Later on, when Materena goes to get some cooking oil, she meets Cousin Mori outside the Chinese store. He's just about to get out of his car. She can't believe Cousin Mori drove to the Chinese store. He lives only two hundred yards away! But some people . . . they're so lazy. Then again, these days Cousin Mori drives his car everywhere. He just wants to show off the painting of the Virgin Mary, Understanding Woman, that Rose's Australian husband painted on the hood.

The two cousins greet each other with the usual Tahitian kisses on both cheeks. Cousin Mori doesn't smell of beer and his eyes aren't red from smoking *paka.* So Materena is going to have a quick chitchat with him, but first she is going to admire the painting on the hood of Mori's car. "Eh, eh," she says. "She's so beautiful, Virgin Mary." Cousin Mori agrees.

Okay, now time for a quick chitchat about this and about that, about how Materena wanted to go to the Zizou Bar but Pito didn't want to escort her and Rita is not home. "I just don't want to be at the Zizou Bar on my own," Materena says. "It's going to look like I'm after an adventure." Mori nods knowingly and then proposes to be Materena's chauffeur and bodyguard.

"You don't mind to be seen at the Zizou Bar?" Materena asks.

Mori, shrugging with indifference, replies, "Beer tastes the same in all bars, and there's going to be girls at the Zizou Bar, *non?*"

So here they are now on their way to the Zizou Bar, and Materena reminds Mori that he is not to start a fight at the Zizou Bar because some *militaires* are special *militaires,* they're legionnaires, and they carry knives. They're trained to defend. They're trained to kill in the event of an attack.

Mori, bopping to a Bob Marley song, laughs.

Materena glances at Mori. He's all dressed up and his hair is twisted into a heavy plait. He reeks of perfume.

"And your car?" she says.

"*Oh, la-la!*" Mori smacks the wheel. "Everybody is always asking me about my car! What's the problem with my car?"

Materena wants to say, "The problem with your car is that it is a bomb, it's always breaking down." Instead she says, "There's enough petrol?"

There is, and so Materena looks out the window and hums to the no-woman-no-cry song, all the while thinking that she's done very well taking some extra francs with her for a taxi in case Mori's bomb breaks down. Or in case Mori drinks too much, although he did swear not to. She's also done very well wearing an old dress that falls all the way down to her knees.

Mori parks his car right in front of the Zizou Bar. He explains that it will be easier for him to check on his car during the night.

"We're only going to be in there less than an hour," Materena reminds Mori. "Nothing is going to happen to your car during that time."

"I just want to be careful, Cousin." Mori locks the steering wheel but leaves the windows opened. He says that he's not concerned about what's in the car since there's nothing to steal, but he's very concerned about somebody stealing the car itself because it is a collector's item now, with that painting on the hood.

"Okay, fine, fine, let's go in." Materena is already marching toward the entrance of the bar. She can hear the *thump-thump* music.

The bouncer politely greets the middle-aged woman dressed like she's off to church, but no way is he letting the big thug in. Looking into Mori's eyes the bouncer says solemnly, "Policy, mate."

Mori, his fists clenched and a mean look on his face, says, "Mate . . . are you telling me that I can't get in because I'm not a *popa'a* but you're going to let my cousin in because she's a woman, even though she's a Tahitian? Is this what you're telling me, eh? You want me to report this to the radio? You want me to start a riot? You want my family to smash this bloody bar down?" After Mori has paid his way in and gotten his hand stamped, the bouncer opens the door and wishes the two cousins a very pleasant night.

The Zizou Bar is packed and Materena can see within one second that the story about only ugly Tahitian girls dancing at the Zizou Bar is an absolute myth. The girls here tonight are young, tanned, full of energy . . . they are stunning! She says this to Mori.

"Oh, I've met lots of beauties in bars," he says, "but for some reason, the next morning they've changed."

Materena reminds Mori that he's her bodyguard tonight and that he'd better not disappear on her. "I'm not paying for your two glasses of beer for you to go drinking with another woman," she says. They head for the bar and Mori gets his beer, then they sit at a table away from the dance floor. Materena, sipping her water, looks around.

She feels strange . . . All those *popa'a* men, those *militaires,* those young men flirting with the young women. The romance in the dark, the French music, the French accent. Materena watches the couples dancing away on the dance floor, cheek to cheek, smiling the smile of love.

Was it like this when Loana was dancing with Tom? When they were young? Tears well in Materena's eyes as Mori finishes his beer and gets up to buy his second.

There's a woman sitting on her *popa'a* lover's knee and they're passionately kissing. Another woman, her back pressed against the wall, is also passionately kissing her lover. There's drunken laughter all around. Mori is now talking to a woman standing against the wall in a dark corner. Well, as long as they're only talking, Materena thinks, but Mori better not disappear.

Five minutes later, while Materena is busy looking at the couples dancing, Mori and the mysterious beauty make a quick exit, and not long after, three *militaires* sit down at Materena's table. They ask her if she'd like a drink, if she'd like a dance, if she'd like to go for a little walk.

Materena's answer is firm. "Thank you, but my cousin, the big tall man over there with the Rasta hairstyle . . . ," she says, looking over to where Mori was standing seconds ago. "My cousin," she continues, smiling at her *militaire* friends, "he's going to be back soon."

Materena thinks that those *militaires* must be pretty desperate, because she knows very well she looks like a middle-aged woman dressed like she's going to clean someone's house.

"You are so beautiful," one slurs. "Are you happy?"

"My eldest son is in France." Materena is trying to divert the conversation. "He's in the army."

"I love older women." This *militaire* is drunk too.

"My youngest son is a chef at the Beachcomber."

"I think I'm in love with you." Another drunk *militaire.*

"My daughter is with her boyfriend in Moorea, he's a dentist and she works with Dr. Bernard." Okay, that's it, Materena is going outside to see what's going on with Mori. But there's no sign of Mori outside. She asks the bouncer if he saw her cousin, the big tall man with the Rasta hairstyle.

He shrugs. "It's not my business what people do outside the bar."

So Materena walks up and down the street, calling out, "Mori! Mori? Mori?" In the end, she gets into Mori's car and waits, all the while muttering about how Mori is going to get it. Bodyguards don't just go walkabout!

But here is a taxi pulling up in front of Mori's car. Two young girls get out, giggling and blowing kisses to the Chinese taxi driver.

Materena is inside that taxi in a flash. "How much for you to drive me to Faa'a?"

The driver turns around and checks his passenger. "For you . . . half price."

Materena gives the taxi driver a smile of gratitude, and to prove to him that she indeed appreciates the special price, she asks him questions about his family, if he's got a wife, children.

"I've got four children," he says.

"Oh, you and your wife are very blessed."

"I'm not with my wife anymore," the taxi driver says.

"Oh really? That's sad, but maybe it was for the best, eh."

"I've got a new wife, and my new wife, she" — the taxi driver glances at Materena — "my new wife, she likes sex, not like my old wife." He goes on about how his old wife only ever gave him excuses and how the new wife is always chasing him all over the house.

Materena is tempted to say, "Well, that's because she's a new wife," but she just nods in the way we nod to show that we totally understand the situation.

"You're married?" the taxi driver asks.

Materena says that she is and that she's been with her husband for more than twenty years now.

"Ah, you must like sex!"

Materena wants to tell that man off, but thinking about the special price, she giggles uncomfortably and looks out the window to show that she's thinking now and not in the talking mood anymore. She doesn't talk about sexy loving with strangers!

But the taxi driver is very interested to talk about sex with Materena. He gives Materena hints that he's a great lover and very soon he's proposing to take Materena to a hotel for a quiet drink.

Materena stays silent, thinking: I can't believe what I'm hearing! Can't he see I'm a respectable middle-aged woman? Ah, if the taxi driver were a big man, she would be very concerned. Luckily the taxi driver is a little skinny man. With one slap, Materena could make him fly all the way to France.

"So?" The taxi driver switches the light on. "We go to the hotel?"

Materena quickly reads the driver's identity card, hanging from the rearview mirror. "Listen, Justin Ah-Kan, Number Fifteen. People don't call me Mad Materena for nothing, okay?"

The light goes off and Materena ponders if she's going to have enough money to pay the taxi fare, considering that Justin is not going to be giving her a special price. Plus, he's driving so slowly now. He slows down at the orange light instead of accelerating, as trucks do, and stops for the red light. Materena, annoyed, looks at the Suzuki car pulling up next to them. The couple inside the car is kissing, full on the lips, and it seems to Materena that she's recognizing Ati.

She hurries to wind the window down and hesitantly calls out, "Eh, Ati? Is that you?"

The kissing ceases abruptly and Ati, shocked, exclaims, "Materena? What are you doing in a taxi at this time of night?"

"Can you drive me home?" Next minute, Materena is in her husband's best friend's car telling him all about her mission and how Mori disappeared on her. Ati listens but his girlfriend doesn't seem to care about Materena's mission, she cares more about kissing Ati on the neck.

"Can you stop your cinema!" Ati says to his girlfriend, sounding very exasperated.

"You didn't mind my cinema before!" the girlfriend says. Materena hurries to say that she doesn't mind all the kissing. "Continue, don't worry about me." The girlfriend does just that, but now Ati is dropping her at her door.

"But you said —"

"Good night, I'll call you tomorrow." Ati speeds away, firing questions at Materena about her night, if she danced a little, if she talked a little. Materena wonders if Ati is interrogating her so that he can report the answers back to Pito. Is Ati playing spy? He's looking at Materena in the rearview mirror with suspicious eyes.

"Ati, I've had lots of men interested in me tonight" —

Materena wants Pito to know this — "but I'm only interested in one person."

"I know what you mean. I'm also only interested in one person."

"You!" Materena laughs. "You think women are like tires."

"That's because I can't have the woman I love."

Materena guesses that Ati is referring to the woman he lost to a legionnaire many years ago. She tenderly puts a hand on Ati's shoulder.

"Ati, you can't go on mourning that woman you lost to a legionnaire, you must —"

"That bitch! I'm not talking about her!"

Speaking softly, Ati goes on about how he's talking about another woman. A woman he has loved for years. She is the only woman Ati wants.

"Well, go get her!" Materena says. "What are you waiting for?"

But the woman Ati loves is married, so he tells Materena. All Materena can say is that another woman is sure to come Ati's way one day, and that woman is going to make the other woman disappear like that. Materena clicks her fingers and Ati laughs a faint laugh.

"Did you know I'm living by myself now?" Ati says.

"What?" That has got to be the news of the century. Materena can't believe Pito didn't tell her about it. "And your mama? She's fine?"

"Oh, she cried, she threw herself on the ground, but I wasn't going to live with her for the rest of my life."

"Ah, true," Materena agrees, thinking: You're forty-two years old, after all.

"I've got a flat in Papeete."

"Ah, no lawn to mow then, eh?"

"I've got heaps of plants in pots."

"Ah," Materena says, thinking, *Aue,* poor plants. She gives them about a week.

"You should come and see my place one day," Ati says, smiling.

"Of course," Materena says, thinking, What's this? Why is Ati trying to cajole me?

"You want to drink a coffee at the airport? I've got a proposition to make to you."

Usually, whenever Ati has a proposition to make, Materena laughs, slaps him on the shoulder, and says, "Ati, you're never going to convert me, okay? You know very well what I feel about Independence. I'm half-French, and I can't change this."

But tonight, Materena would like to find out what his proposition is.

She herself has a proposition for Ati . . . her only connection to Radio Tefana. So Materena tells her husband's best friend that coffee at the airport sounds like a very good idea.

"So," Materena says, stirring her coffee and trying not to stare at the other drunken couples drinking coffee at the airport and looking like they need to wake up a little before they can carry on with . . . whatever. "What's your proposition?"

"You know that I've always liked you." Ati looks deeply into Materena's eyes.

"*Oui,* I know, you like me because I'm the wife of your best friend."

"*Non,* I like you because of you."

Materena smiles and takes a sip of her coffee, thinking how she should have gone home instead of accepting Ati's invitation, but she has an idea and it's really important that she talks about it with Ati.

"I like you a lot," Ati repeats, this time sounding so serious.

"Enough to help me with anything?" Materena asks.

"Anything you want, just ask me."

"Well," Materena begins, "I've got an idea and it's about . . ." Materena's voice trails off. She's a bit embarrassed to talk about her idea to start a talk-back radio show aimed at women. Ati might think she's trying to big-note herself. He might laugh and say, "This is your idea? I thought it was something interesting."

"So?" Ati asks, putting a hand on Materena's. "What is your idea about?"

"I can't tell you about it now," Materena says, taking her hand away. "Maybe after my fortieth birthday."

"What's happening after your birthday?"

"Who knows?"

"Am I in your idea?"

"Indirectly, *oui.*" Materena smiles, but when Ati puts his hand on hers again, she hurries to add, "But it's not what you think." She feels Ati better know this now. She doesn't want to lead him onto the wrong path, so she takes her hand away again. "I love Pito, you know that."

"*Salaud.*" Ati cackles. "I'm jealous."

"But are you still going to be there for me when I'm going to need you?" Materena asks. She doesn't know yet how strongly she feels about her idea, but tomorrow might be a different story.

"Materena," says Ati, keeping both hands in his pockets, "I've known you for more than twenty years. You're like a best friend to me."

Impossible Is Not French

The birthday girl is about to blow the candles out on her triple-chocolate cake. But first she's got to make her wish, eh? Everyone standing around the kitchen table is waiting, and there are so many wishes Materena could make tonight, on her fortieth birthday.

She looks around at all the people who are part of her life, a silent tear falling out of the corner of her eye, and thinks, I can't believe I'm forty years old! *Merde,* life goes fast.

Now, about that wish, what is it going to be?

Well, Materena wishes for Cousin Rita to fulfill her dream of falling pregnant. She wishes for her mother to fulfill her wish of having her son and her grandchildren live in Tahiti. She wishes for Moana to get his wish of buying a restaurant.

She also wishes for:

Ati to meet a very nice woman.

Pito to get promoted.

Rose to find a job in Australia.

Vahine to forget about Tamatoa and move on with her life.

When it comes to wishing, Materena is never out of ideas. She wishes for Tamatoa to remember it's her birthday tonight, she wishes for Leilani to find out what she'd like to do with her life soon, she's been Dr. Bernard's assistant/receptionist for nearly two years now . . .

She wishes for . . .

"Come on, Materena," Pito says, "how hard is it to make a wish?"

Materena blows out her candles.

"*Joyeux anniversaire!*"

They're all singing the birthday song now, making Materena cry her eyes out into her pareu. The birthday song, even when sung with happiness, always makes Materena cry. The next fifteen minutes are spent kissing the birthday girl, and the next hour is spent teasing the birthday girl, who is, as of now, entitled to the title Mama. That's the deal. The day you turn forty, you become a mama. Welcome into the respectable clan of hardworking mothers!

"*Non,* thank you," Materena tells everyone, her husband especially. "I'm Materena, full stop. When you are a mama, the next thing, you are a *meme,* an old woman only good for raking the leaves and minding the grandchildren. I'm not ready for that yet!" As far as Materena is concerned, turning forty is not about turning into a mama, it's about . . . it's about something else. But first things first . . . Materena had best mingle with her guests to make sure everything is fine and to thank everyone for coming.

She thanks Moana for his wonderful effort with the menu. He's been in the kitchen since seven o'clock this morning with his helper, Vahine, mixing ingredients in his bowl, stuffing chickens, stirring soups, chopping onions, tomatoes, and capsicum, marinating fish. "*Merci, chéri,*" she says, hugging him tight. "I'm sure your restaurant is going to become a reality."

Moana hugs his mother tighter and thanks her for believing in him.

She thanks Ati for coming to her birthday party even though he had a very important political meeting to attend tonight, and he says, "Don't forget to tell me about your idea." "*Maururu,* Ati," Materena says, squeezing his hand.

She thanks Leilani for all the decorations in the house and tells her that she's sure she's going to know what she wants to do in her life very soon.

Leilani hugs her mother and whispers in her ear, "I'll have a talk with you later."

"Okay," Materena whispers back.

Materena thanks Vahine for having been so kind as to spend the whole day helping Moana in the kitchen, and tells her that one day she will meet the man who truly deserves her. Vahine squeezes Materena tight and says, "I think I've already found him."

On and on Materena thanks her guests and tells them what they'd like to hear.

Now, time to open the presents.

A book, a statue, some sheets, a quilt, a juicer, a bottle of blessed water from Lourdes . . . "I'm so spoiled!" Materena exclaims each time.

Now, let the party begin!

By two o'clock in the morning, everyone has gone home or fallen asleep. Hotu was the first to leave and Vahine was the first to fall asleep, in her ex-boyfriend's bed, next to Moana's bed.

The only people left are Materena and her daughter, who are both slouched at the kitchen table.

"*Ouf,*" Materena sighs. "That was a good party."

Leilani confirms this.

"So, how's Dr. Bernard?" Materena asks. "He's still your hero?"

"Oh *oui!*" Leilani exclaims. "I love that man."

"What did he do this time?"

The last time Materena asked this question, she found out that Dr. Bernard spent twenty minutes teaching X (Leilani never reveals the identity of Dr. Bernard's patients; X is for women patients and Y for men) about the many contraception methods that her boyfriend wouldn't find out about. Apparently, the boyfriend didn't want X to take the pill. He was firmly against it. X lived in permanent fear that her boyfriend would discover her packet of contraceptive pills. Dr. Bernard said to X, "You're the one who will be carrying his child. *You* decide when." X ended up choosing the *sterilet.*

Materena also found out that Dr. Bernard cried tears of anger when he received the results from the laboratory for Y, a diagnosis of leukemia. But then he was on the phone making one phone call after another to colleagues, and Leilani heard him say, angrily, "Don't you dare tell me nothing can be done! Until proven otherwise, there's hope!"

He spoke softly to little Y, about to receive an immunization shot. "This is going to hurt a little bit, but you need this shot, my boy, to protect yourself from all those nasty germs. Do you understand me? Shall we go for it, then? At the count of three?"

He congratulated X for her strong arms. "These arms have done a lot of good deeds! I've never seen such strong arms on a woman!" X was so proud of her strong arms, she walked out of the surgery grinning from ear to ear, not angry anymore at Dr. Bernard for that strict diet he imposed on her to lower her cholesterol level.

He professed, "Let's never assume in medicine. Everything

must make sense and be proven." So what did Dr. Bernard do and say this time?

Materena is still waiting for Leilani to tell her.

But Leilani asks, "Mamie, do you sometimes wonder what your purpose in life is?"

Oh, la-la, Materena thinks. I'm too tired for an intellectual discussion. Nevertheless, she begins by saying that people don't have just one purpose in life and that purposes can be as simple as helping a child cross the road. Making someone sad smile. Listening to someone's story. According to Materena, a person's purpose in life should be about making a difference, and the opportunity to do so comes to us every single day.

There, Materena hopes this answers Leilani's question.

Well, Leilani is nodding in agreement. It must mean she agrees with her mother's belief. "You know, Mamie," she says, "one of Dr. Bernard's patients told me that when we don't fulfill our purpose in life, we make ourselves heavy in the coffin on the way to the cemetery because we're so angry with ourselves." She goes on about these people, who turn into angry spirits and roam the world of the living, moaning, "I thought I had more time."

Materena shrugs and tells her daughter that you don't have to be dead to moan, "I thought I had more time." Even the alive moan this every now and then. People who are late for appointments moan, "I thought I had more time."

"I don't want to be heavy in the coffin," Leilani says.

"Oh, Leilani! Don't talk about death on my birthday!" Materena chuckles to lighten up the atmosphere a bit. Nobody wants to talk about death on their birthday. Birthdays are celebrations.

"Mamie . . ." Leilani's voice trails off.

Materena waits.

"Imagine you're young."

"Eh ho" — Materena smiles — "what do you mean? I *am* young."

Leilani smiles along. "You're right, you are still young, you've got a whole life ahead of you."

"A whole life — I'm not sure about that. But I know I'm not old yet."

"It's true," admits Leilani. She goes on about how one hundred years ago being forty years old was considered very old, but these days, with all the progress in medicine, being forty years old is nothing.

"I'm sure glad about that!" says Materena, and adds that now that she's thinking about it, there are less mamas around these days because women don't feel old anymore at forty. Not like they used to.

"Mamie, you don't even look forty."

"Really?"

"*Oui* . . . you look closer to thirty-eight, actually."

"*Merci, chérie.*" Materena kisses her daughter's hand. "*Ah hia hia,* I can't believe I already had a child at your age with another one on the way." Shaking her head with nostalgia, Materena confesses how she felt so old at twenty years old. So much older than she feels today at twice the age.

"That's because you had a baby then and you were pregnant. Now that all your children have grown up, you are free to do whatever you want, Mamie."

"Whatever I want," Materena murmurs. "That would be nice . . ."

"Mamie, the sky is the limit for you . . . Do you remember how I used to draw you three times taller than anyone else in my drawings?"

"Oh *oui.*" Materena laughs.

"You're still three times taller than anyone else for me, but you know, Mamie . . ." Leilani's voice trails off again.

"What?" Materena asks.

Cringing, Leilani confesses that there was a time when she was a bit embarrassed about her mother being a cleaner, but that was a long time ago, when she was an adolescent.

"Ah," Materena says, smiling, "back in those days when you hated me."

"I've never hated you, Mamie, I was just a bit *conne,* that's all, and I'm so thankful you're still here today so I can tell you how much I admire you, and love you, and how sorry I am for all the grief I've given you before."

Materena looks her daughter in the eyes. "Don't cry on your birthday!" Leilani says, and pinches her on the arm. "Today is a new day for you! You are forty years old, you are free!"

"Girl, what is this?" Materena smiles through her tears. "Are you on a mission or something?"

"*Non,* I just want to see you fulfilled, that's all."

"But I'm —"

But the telephone starts ringing before she can finish, and Materena is up in a flash, thinking: It better be that son of mine calling to wish me a happy birthday.

"If it's Hotu, tell him I'm asleep," Leilani says.

Nodding, Materena picks up the phone. "*Allo.*"

She hears the *click* noise, meaning the call is from overseas.

"Ah," she says out loud, "it's my son finally remembering to call his mamie. I thought it was impossible."

"Impossible is not French, Mamie." Tamatoa's voice is getting deeper and deeper every time he calls. He can't talk for long, he says, but he promises to call again soon. He just wanted to wish his mother a happy birthday — to say "and may all your wishes come true."

Walking back to the kitchen, Materena chuckles. "May all your wishes come true . . ." What wishes?

As she has done for the past twenty years, Madame Colette has bought Materena a birthday present.

"Oh, Colette," Materena says, taking the small parcel wrapped in silver paper, "you didn't have to." In private, Materena calls her boss by her name, but for Materena's children and relatives, that woman is Madame Colette.

The two women embrace each other, with Materena making sure not to mess Colette's impeccable and complicated chignon.

"Open your present!" Colette says, all excited.

Materena eagerly opens her birthday present, even if she already knows what it is.

"Colette!" And yes, it's another box of chocolates.

Materena thanks her boss profusely. Colette invites her to sit at the table while she makes some coffee.

That has been the ritual for the past twenty years — but only on Materena's birthday.

On the other days of the year Materena jumps into her chores straightaway, ticking Colette's list as she goes. On the other days of the year, Colette has already left for her office by the time Materena arrives. The only day they meet is Friday afternoon, to recapitulate.

But on Materena's birthday, Materena has coffee and chocolate and a ten-minute chat with her friend.

"So," Colette is saying, pouring fresh coffee into the cups, "how does it feel to be forty years old?" Colette will be forty years old in five months, so she's very interested.

"Oh, I feel the same, Colette," Materena replies.

"Really?" Colette sits at the table with the cups. Taking a quick sip she adds, "No midlife crisis?"

"Midlife crisis? Colette, what are you talking about?"

Colette explains. A midlife crisis is like feeling lost. Midlife crises are like wanting more.

"Ah." Materena nods in agreement. "That . . . well . . ."

Colette is waiting, but the words are stuck in Materena's throat. How do you tell your boss you don't want to clean her house anymore? You want to do something else with your life. Here, Materena is going to take a sip of her coffee. This should give her more time to think.

Materena drinks her whole coffee and she still can't tell Colette what she's rehearsed since three o'clock this morning, straight after Leilani left. Words were flying out of Materena's mouth then, in the comfort of her kitchen. Materena had it all figured out. She was going to say, "Colette, here's the situation. After twenty years as a professional cleaner, I feel —"

Colette interrupts Materena's train of thought. "Materena . . . we've known each other for twenty years . . . you shouldn't have to weigh your words when speaking to me."

"Okay then, Colette, here's the situation. After twenty years as a professional cleaner, I feel like a change."

"A change?" Colette asks, sounding worried. "What do you mean?" Before Materena has the chance to explain what she means, Colette, speaking with her I'm-so-stressed voice, is telling Materena that she can't abandon her, not now, not with that mountain of work she has at the office. Not now, with the children still living at home. Not now, with Colette so close to being promoted to company director. Not now, with the networking dinners her husband throws three times a week in their house.

Not now.

"I need you, Materena," Colette says as she puts a hand on Materena's hand. "I'll be lost without you."

Aue, this conversation is so hard for Materena. She loves Colette, but sometimes you've got to love yourself more. "Colette," Materena says, "I've been cleaning houses for more than twenty years, and I *choose* to do something else with my life now."

On Air with Materena

The word in the neighborhood is that everybody who can help Materena is to meet at Loana's house at six thirty tonight. And people are to put their political beliefs aside, because this is not a political meeting, just a family-helping-family meeting. But please arrive before six thirty so that Rita can go through a few things with everyone.

By six o'clock, Loana's house is crowded with relatives, and so is her veranda and garden. Luckily Rita had the good sense to ask her husband to borrow a microphone from one of his musician colleagues.

Anyway, here's Rita standing on a chair, microphone in hand, addressing the audience, beginning with words of gratitude, because today is a big day for her favorite cousin.

So here's the plan, Rita goes on. As soon as Materena starts on air at her new job on Radio Tefana, relatives are to take turns calling the radio on Auntie Loana's telephone to speak to Materena. But don't give out your last name. It's important that the director of the radio doesn't know that the reason his radio is being inundated with calls is because Materena has a lot of relatives who like her. Just give out your first name, but you're free to invent a last name if you want. No problems.

"Everybody is following me?" Rita shouts into the microphone.

"*Oui!*" Everybody is so excited. It's like a spy game. "What name are you going to give?" they ask one another.

"People! Are you listening?"

"*Oui!*"

So Rita continues with the plan's objective, which is, of course, to help Materena get her idea approved by the director of the radio, who unfortunately is not a relative, otherwise nobody would be needed today. But at least he granted Materena one night's trial (with Ati's good word) to see how people all over Tahiti will respond to her program about women sharing inspiring stories with other women on the island. Inspiring, interesting stories worth listening to, stories that will make women listen and call Radio Tefana.

"So call and say something interesting!" Rita shouts, brandishing a fist. "Can we do it?"

"*Oui . . .*" This time the answer is hesitant. Something interesting? the relatives ask each other. Like what? Nothing interesting ever happens to us.

Meanwhile, Rita is looking at the crowd, trying to find someone who has an interesting story. Ah yes, Giselle. "You, Giselle!" Rita calls out into the microphone. "You've got an interesting story. You've given birth in a car three times!"

"Do you think it was interesting for me?" Giselle calls to Rita. "It was only interesting the first time!"

All right, then . . . Rita needs another example. Ah yes, Auntie Tapeta. "Auntie Tapeta!" she calls out. "You've got an interesting story. Your daughter meets an Australian in Tahiti, he gets kicked out of Tahiti when his visa expires, your daughter visits him in Australia and marries him so that her darling boyfriend can live here."

"Do you think it's interesting for me?" Tapeta is cranky. "Imagine you have a daughter, eh? She's so clever, but then she falls in love with an Australian surfer, she leaves school to visit him in his country, she marries him (not even in the church!), then she falls pregnant and leaves Tahiti for good with her husband and your granddaughter (who's not even ten weeks old!). Let's see if you're still going to think this is interesting."

All right, then . . . Rita needs another example, but she's running out of time. *Aue,* she thinks, let's leave it all to destiny.

"Auntie Loana?" she calls out, looking inside the living room. Ah, she's next to the telephone, ready to dial as soon as Ati, presenting Materena tonight, says, "*Call now!*" It has been agreed that the person who will make the first call to Radio Tefana will be Loana, since Materena is her daughter and this is her telephone.

Behind Loana is Auntie Imelda, then another elder, and another elder. All the elders are in the living room sitting in a line, waiting to spill their story.

For the moment they're just going to switch the radio on.

"Georgette!" Rita calls. "You're on!" Georgette, professional dancer, transvestite, and DJ, has brought her hi-fi system to propel Materena's voice into the living room, the garden, and beyond. A reggae song is playing and a few relatives decide to do a little dance. Another song comes on, a *tamure,* and it's party time on the veranda and in the garden.

"People!" Rita calls out. "Think about your interesting story!"

"Rita sure loves that microphone," says a relative.

A roar of excitement greets Ati, opening Materena's program. All the relatives are so excited because soon they're going to hear Materena's voice blast from the speakers. Nothing to do with Ati, even if he's partly responsible for Materena having a chance to test her idea.

"Silence!" Rita herself is very excited, but there's a need to calm the crowd a little.

Meanwhile, back in the Radio Tefana studio, Materena, facing Ati, is breathing deep breaths to relax. She's so nervous. Her heart is going *thump, thump, thump.* Ati is waving one arm in front of her. "I have in the studio with me a very charming woman," he says. "How are you, Materena?"

"Oh, I'm fine, and you, Ati?" Materena grimaces, eyeing all the people behind the glass window staring at her. They rehearsed that line yesterday afternoon, as well as speaking in front of the microphone (not too close — Ati showed Materena how), and it was also a good opportunity for Materena to get used to the earphones.

"Materena will be doing a special edition on the radio tonight," Ati continues. "But before we go on, I must say, Materena, that tonight is quite hot, don't you think?"

"*Ah oui,* Ati, you're quite right about that." Materena feels a bit more relaxed. Ati did explain to her yesterday how they'd do a bit of chitchat before beginning the program to give Materena time to relax and the audience a chance to warm up to that woman they've never heard about before.

"All I can say is" — Ati cackles, winking at Materena — "I hope it's going to rain soon."

"Oh, me too," cackles Materena. "Rain is very good for the . . ." And for some reason Materena's mind goes blank midsentence. For the life of her she can't remember what she's supposed to say now. And here's Ati miming words at her, looking a bit worried.

Back in Loana's house, relatives are shrieking, "The plants, Materena. Rain is very good for the plants. *Aue!* Materena, wake up!"

At the Beachcomber Hotel, Moana, outside the kitchen with one arm around his secret girlfriend, Vahine, is speaking to his mother in his mind: Mamie, the plants . . . the rain is very good for the plants.

In a house behind the petrol station, Pito, the receiver against the radio so that Tamatoa, in a phone booth outside a bar in Paris, can hear his mother doing her cinema on the radio, is saying out loud: "The plants, Materena! You always talk about the plants when it rains, and now you can't! What's wrong with you?"

In a house on top of a hill, Leilani, her head resting on her boyfriend's shoulder, her radio tuned to Radio Tefana for the first time in years, is doing telepathy with her mother: Mamie, say whatever comes to you . . . You always say interesting words anyway . . . Free your mind and the rest will follow . . .

"Rain," says Materena, "is very good for a woman's soul." This sentence just spilled out of her mouth.

"What?" her relatives shout in despair. "The plants, Materena!"

"You know, Ati," Materena continues, not intimidated anymore by the microphone, the earphones, and the people staring at her from behind the glass window, "people always say rain is good for the plants, and that is true, but rain, especially when it sprinkles, is music to a woman's ears and warms the soul."

Totally at ease now, Materena continues to praise the rain.

When it splatters on the tin roof, it makes you feel a bit melancholic and takes you back to some happy days or to those black years you've had but survived because you're a woman and *surviving* is not a foreign word to women from anywhere in the world.

Watching rain is magic. It calms the anxious spirit and the tormented soul. It gives women hope. It reminds us how strong we are. Determined. Courageous. Understanding. And with so much love to give.

Rain is a miracle. Just like a woman is.

"You know, Ati," says Materena, thinking, I hope I'm not raving on too much — Ati's eyes are popping out of his head — "I'm so proud to have been born a woman. And as a proud woman I'm calling on all the women listening right now to share their stories on the radio for other women to learn something and be inspired. People say, 'I've got nothing to say,' but that's not true. Every single woman has something to say. A story. A story about mistakes, obstacles overcome, discoveries, a story. A story that will help another woman take a step forward. A story that will warn another woman before she takes a step backward. A story to reassure all of us that we're not all alone . . ."

"*Call now* — 84-27-17!" Ati, jubilant and showing Materena his thumb up, shouts into the microphone.

Back in Loana's house an hour later, nobody can get through to the bloody radio. It's engaged all the time and it's making Loana very cranky.

"How many lines does that stupid radio have?" she exclaims. Some relatives have walked to the public phone, thinking that there must be something wrong with Auntie Loana's telephone. Other relatives are quite happy just listening to all these lucky women who have managed to get through to Materena. One woman talks about visualizing her children in a tunnel of light whenever she knows they're driving at night, to help guide them safely home.

Another woman told the story of being abandoned by her mother.

Yet another woman told about how she loves her mother with all her heart and soul, and she'll always remember the day she had a splinter in her foot and her mother took it out with a razor blade.

She remembers shouting out in pain and her mother telling her, "But stop shouting like that, people are going to think I'm hitting you! Sing a church song! And what do you want, eh? It's hurting — it's hurting, we're always hurting, us women, it's like that, it's life, we're born to suffer. We suffer but we don't cry. *Au contraire,* we laugh. If we didn't laugh, we'd be spending our time crying into our pareu. We have to be strong in life. When you fall, well, get up, go to work, clean the house, sing a happy song, go do something with your hands! And so? Do you think God is going to ask men to give birth? Do you think it's a man who transformed himself into a breadfruit tree to feed his family? My arse! It's not worth crying about. Let's keep our tears for someone we love who died. Yes, then it's worth crying."

There are all kinds of stories on Radio Tefana tonight — funny, sad, unbelievable, so close to the truth, frightening, inspiring. It sure beats watching TV.

A woman finds her father and tells Materena all about it. Another adopts her husband's dead lover's baby. One confesses her fear of gendarmes (ah, Mama Teta must have gotten through). One caught the plane for the first time in her life, putting aside her fear of flying to visit her daughter living in America.

A woman gave birth in the bathroom while she was showering to be clean for the hospital, but she didn't make it. She didn't make it six times, actually. Her six sons just wanted to come into the world with their mother under the shower.

A woman left her husband for true love with another woman.

A woman calls to tell Materena and all the women listening that her husband uprooted a tree she's planted just because it was dying. He didn't even try to save that tree, he just got the machete out. The woman is sure that when her turn to die comes, her husband will turn the machine off without remorse. She won't have the opportunity to die little by little. She'll be executed, and then her husband will shove her dead body in a coffin and send the coffin back to her island.

After Materena talked about her garden, a woman called to ask Materena for some help with *her* garden. She was particularly interested in cuttings. Materena was more than pleased to share all that she knew about cuttings with that stranger.

Another woman wanted to talk about her beloved uncle, who died last month. She remembers there was a cane basket on top of the fridge and she'd ask him, "What's inside the basket?" And the uncle would reply, "It's a snake that's inside the basket." One day, she was about seven years old, she got a chair, dragged it to the fridge, and looked inside the cane basket. She saw a bottle of wine. She was so disappointed.

Another woman confessed how she's always wanted to be a detective. When she watches movies and there's a mystery, there's a crime, she always knows who the murderer is, and it's a guarantee that it's the one that nobody else suspects, the one who's really well-off and smiles all the time, he helps old ladies cross the road and everything. And she knows all about detective tricks, like how the criminal always comes back to the scene of the crime.

One woman gave her man a black eye because he said that her mother had a pitiful air, and so she threw a mango at her man and gave him a pitiful air. He told his friends and family that he'd been involved in a fight. Apparently, he was walking in town minding his own onions when, out of nowhere, four hoodlums appeared, etc. . . . etc. . . . And he got out his fists, leaped in the air and did a few karate chop-chops, etc. . . . etc. . . . etc.

Within a week of Materena's being on air, she receives a contract from Radio Tefana.

Materena, screaming with joy and crying her eyes out, grips that piece of paper and hugs Leilani, embracing her daughter and her new life.

Before I Leave

The day after Materena receives her contract in the mail, Leilani invites her for lunch in town to celebrate the wonderful event and also because Leilani has an announcement to make.

"A good announcement or a bad one?" Materena asks.

"I'll meet you at Chez Patrick at twelve o'clock." That's all Leilani is prepared to tell her mother on the telephone.

By twelve thirty, at table 7, which her daughter has reserved, Materena is still waiting and looking very much like she's been stood up by her boyfriend. She's drunk all the water in the carafe and eaten all the olives on the plate, and she's getting crankier by the second.

This announcement of Leilani's better be important, she growls in her head, smiling to the people happily stuffing themselves. Meanwhile, the waiters (four in total) are busy taking dishes to tables, and none of them notices Materena's discreet wave. She'd like more olives if possible. She only ate a little piece of bread this morning, saving herself for the restaurant food, but the waiters are so preoccupied, she understands. *Ah, la-la,* and plus it's so hot in here. And the jazz music is a bit too loud. But the nets on the ceiling are nice, they give the restaurant a bit of a Tahitian atmosphere. Materena makes a mental note to tell Moana about the nets. He might be interested in this idea when he opens his own restaurant.

Materena wonders what Leilani's announcement is about.

Could it be a marriage announcement? Leilani and Hotu are still madly in love (so their neighbor is always kind enough to report to Materena). As a matter of fact, last week the neighbor saw Hotu and Leilani dance cheek to cheek on the veranda. They were dancing to "A son insu je caresse son ombre." That woman sure has big eyes and ears. Materena is not complaining.

Now, where's that girl of mine? Materena asks herself yet again. She hopes Leilani hasn't forgotten the rendezvous. Leilani could be having lunch in the park with her boyfriend right now, as they've been doing for the past two years, leaving her poor mamie stuck in this restaurant.

But wait a minute, how long is a person allowed to wait at the table for? What's the protocol? The man with the bushy eyebrows sitting behind the cash register doesn't look too happy, considering the glances he keeps throwing Materena's way. He's not doing Materena's cranky mood any service.

Ah, finally! Here she is, that *cachottière!*

The mad mood of Materena disappears in a flash. First, because she's going to be eating soon, and second, because Leilani is her daughter.

"Mamie!" Leilani calls out, walking in. "I'm so sorry! We had an emergency at the surgery, a kid fell off his bike. Eight stitches!"

All heads turn to Materena's daughter. She's young, she's loud, and she's just had an emergency at the surgery. Nothing to do with the very conservative brown pants and top she's wearing. She looks so much older than her age in this outfit, but then again, as Rita pointed out many years ago, Leilani could wear a potato sack and still get attention because she has long legs and a beautiful face.

Leilani gives her mother a big embrace, falls on her chair, and calls out to one of the waiters, "*Ouh-ouh!* Excuse me!" The waiter promptly attends to Leilani.

"Could we have more olives, please?" she says, flashing her white teeth. "And some water too, that would be great, *merci.*" Then, turning to her mother, she asks, "So? What do you feel like eating?"

"What's the announcement?" Materena is too curious to wait for Leilani to be ready to spill the bucket.

"Let's eat first, Mamie." Leilani is already looking at the menu.

"Is it a good announcement or a bad one?" When it comes to announcements Materena is very impatient. Never tell her you've got a surprise for her either. She'll hound you until you crack, and then she'll be cranky at you for telling her about her surprise.

"Do you feel like chicken?" Leilani asks. "Or meat . . . Fish? I think I'll have the grilled mahimahi served with salad."

"Me too."

"You don't have to order what I order."

"Leilani, you're not the only one who likes fish."

The grilled mahimahi rates ten out of ten with both Materena and Leilani. Their only criticism is that the portion is too small. In fact, according to Leilani, that dish should have been called salad served with mahimahi. Materena agrees on that one. But anyway, at least there was lots of bread and Materena isn't famished anymore.

"So?" she says picking at a tomato. "What's the announcement?"

Leilani fills her glass with water, along with her mother's glass. "A toast to you, Mamie," she says. "You are the most inspiring woman I know."

Aue, Materena is going to cry in public, and plus, everybody is looking at her. Leilani talks so loud that they all know now that she's an inspiration for her daughter. *Aue* . . . what pride. Materena raises her glass, her other hand on her chest. "*Tchin-tchin.*"

"*Tchin-tchin.*"

Mother and daughter gently knock their glasses together. Then they go on drinking their water. There, done.

"So? The announcement?" asks Materena.

"Mamie, I'm leaving."

"Pardon?" Materena wasn't expecting that kind of announcement. "Leaving . . . leaving what? Your job? Your boyfriend?"

"I'm leaving Tahiti."

"To go where?"

"Mamie" — Leilani places a hand on her mother's hand — "you know how you always tell me that things happen for a reason?"

"Things happen for a reason sometimes, not all the time," Materena replies. "What happened to you?"

Leilani recapitulates:

She's called after Leilani Bodie, a medicine woman.

Biology and chemistry were her favorite subjects at school.

She met a boy with whom she could explore these subjects.

She got a job at a doctor's surgery facing her boyfriend's surgery.

Under the guidance of the wonderful Dr. Bernard, Leilani grew very fond of dealing with people in need and helping them.

Leilani now has all five of her left-hand fingers down, and she gives her mother the see-what-I-mean look.

"And . . . ," Materena says.

"Mamie, I've found my purpose in life!"

"To be . . ."

"But to be a doctor!"

"A doctor!"

"*Oui!*" Leilani takes her mother's hands and squeezes them tight, grinning from ear to ear. She goes on about how she owes Dr. Bernard so much. He's the one who made her fall in love with a career in medicine. Watching Dr. Bernard and listening to him talk with his patients made Leilani realize how fulfilling life as a doctor can be. "Doctors don't just write prescriptions and sign death certificates," says Leilani. "They investigate, they repair, prevent, nurture, educate, warn, help, love . . . Being a doctor, a good doctor, is a mission, not just a job. It's a purpose in life, you know, Mamie . . . it is mine."

Materena is very happy her daughter has found her purpose in life, but . . . "How long does it take to become a doctor?" Materena hesitantly asks.

"Seven years."

"Seven years!" Materena guessed it was something like that. "That's so long."

"Mamie, I don't want to be forty like you and realize I should have done what I wanted a long time ago." Leilani continues about how she's never seen her mother so happy since she got that job at the radio. "Look at you, you're radiant, you're beautiful, you're so happy."

"I was happy before."

"You're the one who's always pushed me to know what I want and to make it happen." Materena nods in agreement. But seven years . . .

"What about Hotu?" she asks. "What does he say about it?"

Leilani confesses he's very upset but he understands that this is what she wants to do. The same as she understands that he won't be following her to university in France, having already spent five years of his life there pursuing his own studies.

Materena looks down at her salad, thinking that young people today are so understanding. "It's finished between you two, then?" she asks, even sadder now. Despite his annoying habits, like chewing food for such a long time, Materena has grown very fond of Hotu over the past three years. He's like family. And he's such a good man. Three times Materena has looked at him, thinking, what a wonderful father he's going to be for my daughter's children.

Leilani informs her mother that it is indeed finished.

"Aren't you sad?" Materena asks, looking at Hotu's initials tattooed on Leilani's hand.

"Of course I'm sad! I've been crying for days!"

Materena looks up. She doesn't think Leilani looks like she's been crying for days. When you cry for days your eyes swell, and Leilani's eyes aren't swollen at all.

"Mamie, we both cried, Hotu and me. But there's no other solution than to go our own ways." Leilani explains that Hotu's life plan is to enjoy his work, row three days a week (which he loves so much), continue to rediscover his island, and start a family. And she refuses to ask him to consider altering his plans to suit her plan.

"I thought it was you he loved," Materena says, wishing Leilani had made her announcement at Materena's kitchen table and not in this crowded restaurant.

"He hasn't asked me to change my plan," Leilani snaps. "This is the best proof of his love for me."

"What about his initials tattooed on your hand?" asks Materena.

"I'm keeping them . . ." Leilani's voice trails off. She looks away for a second and adds that he'll always be a part of her life.

Materena looks down at her salad again. Tears are falling into the lettuce. "Seven years," she whispers sadly.

"Why are you sad? What would you have preferred? That I left you for a man?"

"Leilani, stop."

"Please be happy for me," Leilani pleads, her voice breaking up. "I will be leaving all the people I love behind . . . If you think this is easy for me to do, it's not, *merde.* Mamie, it'd be easier for me to go on doing what I'm doing, but you showed me the way . . . Please say you're happy for me." Leilani bursts into tears.

Materena is on her feet. Mother and daughter fall into each other's arms.

"I'm happy," Materena says, crying, "but I can't help it if I'm sad." She goes on about how it's like that when you're a mother. Sometimes you cry but deep down you're happy.

Materena goes on agreeing with her daughter that it makes sense that she wishes to give something back to the world, having had such a fortunate childhood.

Before she walks through customs, Leilani, struggling with her shell necklaces, turns around to look at all the people who have come to wish her well in her journey.

She sees her father hiding behind a pillar.

Auntie Rita is rocking her adopted three-month-old baby girl to sleep.

Moana and Vahine are holding hands.

Grandmothers Mamie Loana and Mama Roti are competing to cry the most tears. There's Mama Teta, Mama George, Auntie Teresia, Giselle, and another auntie, and another auntie, and more mamas. Nieces and nephews are yawning because they're not allowed to run around and because everybody is crying. It's so boring.

Leilani sees the man who will always be her inspiration in her journey as a doctor — Dr. Bernard, who never assumes anything.

Her ex-mother-in-law, the one and only Constance, is all made up and the only one not crying.

She sees the man of her life and her heart feels like it's being crucified. She wants to run out to him and say, "Come with me, I beg you." But like that song says, if you love somebody, set them free. Sometimes, people who are so meant for each other don't meet at the right time.

She sees her mother presently, holding on to Uncle Ati, and Leilani bursts into tears. She walks to her mother, arms opened, for one more of her legendary hug-and-kisses.

"I will miss you, Mamie."

"Go on," Materena says, smiling through her crying and holding her daughter tight. "*Faaitoito,* girl, be strong. We're not women for nothing, eh? Bless the day you came into my life."

Acknowledgments

This book follows the challenging yet rewarding relationship between a mother and her daughter. It also celebrates the strength, beauty, talent, humor, and commitment of women. I was blessed to have a whole team of such women behind me during the writing of *Frangipani.*

My mother, strong and passionate woman, thank you for your patience with me. I must have driven you crazy with my questions!

My daughter, who fed me (sometimes without even knowing it) many ideas. My sisters, Turia and Virginie — I love you! Friends Terri Janke, Jo Buckskin, Santi Mack, Leonie Higgins, Hayley Hansen, and Lisa McKeown.

Then there's Louise Thurtell, friend, editor, and agent with a mission. I will always remember our rides in the truck in Tahiti, walking through the streets of Papeete, chitchatting with the mamas, and that famous snorkeling session! Thanks to you, my book landed in the hands of a first-class publishing house, and I got to work with yet another passionate and dedicated editor, Amanda Brett. Mandy, your mind amazes me, it is always thinking and thinking, but I love your energy, you gorgeous girl!

As for Patty Brown . . . well, *vahine nehenehe . . .* beautiful woman from the outside and the inside, you're like an auntie to me!

To you all, *maururu . . .*

Back Bay Readers' Pick

Reading Group Guide

Frangipani

A novel by

Célestine Vaite

A conversation with the author of *Frangipani*

Célestine Vaite talks about writing, about family, and about her native Tahiti

You grew up in Tahiti and lived there until you were a young woman. Can you talk a little bit about your family, and about where you lived as a girl?

I'm the eldest of four children — born from different fathers and all *popa'a* — raised by a strong, passionate, and loving mother, a professional cleaner with a vision. I grew up in Faa'a, in the Mai quarters, in a fibro shack behind a petrol station next to the international airport, the church, the Chinese store, and the cemetery, and with breadfruit trees galore growing nearby. And relatives (also living in shacks) by the hundreds. When I look back on my childhood, I feel very blessed to have had so many extraordinary women as part of my life. Telling stories, laughing, minding babies, raking, working on quilts, dancing, singing at Mass, cleaning, crying, climbing the breadfruit tree to put food on the table, growling at dogs, worrying, sitting quiet and exhausted. Often in interviews I'm asked, "But where were the men?" Who knows! Probably drinking by the side of the road and counting cars driving past.

The Tahiti you write about is an amazingly matriarchal place, and a place deeply rooted in folklore and traditional wisdom. Is this the

Tahiti of your childhood or the Tahiti of the present day? Has Tahiti changed a lot in recent years?

The Faa'a of my childhood has physically changed; the fibro shacks are run down, the trees are either huge or gone, the cemetery holds more dead, the church has more followers, the little Chinese store is a big supermarket; but the everyday life is still the same. Women share stories, inspire one another, fall and get up stronger. Young men come and go. Older men become fabulous grandparents. And children are gifts from the sky.

In what ways was your mother like Materena when you were growing up? Was the "welcome to womanhood" talk Materena has with Leilani in Frangipani *similar to a talk your mother had with you?*

Like Materena, my mother loves her broom — she calls it her faithful companion. Both women left school at fourteen years old for a career as a professional cleaner, and both women have a vision for their children. My brother, for example, is a fabulous cook (his chicken curry melts on your tongue!), and he's never stayed at the Five Star Hotel, our polite name for prison. And our house was the only fibro shack in the neighborhood with an encyclopedia set. I loved my encyclopedia set! When the electricity was disconnected, no worries, Mum had the candles and flashlights under control.

My welcome into womanhood lecture began with the usual line — don't wash your hair during your period, otherwise the blood is going to turn into ice and you're going to be mad — moved to social etiquette, customs, and how being a woman was an honor. Then it was straight to the hormones, and contraception, contraception, contraception! "If you're going to play around in the dark, be armed!" Mum drove me mad about my hormones, but when they did start to kick in, I was armed. Though Mum often said that her unplanned children were gifts from the sky, she wanted her daughters to have different kinds of gifts, like papers, degrees, a job that had nothing to do with a scrubbing brush.

Who were your idols when you were a girl?

My mother. I had a picture of her in my copybook. It always made me refocus whenever I was tempted to do something stupid like wag school. She was my idol because I had watched her overcome so many obstacles, but always with gusto. Nothing was a problem, only a chance to grow stronger. She didn't wait for help to fall from the sky (I must mention here that although Tahiti is a French colony, there was no financial help from the government), and she didn't need any man in his shiny armor to rescue her. She just took matters into her own hands. I was in awe of my mother, the hardcore feminist!

You have children of your own now, and your experience with motherhood must have had a lot of influence on this book. Can you talk about that a little?

The idea to write a mother-daughter story came to me a few days after my daughter, Turia, became a woman. I decided then to dedicate the book to Turia but changed my mind about this many times during the writing of *Frangipani.* My daughter has always been a strong-willed child, but turning into a woman really went to her head! Her Royal Highness became very good at dismissing me with the back of her hand, and as in the book, we had a major screaming match about a pen. Writing about it was very therapeutic! Meanwhile my mother was reminding me that, as an adolescent, I was very good at dismissing her with sharp nods, and she advised me to foster this new strong woman because being a strong woman is a blessing, not a curse. By the time *Frangipani* was completed, I had accepted my very strong-willed daughter and was even finding her very inspiring. When Turia read the book, she burst into tears at the passage of Materena crying in the church, and said, "Mum, is this how you used to feel?" I replied, "This is how mothers all over the world feel!"

Rights to your book have sold throughout the world, so clearly the story you tell has a kind of universal appeal that transcends its Tahitian setting. Does this surprise you at all?

I write about people, they just happen to be from Tahiti, and though there is a strong Tahitian influence, these people have the same desires and hopes as any other people in the world. Tahitian readers always recognize themselves or relatives in my books the same as Australian readers do. The only difference is that the Australian readers find the insight into Tahitian culture fascinating, whereas Tahitian readers don't make much fuss about it.

How did your family and friends in Tahiti react to your writing? Does your mother enjoy your work?

Relatives were very intrigued when *L'arbre a Pain* (*Breadfruit*) was released in Tahiti, and many commented on the thickness of the book. "Almost as thick as the Bible!" The tribe was present at the book launch in Papeete, dressed up in their best clothes and sporting their best behavior. Patiently, they waited in the queue for their turn to have their book signed and made sure that the other people understood they knew me very well and that, unlike "you people," they weren't just fans. So one auntie loudly mentioned as she hugged me tight that once as a baby I ate a peg and it came out of my *caca* three days later. Thanks, Auntie! Copies of *L'arbre a Pain* are now proudly displayed all over the neighborhood where I grew up, next to the Bible and the statue of the Virgin Mary Understanding Woman.

When *Breadfruit* was released, my youngest sister, Virginie, orally translated it to our mother, every night, as Mum sat there sipping her glass of wine. It was quite painful for Mum to listen to her mother's story (the chapter "Kika" is about my grandmother), and she was a bit annoyed that I had made her teacher a smoker when he had never smoked in his life (the chapter "Teacher"), but the lesbian scene was fine. In Mum's own words, "Oh, it happens, you know."

What is it like to go back to Tahiti now that you've been living in Australia for so long?

During my absence, my mother briefly keeps me informed of what's happening in the family. Who's pregnant, who gave birth, who's dying, who's not talking to whom (until Sunday at Mass when the two will reconcile with the peace-be-with-you embrace), my sisters' follies, my brother's cooking, the nephews, the nieces, the cousins, the oranges are really sweet this year . . . so in a way I'm still home. But the second I step out of the airplane is when I cry out with joy because I'm truly home. I love my island and my family with a passion. Everything fascinates me — the majestic mountains, the hibiscus hedges, the rides in the truck, the people and their stories. Had I never left, I'm sure I wouldn't be as fanatical and enthusiastic.

How did you begin writing? Did you start to write thinking that you'd try to get your work published, or was it more gradual than that?

Pregnant with my third child and feeling very homesick, I began to write a short story — "The Electricity Man" — about a woman, Materena, telling off the electricity man for daring to disconnect her electricity when she didn't even receive a disconnection notice. I'd lived that scene so many times in my childhood that I knew it by heart. Writing it made me feel very good, it was like I was back home. I kept on writing (since it was making me so happy) and at my husband's suggestion sent my stories to literary journals. Within weeks these stories were published in various journals, a few from universities, with requests for more stories. Months later, a publisher rang to ask me if I had a novel in mind. She particularly wanted to read more about Materena. And *Breadfruit,* which tells the lives and loves of an extended Tahitian family, with the delightful Materena as the main character, came to life. I remember pushing my beautiful baby boy into the world thinking, "I have to finish my book before Mamie dies!"

Questions and topics for discussion

1. *Frangipani* is, at its heart, a mother-daughter story. Did the novel remind you at all of your own mother? Which scenes between Materena and Leilani were the most meaningful to you?

2. In Tahiti, a woman is considered wise to have a child with a man first, before she marries him, to see if he'll make a good father. What were some of the other cultural norms depicted in the novel that impressed or surprised you?

3. What do you most admire about Materena's character? Do you find her inspiring? At what points is she at her best in the novel?

4. Tahitian society is obviously very different from ours, but a lot of Materena's struggles (making ends meet while raising three children, getting along with relatives and in-laws) seem familiar in general terms. Which aspects of the narrative did you like best, the familiar parts or the more exotic details?

5. Did you ever get (or give) a "welcome into womanhood" talk? What do you think of Materena's many nuggets of wisdom?

6. The Tahiti that Célestine Vaite describes is a matriarchal place. Women are the ones with common sense, the ones who make the tough decisions and see to it that the family holds together. But at the beginning of the book Materena has an impossible time trying to convince Pito that she should be allowed to pick up his paycheck so that he doesn't spend it all at the bar. Discuss the roles of the women and men in this story. What do you think of Materena and Pito's relationship?

7. There's a lot of hardship in this novel, but *Frangipani* is notably void of sadness and self-pity. Do you think there's a lesson to Vaite's story in that respect? How does reading her book make you reflect on American culture?

8. Vaite's love for Tahiti is completely evident in this novel, even though she pokes fun at many aspects of island life. What kind of story would you tell if you were to draw on your own childhood and upbringing as Vaite does in *Frangipani?*

Célestine Vaite on her own life as a reader

Since becoming an avid reader at the age of eleven, my reading has gone through several stages.

At eleven, I was hooked on the works of Balzac, Zola, Dostoevsky. Novels thicker than the Bible with pages and pages of description and countless characters coming in and out (brothers, sisters, cousins . . .), but I had all the time in the world for family sagas! And I really didn't mind reading four paragraphs about a tree.

Eight years later, a mother and a university student with very limited reading time, thick novels were out. Paragraphs of description got on my nerves. Too many characters tired and confused me. I wanted to be entertained, fast, in between studying, breastfeeding, washing, etc. I fell in love with Guy de Maupassant's short stories. He is a master of short fiction and shows a deep knowledge of human nature whether he writes about *paysans,* courtesans, barons, abandoned children . . .

By the time I moved to Australia at the age of twenty-two to follow my husband, the father of my two children, Guy de

Maupassant was still my hero, but I felt that to survive in this foreign country, I had best master the English language. So for about two years I was a magazine reader. Mostly women's magazines such as *New Idea, Woman's Day, Women's Weekly,* etc.

As I grew a bit more confident, I started to read poems by the Australian writer Banjo Patterson, short stories by Roald Dahl, and novels with short chapters — *The Color Purple* by Alice Walker, *Fried Green Tomatoes at the Whistle Stop Café* by Fannie Flagg.

Later, much more confident and missing my big extended family, I started to read books about families and other cultures: *The Joy Luck Club* by Amy Tan, *Like Water for Chocolate* by Laura Esquivel, *The Color of Water* by James McBride, *Once Were Warriors* by Alan Duff, *Hanna's Daughters* by Marianne Fredriksson.

I'm still hooked on novels that give me an insight into another culture. I just can't get enough of them! I love the unusual way the characters speak, the settings, the family stories. Some favorites: *A Kiss from Maddalena* by Christopher Castellani, *The Almond Picker* by Simonetta Agnello Hornby, *Mao's Last Dancer* by Li Cunxin, *Falling Leaves* by Adeline Yen Mah.

Michael Pitt

About the Author

Célestine Vaite was born and grew up in Tahiti. At age sixteen, she fell in love with a spunky Australian surfer. They now live on the south coast of New South Wales, Australia, with their four children.

Frangipani is Vaite's first novel to be published in the United States. It will be followed by two other novels about Materena Mahi and her family: *Breadfruit,* which has already been awarded the Prix littéraire des étudiants (Vaite is the first native Tahitian ever to receive this prize), and *Tiare.*